AN
AMISH
Christmas
KITCHEN

AN
AMISH
Christmas
KITCHEN

*Three Novellas Celebrating
the Warmth of the Holiday*

An Amish Family Christmas
BY LESLIE GOULD

An Amish Christmas Recipe Box
BY JAN DREXLER

An Unexpected Christmas Gift
BY KATE LLOYD

BETHANYHOUSE
a division of Baker Publishing Group
Minneapolis, Minnesota

Published by Bethany House Publishers
11400 Hampshire Avenue South
Bloomington, Minnesota 55438
www.bethanyhouse.com

Bethany House Publishers is a division of
Baker Publishing Group, Grand Rapids, Michigan

Printed in the United States of America

Library of Congress Cataloging-in-Publication Data
Names: Gould, Leslie. Amish family Christmas. | Drexler, Jan. Amish Christmas
    recipe box. | Lloyd, Kate (Novelist). Unexpected Christmas gift.
Title: An Amish Christmas kitchen : three novellas celebrating the warmth of the
    holiday : An Amish family Christmas by Leslie Gould : An Amish Christmas
    recipe box by Jan Drexler : An Unexpected Christmas gift by Kate Lloyd.
Other titles: Amish family Christmas | Amish Christmas recipe box | Unexpected
    Christmas gift
Description: Bloomington, Minnesota : Bethany House Publishers, 2019.
Identifiers: LCCN 2019019122| ISBN 9780764233838 (trade paper) | ISBN
    9781493421732 (e-book)
Subjects: LCSH: Amish—Fiction. | Christian fiction, American. | Christmas stories.
Classification: LCC PS648.A45 A3435 2019 |DDC 813/.6080334—dc23
LC record available at https://lccn.loc.gov/2019019122

Cover design by Koechel Peterson & Associates, Inc., Minneapolis, Minnesota/Jon Godfredson

Leslie Gould is represented by Natasha Kern Literary Agency.
Jan Drexler is represented by WordServe Literary Group.
Kate Lloyd is represented by MacGregor Literary, Inc.

19 20 21 22 23 24 25   7 6 5 4 3 2 1

CONTENTS

AN
AMISH
FAMILY
Christmas

LESLIE GOULD

For my husband,
Peter,
who makes Christmas
magical every year.

CHAPTER ONE

The vase slipped through Noelle's hand and shattered on the *Kicha* floor.

Just as her heart had been broken.

"What was that?" *Dat* asked from his chair in the living room.

"Just an old vase." Noelle stared at the shards of red glass. "Nothing, really." The vase was a gift from Jesse King before he moved to Montana.

Just the night before, as Noelle moved the last of her things out of the *Dawdi Haus*, her oldest sister, Salome, said she'd heard Jesse had returned to Lancaster County from Montana. *"He's hoping to get a job at the Christmas Market,"* Salome had said.

Noelle felt ill as she stepped around the glass and headed for the broom closet. After three years, just like that, Jesse King had returned.

After she dumped the glass in the trash, she returned to the boxes stacked on the counter. The next one was the set of china her parents had given her back when she was courting Jesse. She slammed the lid down. The box would go in the back of her closet. She'd label it "Do Not Open Again." She moved on to a box of whisks, wooden spoons, and measuring cups.

The new house smelled of wood and fresh paint and the sweet creamsticks she'd just pulled out of the *Offa*, from a recipe that called for baking them instead of frying. She and Dat had their rooms set up, but she had a lot of unpacking to do in order to truly make it a home. And most importantly of all, she needed to get the kitchen set up. It had always been the heart of their home, and even though *Mamm* was now gone, that wouldn't change.

The Christmas Market, all five weeks of it, was the Schrock family's busiest time of the year. From March through the weekend before Thanksgiving, they participated in the Country Market on Saturdays, which was lucrative. But the Christmas Market, held at the same place and on Thursdays, Fridays, and Saturdays, brought in as much money as the other months combined. The family baked goods business had to go on, even though Mamm was no longer here to make sure it all ran smoothly.

It had been three months since Mamm died, and the grief was still as sharp as the broken glass. The pain hadn't lessened one bit; in fact, it had only grown stronger, much to Noelle's embarrassment. She'd been taught to accept the ways of God, to know He knew best with life and death. But every minute of the day, Noelle missed Mamm. It was the worst when she baked. She'd imagine Mamm beside her, her gray hair tucked under her *Kapp*, her wrinkled hands kneading bread dough, rolling out piecrusts, mixing fillings. The memories pierced her heart—but not enough to avoid baking. *Jah*, she missed Mamm, but she also felt her love and comfort the most clearly in the kitchen.

No doubt about it, she'd had one loss after another. Mamm's stroke. Noelle's fight with Jesse. Jesse going to Montana. Jesse staying in Montana. Her estrangement from her niece, Moriah. And then Mamm's death just before it was time to harvest the corn. At times, it all felt like too much.

Of course, she told others that she was doing fine. That God was in control. That she missed her Mamm, but the Lord giveth and the Lord taketh away.

And if anyone asked, she said she was long over Jesse. She tried to convince herself of that too. But in truth, she doubted she ever would be. He'd hurt her too deeply.

Dat shuffled unsteadily toward her, his long white beard flowing over his belly. He carried his empty coffee cup in one hand, and she quickly took it from him.

"If only I would have known how much I was going to need you back when you were first born," he said.

Her Dat had a way of reminding Noelle, over and over, what a surprise she'd been nearly twenty-two years ago. Before she could form a reply, footsteps fell on the front porch and then a knock landed on the door.

She opened it to find her brother-in-law, Ted, leaning on his cane as a gust of icy wind assaulted her. Behind him, their Lancaster County farm looked like a Christmas greeting card, flocked in *Shnay*, as the first rays of light fell over the landscape. It was Noelle's favorite time of year.

She squinted. A van idled in the driveway.

Ted gestured toward it. "Salome threw her back out. She needs you to run the booth today."

Noelle shuddered. What if Jesse was at the market? "I'm unpacking," she said. "Can Moriah do it?"

Ted shook his head. "She needs to help Salome." Moriah was Ted and Salome's twenty-two-year-old daughter. Noelle and Moriah were practically raised as twins, which made their current conflict all the more unsettling.

Noelle squared her shoulders. She wasn't used to challenging her brother-in-law. "I don't want to leave Dat alone when—"

Dat cut her off. "Go ahead. I will be fine."

Noelle's shoulders slumped. She'd avoided helping with the booth for a few years now. She was horrible at selling. Her job was to do the baking. And, above all, she didn't want to see Jesse.

However, missing the second Saturday of the Christmas Market would be a big hit to the business. She had to go—it was her duty to help her family. "Just a minute. I'll change my apron."

Ted gave her a nod, rubbed his hands together, and then headed toward the kitchen counter. "Mind if I have a cream-stick?"

"Go ahead," Noelle answered as she headed down the hall to her room.

She put Jesse out of her mind, as best she could. But she dreaded bumping elbows with a crowd of local *Englischers* and out-of-state tourists all day too.

She put on a fresh Kapp and a clean apron and determined, regardless of her stomach, which was growing more and more upset, to do what she needed to. When she came back down the hall, Dat stood at the kitchen counter with two slices of bread and a jar of peanut butter spread in front of him. "You will need a sandwich," he said.

Surprised, Noelle answered, "*Denki*." It wasn't like her father to think of her needs.

He made the sandwich while she put on her boots, slipped into her coat, and grabbed her purse. Then Dat handed her a brown bag. "I put an orange in it too."

She thanked him again and met his eyes. "The market doesn't close until six."

Dat nodded. "I will be fine. We will eat when you return."

She stepped out the door. The exhaust from the van billowed out into the cold, and the icy wind stung her face. The weather forecast was for a weeklong cold spell with more snow.

Ted sat in the passenger seat of the van, licking his fingers, so Noelle climbed into the middle seat. She didn't recognize the driver—a woman Ted introduced as Pamela—but he seemed well acquainted with her. The driver dropped him off at the Dawdi Haus behind the original farmhouse on the Schrock property.

"I'm sorry about your mother," Pamela said as she turned the van around. "Salome said you were a big help in caring for her."

Noelle wasn't sure what to say. It worried her to know Salome talked about her to a stranger. Her sister was known for her constant gossiping, and Noelle didn't trust her.

Plus Salome had used the word *help* in talking with Pamela, as if Salome had been in charge of Mamm. It was Noelle who had seen to her care, along with Dat. True, Salome liked to barge in as if she were in charge, but it was Noelle who'd done all of the work.

Pamela turned onto the highway. "So you and your father just moved into the new house?"

"That's right," Noelle answered, soaking in the view of the snowy fields on either side, appreciating the winter wonderland around her. Salome and Ted's oldest, Paul, now farmed the land. Paul and his wife already had four little ones, so it made sense for them to live in the big house. The new house, the one she and Dat had just moved into, was essentially a second Dawdi Haus, although it sat by itself on the southeast plot of land.

Noelle had lived in the big house as a baby. By the time she was in school, Ted and Salome and their children occupied it, because Noelle and her parents had moved into the Dawdi Haus after the last of her eight older sisters left home. By then Noelle already had a score of nieces and nephews.

Now all of the older ones were married, except for Moriah, who was a widow. Of course there were many who were younger than Noelle was too, all the way down to infants, and now there were great-nieces and great-nephews too.

Time seemed to march on for everyone but her. Family and friends all around her were growing up, getting married, and starting families while she'd been frozen, as solidly as the icicles hanging from the eaves of the farmhouses they passed by, for the last three years.

They arrived at the market by eight-thirty, parking in the back among the other vans, cars, and buggies. Noelle only had a half hour to unload and set up the booth. Thankfully, Pamela grabbed a dolly just outside the door of the market and began stacking plastic crates, explaining, "Salome pays me extra to do the heavy lifting. She's been having pain in her back for a while."

Noelle grabbed a crate of whoopie pies and followed Pamela. Salome had complained some about her back, using it as one of her excuses to not help lift Mamm, but Noelle hadn't realized it was affecting her ability to carry crates in and out of the market or perhaps do things at home. And now she'd injured it worse.

A threshing accident had left Ted disabled over a year ago. Then Moriah's husband died. Jah, it had been a hard year for all of them.

Pamela pushed through the back door into the building and then led the way past a big dining area with a kitchen to their right. The door was open, showing a large range, double sinks, and lots of counter space. Noelle couldn't help but be impressed by the kitchen. The dining area was also new since the last time she had been to the market. She'd come with Jesse not long before he'd left.

She followed Pamela into the large hall with booths of pretzels, popcorn, sausages, candles, soaps, quilts, furniture, baskets, and dried flowers. She caught whiffs of lavender potpourri as she hurried past. Finally, the woman stopped at Salome's booth, toward the back. "You start setting up," she said. "I'll keep unloading."

"Denki," Noelle replied.

Noelle had started helping Mamm with the baking for the business by the time she was nine. Of course, everything had to follow regulations, and Mamm made sure to teach Noelle all of their mixing and baking techniques, along with their ingredients. But working with Mamm in the kitchen had always been her favorite thing to do. Her mother was a wonderful baker: whoopie pies, loaves of bread, sticky buns, fruit pies. "Keep it simple" was Mamm's motto.

Mamm didn't mind working in the market, but Salome hated to bake and agreed to do the selling, even though it meant interacting with the Englischers that she seemed to disdain. She'd come home with stories about how hopelessly impractical they were, how it took them forever to make a simple decision between something as mundane as choosing either a blueberry or peach pie. How they fretted if their children would prefer the chocolate whoopie pie or the peanut butter one. *"It's no surprise,"* she once said, *"that our word for anxious is* Engshtlich. *Don't you think it was inspired by the word* Englisch?*"* Noelle responded that she had no idea.

And she had no idea if her sister was accurate in portraying the Englisch. She hadn't spent enough time around any to know, except for nieces and nephews who hadn't joined the Amish.

Salome would go on and on. Not only were the Englisch anxious, but they always bought more than they needed—of everything. Still, Salome never balked at working at the market. Noelle asked her once why she agreed to do it when she seemed to despise the Englisch.

"Oh, I don't hate them," she'd said. *"Quite the contrary. I find them highly entertaining. I enjoy spending time among them. And I find getting them to buy our goods quite rewarding."*

And she was good at selling, which meant Mamm and Noelle could do the baking without any pressure to go to the market. Noelle had hoped to continue with the arrangement after Mamm died.

She sighed. There was no reason to think Salome wouldn't soon be back at the market, and Noelle back in the kitchen. As Noelle stacked the pies, all securely packaged in cardboard boxes, she caught a whiff of chocolate. She had her back to the aisle as she looked to her left, to the soap booth. Then to her right, to the quilt booth. She turned around. Sure enough, a candy booth was directly across from her.

A young woman, probably around Noelle's age, pulled trays of handcrafted chocolates from a plastic crate. She already had five candles, four purple ones with a white one in the middle, set up on the front counter, along with a stack of super-thin boxes that had a picture of a nativity scene on the front.

A young man arrived with another plastic crate. "That's all," he said. "I'll see you at five-thirty."

"Thanks." The young woman flipped her long dark hair into a hair band and then knotted it into a bun high on her head. "Have a good class."

"I'll try." The young man's dark eyes sparkled as he turned to go.

"Carlos." The girl's voice was commanding. "Don't forget to call Mama on your way."

"I won't." He glanced over his shoulder. "I'll tell her you'll call this evening."

Realizing she was staring, Noelle turned her head.

As the young man walked away, the girl called out to Noelle. "Hey, where's Salome?"

"She hurt her back."

The girl stepped into the aisle, her hand extended. "I'm Holly."

Noelle met her and shook her hand. "Noelle."

"Really?"

Confused, Noelle nodded.

"Any chance you're a Christmastime baby? I mean, with a name like that . . ."

Noelle couldn't help but smile. "You too?"

Holly laughed. "Christmas Eve."

Noelle wrapped her finger around the tie of her Kapp. "Same."

Holly held up her hand. It took Noelle a half second to realize she wanted to high-five. Awkwardly she slapped her palm against Holly's.

The girl said, "I'm turning twenty-two."

Noelle smiled in surprise, again. "So am I."

"We're twins." Holly beamed. "I was born at Lancaster General. How about you?"

"A birthing clinic." Her Mamm had been forty-seven, a little old to have a baby. But all the tests, including an ultrasound, had indicated her baby was fine and the birth would be low risk.

"Ah well. We're still twins."

Noelle fought the urge to laugh. Clearly they weren't, but she enjoyed the thought of it. A twin would have been lovely. She wouldn't have felt like the odd one out, the tagalong, the after-thought child.

"I've always wished my parents named me Noelle instead of Holly. It's the perfect Christmas name."

"Oh no," Noelle said. "I've always loved the name Holly." It was true, she had. Mainly because her Mamm had been sure that her last baby, this Christmas surprise, was going to be a boy. In fact, that was what the ultrasound technician had told her. After having eight girls—she'd finally have a boy. She'd make the best of the shock and name the baby boy Noel.

When a little girl arrived instead, she couldn't think of another name, so Salome convinced their mother to add "-le" to the end. At least that was the story Noelle had heard her entire life.

Of course, she didn't tell Holly all of that.

Pamela arrived with another crate. Holly said, "We'll chat later . . . twin." The girl's melodic laughter warmed Noelle's heart.

The market opened by the ringing of Christmas bells. Salome had told Noelle all about them, saying the manager thought they added class. Salome thought they added chaos. Noelle listened carefully, thinking she liked the sound of the bells as they reverberated under the open timbers of the hall. Granted, they had to be a recording. There were no bell ringers on the premises. But she still appreciated the sound.

She turned her attention to her products—whoopie pies, bread, rolls, and pies. All things she'd made in the Dawdi Haus kitchen yesterday morning, before several of her nephews moved most of her and Dat's things, while she packed up the kitchen and then moved the rest.

Now she needed to sell what she'd made. A few customers trickled by, but no one stopped to buy anything the first half hour. However, several people stopped and bought the thin boxes Holly was selling.

Finally, Noelle's curiosity overpowered her shyness. "What are those?"

"Advent calendars," Holly answered.

Noelle's expression must have given away her confusion because Holly continued, "Advent . . . the pre-Christmas tradition?"

Puzzled, Noelle shook her head.

"I know—the Amish don't celebrate Advent. Neither do the Mennonites, which we are."

Noelle was surprised.

"My mom grew up celebrating Advent, but then as a teenager in Mexico, she joined a Mennonite Church. Now we go to one a few miles from here."

Obviously it was a liberal one. The girl was dressed in jeans and a sweatshirt.

Holly continued. "Advent celebrates the coming of baby Jesus, during the four weeks before Christmas . . ." She pointed toward the five candles on the counter, all unlit. "The purple candles are for hope, joy, peace, and faith. And the white one symbolizes Jesus. That's what my mama taught me. We light one each Sunday before Christmas." Holly grinned. "Or flip the switch, for the battery-operated ones because we're not allowed to light candles in here. I'll"—she made air quotes—"'light' the one for hope tomorrow, the first Sunday of Advent."

Holly held up one of the calendars and pointed to the numeral one. It wasn't a normal calendar with grids. Instead it had little cardboard doors arranged around the painting. "Each of the twenty-five flaps has a verse printed on it, and inside is a piece of chocolate." She put the calendar back down on the counter. "It's a fun countdown to Christmas, but it also helps kids stay focused on the reason for the season." She grinned again.

Noelle appreciated the lesson. She liked Holly. And not just because they shared a birthday.

Business picked up gradually with each passing hour, but it wasn't as packed as Noelle remembered from when she helped before. Holly was keeping busy, but sales were slow for Noelle. An older Englisch woman stopped at her booth and asked what Noelle was selling. In her typical low voice, she explained. The woman proudly announced she was visiting Lancaster County and reached out and patted Noelle's hand. "Try to smile and sound a little more enthusiastic, dear."

Noelle grimaced.

The woman bought an apple pie, sticky buns, and a loaf of bread. "I'm going to compare your baking to mine." Her eyes twinkled.

Noelle knew she should come up with a snappy comeback, but she couldn't think of a thing to say except for "Have a nice day."

The tourist gave her a smile and then joined another Englisch woman at Holly's booth.

When Noelle and Jesse courted, she'd been more confident. She always felt more outgoing with him, and she had plenty to smile about back then. When he left, she grew even more shy than she'd been before. Mamm had told Noelle, or tried to in her post-stroke speech, not to let embarrassment isolate her. But Noelle couldn't seem to help it. Her shame sucked all of her energy, except what she needed to care for Mamm and continue with the baking for the business.

Noelle stayed in her booth without a break, not wanting to miss any customers. She took bites of her sandwich as she stood, hoping for more customers, while Holly grew busier and busier as the day continued.

Finally, in the midafternoon, the girls watched each other's booth so they could each take a quick trip to the restroom and grab a cup of coffee. Holly gave Noelle a truffle, and Noelle returned the favor with a sticky bun.

Noelle enjoyed interacting with the girl. Her best friend had been her niece Moriah, who was a couple of months older than Noelle. Her husband, Eugene, had been good friends with Jesse, and the four of them had gone on buggy rides and hikes together. But Noelle's relationship with Moriah had grown strained in the last few years, especially after Eugene had died nearly a year ago. Noelle had tried to console her niece but to no avail.

Most of Noelle's friends from school were either married or would be soon. Spending time with them just reminded her of what she didn't have. After Jesse stayed in Montana, Noelle was too embarrassed to go back to the *Youngie* singings and volleyball games. She saw enough pity in the expressions of others at church. Soon, Moriah told Noelle that she'd heard, through the grapevine, that Jesse was dating an Englisch girl in Montana.

Noelle felt as if a half-grown calf had kicked her. Before that, she still hoped Jesse would come home, that they would make up and join the church together. And then marry.

But obviously those were no longer his plans.

She'd joined the church the next spring. Mamm and Dat thought that meant she'd forgotten Jesse, that she was willing to marry someone else. It meant nothing of the sort.

It just meant she was resigned to a life alone.

By midafternoon, Noelle had sold a quarter of the pies. She hoped the rest would sell and moved the boxes to the front of her booth, sure Salome would be nearly out of product by now. It appeared that Holly was out of calendars.

As Noelle bagged a pie, someone off to her right caught her attention.

Her worst fear had come true.

Jesse.

He wore Amish clothes and a beard that matched his sandy hair. Unintentionally her eyes met his. They were as bright blue as ever. She stepped backward, struggling to catch her breath.

Not only was he at the market, as she'd feared, but as indicated by his beard, he was both Amish and married.

She finished the transaction as her heart thumped in her chest. She hoped she could continue to function without crying.

As the customer stepped away, Jesse took the woman's place. He held something in his arms. Noelle stepped backward again. A sleeping *Boppli*, wrapped in a pink woven blanket. The baby's head was partly uncovered, but her face was turned toward him.

Noelle clenched her trembling hands. Jesse was a father.

Feeling as if her heart might stop, she turned away from him and toward a customer. Thank goodness her booth was the busiest it had been all day. "May I help you?"

As she handed the customer a boxed blueberry pie, Noelle looked behind Jesse, trying to spot his wife. Obviously he'd married an Amish woman—not the Englisch girl he'd been dating. But there didn't appear to be anyone with him.

A man wearing a Pittsburgh Steelers hat stepped in front of Jesse. "Are you Noelle Schrock?" he asked.

She nodded.

"I'm Steve Browne—the manager of the market." She guessed he was in his forties. "Your driver called. She can't give you a ride tonight. Some sort of emergency came up."

Noelle rubbed the back of her hand over her forehead, wishing Jesse would go away. She didn't have any idea what to do now, and she couldn't think with him so close.

Jesse stepped to the man's side. "We can give you a ride."

We. She shook her head but didn't speak.

Steve, who seemed to sense her discomfort, nodded toward Holly. "I'll ask if Carlos can give you a lift."

Before Noelle had a chance to say anything more, Steve disappeared into the crowd and Jesse stepped forward again. "Let me give you a ride."

The last thing she wanted in all the world was to talk with Jesse King.

"Noelle."

She couldn't fathom how he could seem so familiar and so foreign all at the same time. The line of his jaw. His baby blue eyes. The way his hair curled along his forehead, ruining his bowl cut. It was as if he'd never been away. But he'd left her and married someone else. And now had a baby daughter in his arms. She turned toward the customer to her right, willing herself to remain calm.

Jesse stayed put, even after Steve returned and announced that Holly said Carlos could give her a ride. Noelle thanked the man and helped the next customer. A baby cried and Noelle realized it was Jesse's. Where in the world was his wife?

A few minutes later, he finally left, without saying another word. God willing, Salome would recover quickly, and Noelle would never have to see Jesse again.

CHAPTER TWO

At six o'clock, when the bells rang to signal the market was closing, Noelle tucked the money box into her purse and then quickly packed up the leftover loaves of bread, sticky buns, and pies—far more than what she'd hoped for. It was obvious she wasn't as good at sales as Salome. She'd only sold a couple of loaves of bread and a few boxes of sticky buns.

The manager wandered down the aisle, asking vendors if they needed help. His baseball cap was backward now, and it appeared he was as eager to go home as everyone else. Noelle grabbed an apple pie, surprising herself, and held the box out to him. "I have an extra," she said. "Would you like it?"

"Wow." He took it from her. "Salome has never given me a pie."

Noelle winced. That was because Salome was a better businesswoman.

Steve smiled. "Thank you. My wife and kids will be thrilled."

She nodded and then said, "I appreciate you asking Holly if they could give me a ride."

"No problem. Tell Salome hello."

Noelle said she would and then, as he continued on, turned her attention to across the way, where Holly was packing the last of her chocolates into her plastic crates as Carlos arrived. She didn't have nearly as much left as Noelle.

Holly slapped her brother on the back. "We're giving Noelle a ride."

"Noelle?"

"Over there," Holly said. "Salome's sister. Is that all right?"

Carlos turned toward Noelle, a smile on his face. "Sure," he said. "I'll take out our crates and then come and help you too."

Noelle slipped into her coat and finished tidying up the booth. When Carlos returned with the dolly, the three of them managed her boxes in one load. Carlos led the way, followed by Noelle and then Holly. As they neared the back door, Noelle spotted Jesse sitting on a bench, talking with the owner of the furniture booth as he gave the baby a bottle.

She quickened her pace.

But when Jesse saw her, he stood. "I'll be at church tomorrow." He effortlessly balanced the baby and bottle. "Could we talk then? About what happened?"

Noelle stopped abruptly, causing Holly to run into her, hitting her with a box. "Oops. You okay?"

Noelle ignored Holly and spun around toward Jesse. In a raw voice, she stammered, "I have nothing to say to you."

In a calm and steady tone he said, "It's apparent you haven't changed your mind about me."

Her voice shook as she asked, "What are you talking about?"

"You know."

Noelle's jaw dropped. "Actually, I have no idea." He hadn't come back. He'd dated an Englisch girl. Then he'd married someone else.

And now he was blaming her. Noelle stomped away, the heels of her boots clicking across the linoleum, without waiting for a response.

Holly followed, squeaking "Oops" again, this time to Jesse as she passed by.

When they stepped out into the cold, Holly asked, "Whoa, who was that?"

Noelle's voice still shook as she said, "A guy I used to know."

"Do you despise him? Or love him?" Holly raised her eyebrows. "The two can be so hard to distinguish between at times."

Carlos shot his sister an exasperated look and said, "Ignore her. I'm still trying to teach her some manners."

Holly shook her head and then stepped ahead to an old white pickup.

It had a canopy over the bed, and once they'd loaded the boxes, Noelle climbed into the back seat of the cab while Carlos and Holly sat up front. Noelle gave Carlos the address of Ted and Salome's Dawdi Haus, where the boxes and products were stored, for now. They'd most likely move them once Noelle had the kitchen unpacked in the new house.

After Carlos entered the address into his phone, they were on their way. Soon the siblings' conversation fell to their mother.

Noelle leaned her head against the cold glass of the window and looked out into the darkness, half listening to the brother and sister, envying how close they were.

Fifteen minutes later, they reached the Dawdi Haus. Both Holly and Carlos jumped down to help her unload. Noelle took out the money she'd intended to pay Pamela and handed it to Carlos. He wouldn't take it. She tried to give it to Holly.

"Don't be ridiculous," Holly said. "This is practically on our way. Besides, we'd do whatever we could to help you. Salome, too."

As Carlos started pulling Noelle's boxes out of the truck, Holly handed her an Advent calendar. "I held one back for you."

"Oh, that's so nice." Noelle felt a surge of gratitude, thinking of the candles. Hope, joy, peace, faith. She needed all of those in her life this Christmas season. She just wasn't sure where she'd find them.

"Start tomorrow," Holly said. "And no cheating." The girl's grin was so infectious that Noelle smiled back. She couldn't remember the last time she'd smiled as much as she had today, regardless of seeing Jesse King.

Holly and Carlos followed her up to the door of the Dawdi Haus. Noelle knocked and then opened it.

Moriah, tall and slender like her mother, stood amidst boxes in the middle of the living room. "There you are." She explained that Salome was resting and that her father was at the big house, eating supper.

Noelle quickly introduced Holly and Carlos to Moriah, as they stacked the boxes next to the living room window. After she thanked the two, Holly said she hoped she'd see Noelle again.

"It will depend on Salome's back. . . ."

Holly grimaced. "Well, I hope she recovers quickly. Perhaps you could come with her sometime."

Noelle doubted she would, especially not with Jesse around, but she didn't say so.

Once the front door closed behind them, Moriah stepped to the window. "Mamm's mentioned Holly before."

"Oh?"

"I don't think it was exactly positive." Moriah's brown eyes widened.

Noelle couldn't imagine what could be negative about Holly, but leave it to Salome to come up with something.

"I need to talk with you about something else," Moriah said. "Actually two things."

"Oh?"

"I know how much you like Family Christmas, so I want

to warn you that Mamm's afraid she's not going to feel up to putting it together this year."

"What?" Noelle shuddered. Family Christmas, when her parents and all of her sisters and their families gathered, was her favorite few hours of the year.

"Jah," Moriah said. "She's in a lot of pain and overwhelmed with the move."

"She won't have to do anything. The rest of us can do it all." Everyone usually pitched in with food, the setup, and the cleanup. No one expected Salome to be in charge.

Moriah's shoulders slumped. "It's not that I agree with her, but she seems pretty determined. . . ."

"There's no reason to cancel it." Noelle couldn't imagine not celebrating Christmas with the whole family. They hadn't all been together since Mamm's service.

Moriah sighed. "I just wanted to give you fair warning is all."

"Denki. I appreciate it." Noelle crossed her arms. "What else did you want to talk about?"

"Jesse stopped by today. Did he find you?"

She concentrated on keeping her voice level. "He stopped by the booth."

Moriah wrinkled her nose. "Did you see his baby?"

Noelle's chest began to ache. It felt as if it were only yesterday that Jesse had left her. "Jah," she said. "I saw the baby. But not his wife."

"His wife?"

Noelle nodded.

"There is no wife," Moriah said. "She died seven months ago."

The next day, Noelle went to Sunday services with her father at the farm of Ben King, who happened to be Jesse's uncle.

When Jesse was fourteen, his father died and then his mother left the Amish. Ben and his wife, Barbara, took Jesse in and finished raising him.

Thankfully, when she and Dat arrived, Noelle didn't see Jesse. Everyone congregated in the Kings' cleaned-out shed that had several kerosene heaters running to ward off the cold. Noelle hoped her father was warm enough.

Despite the chill, she yawned through the singing and the scripture reading. But when the sermon started, her heart raced at the sight of Jesse slipping down the outside of the men's side, his baby asleep in his arms. Noelle shifted her eyes forward, hoping no one had seen where her gaze had momentarily landed. Her racing thoughts matched the accelerated beat of her heart. How had Jesse's wife died? How long had they been married? How devastating it must have been for him to lose her.

It put Jesse wanting to talk with her in a new light, but she felt the same as she did when she saw him at the market. She wanted to avoid him at all costs.

Noelle couldn't concentrate on the preaching, although now she wasn't having a hard time staying awake. However, the last scripture reading caught her attention: "Now the God of hope fill you with all joy and peace in believing, that ye may abound in hope, through the power of the Holy Ghost." *Hope.* That was what the first candle in Holly's Advent wreath represented.

She hadn't felt any hope for a long time. Not since Mamm had her stroke. Not since Jesse left. Certainly not since Mamm had died.

Could God fill her with hope again?

After the service, they all filed out of the shed and into the big, sprawling farmhouse, where it was much warmer. Jesse's *Aenti* Barbara held the baby while Jesse helped set up the tables. The little one was awake now, bright-eyed and smiling. Her dark hair stuck up all over her head, and, by her size, Noelle guessed she was seven months or so, which meant she was a newborn when her mother died.

When Moriah approached Noelle, she quickly looked away from the baby. Moriah crossed her arms. "Mamm's back isn't doing any better. You'll need to do both the baking and the selling this week."

Noelle didn't answer. It wasn't a request. It was a command, sent from Salome. Moriah added, "I can come over and help on Wednesday."

"Denki." Noelle would need to get the kitchen unpacked on Monday and the shopping done. She could then start baking on Tuesday and finish up, with Moriah's help, on Wednesday.

Moriah continued to stand with her arms crossed. Noelle wasn't sure what to say. They used to be close—the best of friends. But then Moriah had married about the time Jesse left for Montana. Perhaps Noelle, deep in her own grief, hadn't been as happy for Moriah as she should have been. And then when Moriah's husband had died a year ago, their relationship had grown even more strained.

When Moriah drifted off toward a group of women, Jesse headed toward Noelle. In her experience, no one was as determined as Jesse King when he put his mind to something.

"Could we talk?" He nodded toward the window seat on the enclosed porch, in the nook that used to be their special spot.

As much as Noelle wanted to flee, she was curious to hear Jesse's side of the story. She followed him to the window seat but sat as far away from him as possible and crossed her arms.

Jesse exhaled. "I need to know why you didn't want me to come back."

Was he trying to pin their breakup on her? "You chose to stay in Montana."

"You were angry with me," he said.

Noelle shook her head, baffled. "Of course, I was angry with you. We'd had a fight and you left in the middle of it."

"I had a train to catch."

Noelle stared at him until he looked away.

"Jah, I shouldn't have gone. I see that now. I didn't realize how bad your Mamm was at the time." His eyes stayed on the floor.

She tried to choose her words carefully. "Even though we'd had a fight, I expected you to come back."

He crossed his arms and met her eyes again. "That's not what I heard."

She stood.

"Noelle." His voice sounded defensive.

The Jesse she used to know was honest and willing to take responsibility for his actions. Now he was being deceptive—and manipulative.

She fled, slipping into the kitchen. Ten minutes later she managed to eat with the first sitting. Thankfully, Dat did too.

After the meal, he was tired and wanted to go home. Relieved for an excuse to leave, Noelle told Barbara good-bye, ignoring the baby still in the woman's arms. Barbara gave her a sympathetic look but didn't say anything. Noelle's face grew warm, and the shame burned straight through her all over again. Why hadn't Barbara told her he'd married? And then that his wife had died?

Dat was quiet on the way home. When he closed his eyes, Noelle assumed he'd fallen asleep. But then he said, "If we love, we grieve. It cannot be helped."

Had he seen her outburst? When Dat didn't say any more, Noelle's thoughts returned to Jesse. She had loved him. Then grieved him. And then here he came, stirring everything up again.

"The challenge," Dat added, "is not to close off our hearts to love. We have to find ways to embrace hope and joy in our lives."

Noelle stared straight ahead at the horse's sloped back. Hope. Joy. Love. All included in Dat's brief words—all included in Holly's Advent story. Wise words. But also impossible words. She couldn't imagine what it would take for her to open her heart again.

After Dat had settled down for a nap, Noelle wished she could get started on unpacking the Kicha, but no work was allowed on Sunday. Dat might not notice when he woke up, but Ted could stop by at any moment. Or Salome. Both would rebuke her for her sin of working on the Sabbath, with no hesitation.

Instead, she stood at the living room window and watched the sunlight sparkle on the brilliant landscape. Out in the field was the frozen pond where she and Jesse used to skate. She thought of the snowmen they'd built and the snowball fights they'd had. Racing across the ice. Making snow angels. Going for moonlight rides in his sleigh. There was no season she loved more than winter, and nothing she'd loved more than spending frosty days with Jesse.

She'd feared Jesse would grow bored with her, since she was so quiet and shy. Because he was so gregarious, outgoing, and such a people person, she was always surprised that he wanted to be with just her. But, at the time, it seemed he genuinely did. It wasn't that they didn't spend time with others. They did. At Jesse's side, she enjoyed the interaction with others.

But it seemed he'd been bored with her all along, causing all of her hopes and dreams to shatter. Without even an explanation.

Her mother had told her, in the unsteady way she spoke after her stroke, that the pain would ease with time, and it partly had. Noelle had stopped thinking about Jesse every moment of the day, stopped mulling over the fight they'd had that morning he came to take her to the train station. Stopped searching her memories for what had gone wrong.

But as she stared across the frosty expanse, it all came tumbling through her mind again.

Mamm had her stroke the day before, and Noelle had left a message for Jesse saying she couldn't go and asking him to stay too—but he hadn't received it. He came bouncing up the sidewalk to the Dawdi Haus, excited for their trip together. A cousin on his mother's side had moved to Montana the year before and had asked Jesse to ranch with him. Jesse wanted Noelle to see the place, to decide if she thought she could live that far away from her parents. If so, once they returned, the two of them planned to join the church, marry, and move to Montana. If she didn't think she could live that far from home, they would still come back and join the church and marry, but figure out a way to make a living in Lancaster County.

But once Mamm fell ill, Noelle couldn't leave. That morning, she'd asked Jesse not to go, but he insisted he should. He believed because her mother had survived her stroke that everything would be all right. *"I need to do this for us,"* he said. *"I'm fine with you staying, but I need to go."*

When she'd yelled at him, *"Go then, just go!"* he'd turned away from her, puzzled, and did just that, promising he'd be back in a few weeks. When he didn't return and instead dated an Englisch girl, she was crushed. That wasn't the Jesse she knew, the one she'd given her heart to. He'd abandoned her.

For the first two years, memories of him stalked her. She willed them to stop, even begged God to take them away, but they wouldn't leave her. Finally, as Mamm grew worse, the memories became less vivid. And then when Mamm died, Noelle felt doubly abandoned.

And now, with Jesse's return, she couldn't deny that the hollow, unsettled feeling she'd fought for so long to banish was growing stronger again.

As she turned away from the dazzling sunlight reflecting on the snow, she remembered the Advent calendar from Holly and headed to her room. She opened the first little window with a star on it, in the top left-hand corner, popped out the piece of chocolate, and then read *Why? John 3:16.* She didn't know a lot of verses by memory, but she knew that one. She didn't need to look it up in the Bible Mamm and Dat had given her when she'd joined the church. *For God so loved the world, that he gave his only begotten Son . . .*

She slipped the chocolate into her mouth and then let it melt. Literally. A creamy warmth flowed through her. Holly was blessed with good ideas, an amazing talent, and the ability to sell. If only Noelle could say the same about herself.

Over the next three days, she accomplished all of her tasks, while caring for her father too. As she and Moriah packed the cardboard boxes on Wednesday evening, Noelle asked her niece if she'd go with her to the market.

"*Nee.*" Moriah placed the last apple pie in the box. "I have other plans."

Noelle bristled but then remembered it was nearing the one-year anniversary of Moriah's husband's death. Eugene had been herding cows across the highway when a truck came over the hill. The driver slammed on the brakes but still plowed into him. He'd died instantly.

Perhaps Moriah was thinking about him too because she said, "I feel so bad for Jesse, losing his wife."

Noelle didn't respond. She felt badly too, but her emotions still churned. She didn't trust herself to say anything.

Moriah's eyes glistened. "When Eugene died, Jesse sent me

a sympathy card. He would have been married by then, but he didn't say anything about that, just how sorry he was for my loss."

That sounded like Jesse—at least the man she once knew.

Moriah brushed at her eyes. "Did I tell you I found out when his wife died?"

Noelle shook her head as her chest tightened. Jesse had been married. They had a baby. His wife had died. She could hardly comprehend it all.

"Right after giving birth."

Noelle gasped.

Moriah nodded. "Isn't that awful? Jesse lost his wife and became a single dad all in one day."

Noelle struggled to catch her breath.

"You're not still mad at him, are you? Not after everything he's gone through."

Forgive and forget was what Noelle had been taught her entire life. But, despite the pain he'd gone through, she hadn't forgotten what Jesse had done to her. And what was even more surprising was that he, because his mother had left him, had asked her several times if she was serious about her love for him, trying to confirm she would never leave him, never reject him.

Then he'd left her. And rejected her too.

Before she could figure out how to answer Moriah's question about being mad at Jesse without revealing her own pain, the front door swung open and Salome stepped into the living room. She peeled off her bonnet and shook the snow from it, revealing her gray hair under her Kapp. She called out a hello to Dat as she slipped off her coat.

She waved at Noelle and Moriah. Then she marched, her hips swaying, over to Dat's side. "My chiropractor said it would do my back good to walk a little, so I decided to come over and see you."

He smiled up at her, his faded hazel eyes heavy. He'd been twenty-nine when Salome had been born and fifty-five when Noelle came along. Now, at seventy-seven, he was all tuckered out after a lifetime of farming. Of course, grief had worn him down too. He'd been lost since Mamm had her stroke and even more so since she'd died. "Sis," Dat said. Salome was the only one he called that. Probably because she was the oldest. "How are plans coming for our Family Christmas?"

Noelle turned toward the living room, not wanting to miss a single word.

"Do you think you feel up to it?" Salome asked. "Wouldn't you rather have a quiet Christmas with just us?"

"Why?" Concern filled Dat's voice. "Do the other girls not want to gather together?"

"Oh, I don't know about that," Salome said. "I just thought it might be too much for you."

Noelle glanced at Moriah, but her niece just shrugged. What was Salome up to? First her reason was that her back was bad, but now she was insinuating Dat wasn't up to Family Christmas.

"Besides," Salome said, "maybe it's time for each family to start doing their own thing. Of course, you'll come to my house for Christmas, so there's no need to worry about that."

Noelle bristled. Where would she go?

"No," Dat said. "We do not want to stop having Family Christmas. Especially not this year."

"Well, we may have to." Salome's voice grew louder, as if Dat might not be hearing her clearly. "We don't have a place big enough anymore."

"The shed," Dat responded.

"But it's so cold. And, honestly, we've grown by twenty or so between marriages and new babies this year. There are over a hundred of us now. We'd be crowded in there."

Noelle knew that was false. They held church in the shed once a year. And they'd had last year's Family Christmas there.

Dat said as much.

"That's true," Salome replied. "But we're too big to sit around a circle like we've always done." She patted Dat's hand.

"Then find a bigger place." Dat pulled his arm away.

"Like where?" Salome asked. "And on Christmas Day? Who's going to have a place we can use?"

Noelle couldn't stay quiet any longer. "We'll figure out something."

Salome pursed her lips together, turned toward Noelle, and then said, "Let me know when you do."

CHAPTER THREE

*T*he weather had warmed on Wednesday night, turning the snow to rain. All of the world seemed to be dripping and melting and colorless as Noelle rode with Pamela to the market on Thursday morning. She turned her face toward the window, as if she were entranced with the dreary scene. She wasn't. In reality, she was trying to calm her nerves about working at the market again.

It didn't help that Holly's booth was empty when she arrived and remained that way until long after the market had opened. Seeing her was the only thing Noelle had been looking forward to.

But someone else was present. *Jesse.* He wore a forest-green shirt with his black pants, suspenders, and a pair of work boots. Noelle guessed Barbara was watching the baby. He worked all alone in the furniture booth, kitty-corner from Noelle and behind Holly, selling rocking chairs, hope chests, and bookcases. Why couldn't he be on the other side of the market, if he had to be around at all?

Several times Jesse tried to catch Noelle's eye, but each time she shifted her gaze. There wasn't anything more she wanted to talk with him about. In fact, she wished—with all of her heart—that he would go away.

But neither of them had much business, so when he strode over to her booth she couldn't ignore him.

He spoke softly and kept a good amount of distance between the two of them, which she appreciated. "Look," he said. "I just wanted to say hello. And to say how sorry I was when I heard about your Mamm. I should have said that when I first saw you again and at least by the second time. She was a wonderful person—and I know how important she was to you."

Noelle swallowed hard, trying to dislodge the lump in her throat. Finally she managed to say, "Denki. I heard about your wife. I'm really sorry for you and your baby."

For a moment it appeared he might cry, but then he managed to smile a little. "I appreciate your kindness."

Noelle tried to breathe, but the air felt thick and heavy, and it filled her throat.

"I know our conversation didn't go well on Sunday, but I'm hoping we can—"

"That's not a good idea."

"What's not a good idea?"

Noelle turned. Holly stood in the middle of the aisle, a plastic crate in her hand.

"Nothing," Noelle muttered.

Holly introduced herself to Jesse. He greeted her and then returned to his booth.

"At least you two are talking, right? That's a step in the right direction." Holly's eyes lit up.

Noelle ignored the comment. She knew Holly was joking—and that she had no idea how much it hurt. "I was afraid you weren't coming."

"We had to stop by the college so I could turn in my final paper."

"College?"

"Lancaster Community College," she said. "I'm on the slow track. I only take two classes a term. Next week is finals, but my big paper was due today." She jerked her head toward her brother, who had just shown up, carrying two more crates. "Carlos didn't have any big papers due this term, which isn't fair. Right?"

Noelle nodded in agreement, even though she wasn't sure if it was fair or not. Because she had no one stopping by her booth, Noelle offered to help. Holly gave her the four purple candles, white candle, and wreath to set up. Noelle did so, carefully placing the wreath on the counter and then inserting the candles into the holders. She took a step backward. The purple candles were so rich, and the white such a stark contrast.

Noelle asked Holly if she had any more Advent calendars.

"No, silly," Holly answered as she switched the light on one of the purple candles. "No one wants those after the first Sunday of Advent. We only sell those in November."

"Oh," Noelle said. "I'm enjoying mine."

"Oh yeah? What's the verse for the day?"

"Isaiah 7:14. 'Therefore the Lord himself shall give you a sign . . .'" She couldn't remember the rest.

But Holly did. "'Behold, a virgin shall conceive, and bear a son, and shall call his name Immanuel.'" She grinned again. "How do you like the chocolate?"

"It's delicious. Did you make it?"

Holly shook her head. "My mother does the Advent calendars. She made them before she left."

"Where'd she go?"

"To be with our grandmother."

"Oh." Noelle paused but then asked, "Is she coming back? For your birthday? For Christmas?"

Holly shrugged and glanced at Carlos.

"We'll see," he said, his voice deeper than usual.

Noelle wasn't sure if she should ask any more questions, so she didn't, but she wondered about the rest of Holly's family. Where was her father? Did she have other siblings? Aunts and uncles? Cousins?

Salome had said one time that there were more Hispanic people in Lancaster County than Amish people, and that their population had grown rapidly in the last ten years. Noelle had the feeling Salome viewed it in a negative way, but at least she hadn't been overt about her opinion, for once.

Hopefully Holly had more family around than just Carlos.

In the afternoon, Noelle's nephew Paul and his wife, Lu-Anne, stopped by the booth, taking Noelle by surprise.

"We're Christmas shopping." Paul was large like his Dat. "Moriah's watching the kids so we can shop. We're going in with Moriah to buy a clock for the folks."

Paul had always loved shopping for Christmas, even though the Amish didn't give much. A clock for Salome and Ted was a big item.

"We're also looking for little gifts for Family Christmas," Paul said.

"Your Mamm didn't tell you she doesn't want to have it this year?"

Paul's voice boomed. "What?"

Noelle's face grew warm. "Jah," she said. "She thinks each family should just do their own celebration." Noelle didn't have the heart to list all of Salome's reasons.

"But what about you and Dawdi?" Paul's voice had increased in volume.

Noelle shrugged. She was too embarrassed to say that Salome had invited Dat for Christmas but not her. Instead, she explained Salome didn't feel any of their houses were big enough.

"We can have it at our house." He turned toward his wife. "Right?"

"Except my family is coming for second Christmas. That would be a lot to host two big gatherings back-to-back." She gazed up at him. "How about next year . . . ? Although there will probably be ten new in-laws and as many babies."

Noelle kept herself from dropping her eyes to LuAnne's belly. Was she pregnant again?

"Is it really the lack of a building?" Paul asked. "Or does Mamm just not want to do it?"

"The former, according to what she said. She told me if I came up with a building to let her know."

"I'll ask about the school." LuAnne seemed happy to help.

Paul stopped listening. He'd spotted Jesse. "Hey, what's he doing here?" Before Noelle could answer, her nephew was striding toward Jesse, his hand extended. They shook hands, slapping each other on the back as they did. Everyone loved Jesse.

LuAnne leaned toward Noelle. "Are you doing okay?"

Noelle nodded.

"It's not too awkward having Jesse around?"

They'd all seen her suffer when he left, but she wasn't going to admit to anyone how hard it was to have him back. Only to herself.

LuAnne was as easily distracted as Paul. She spotted Holly's chocolates and scurried across the aisle. After a minute, she turned toward Noelle, holding up a small box. "Look at these mini sleighs. Aren't they cute?"

Noelle nodded. She'd noticed the Englisch seemed to like to buy small things, too, as she observed them in the market. Small squares of soap instead of bars. Small candles. Small greeting cards. Small jars of jam. Even small quilts.

The appeal was a mystery to her. But LuAnne seemed to share it.

Noelle turned her attention to her pies and pans of sticky buns. Maybe her servings were too big.

A few minutes later, a woman stopped to browse at Noelle's booth, carrying a small candle in a tin. Noelle worked up her nerve and asked the woman why she chose it.

She held it up. "It's just so cute, don't you think?"

Cute. Noelle nodded. "But it's not very practical."

The woman laughed. "It makes me happy—that's what matters."

"*Ach*," Noelle said. "I see." But the truth was, she didn't. Not at all.

Holly insisted that Carlos give Noelle a ride home, so she called Pamela in the early afternoon and left a message on the woman's phone. By the time the market closed, marked again by the ringing of the bells, Holly was practically out of her chocolates.

"I'm going to have to go home and make more," she said as she packed the few boxes that were left.

Last year during the Christmas Market, Noelle baked more each day for Salome to sell. Obviously, she wasn't selling nearly as much this year though. She sighed at the thought of letting her family down.

"What's the matter?" Holly asked as she unwound her hair from her bun.

"Just a little tired is all." Noelle placed more product into a crate.

Jesse pushed a cart by, loaded with three bookcases. Noelle ducked her head so she didn't have to say hello.

"What is going on with you two?" Holly crossed the aisle and stepped into the booth.

"Nothing," Noelle whispered.

"Oh, I get it." Holly had her hands on her hips and spoke loudly. "It's a taboo topic, right?"

Noelle nodded.

"Which means you two used to—what do you call it? Court?"

Noelle nodded again.

Holly dropped her voice to a whisper. "I can't blame you. He's gorgeous."

Noelle's face grew warm.

"Okay, okay, I'll knock it off. I know I can be incorrigible. Carlos tells me so all the time." Holly's brown eyes danced. "Give me a box. I'll help you pack."

Instead of dropping her off at the Dawdi Haus, Noelle asked Carlos to take her to the new house.

"How many houses are on this property?" he asked.

"Just the three," Noelle answered.

Holly's voice wavered uncharacteristically. "Do you realize how lucky you are? To live right next to family?"

Noelle hadn't given it much thought. Every Amish person she knew lived near family. "I don't live close to all of my relatives," she said. "I live with my Dat. Salome and her husband and their daughter live in the Dawdi Haus, while my nephew Paul and LuAnne and their kids live in the big house. My other seven sisters and their families are scattered all over the county, and a couple live in Chester County."

Holly whistled. "There are nine girls in your family?"

"Jah," Noelle answered.

"How many brothers do you have?"

"No brothers."

Holly jabbed Carlos. "Lucky." By her voice, Noelle could tell she was teasing.

"Do the two of you have other siblings?" Noelle asked.

Carlos shook his head. "It's just us." He jabbed Holly back. "Although I prayed she'd be a brother."

"You prayed that when you were two years old? I don't think so." She laughed. "But nice try."

Holly and Carlos helped Noelle carry her boxes again. After they'd put everything down in the entryway, Holly pulled a white box of mini chocolates from her coat pocket and gave it to Noelle, who, in return, gave her a cherry pie.

"Thanks!" Holly gave her a quick hug, and Noelle forced herself to hug her back. She wasn't used to hugging anyone. Not even her parents.

"Noelle, is that you?" Dat came padding down the hall.

"Jah, Dat. And my friends, Holly and Carlos. They gave me a ride."

Dat leaned on his cane as he reached the three of them and then shook Carlos's hand. "Nice to meet you," Dat said. But he didn't thank them for their help.

"See you tomorrow!" Holly said as she headed to the door. "And count on us giving you a ride home again."

"Thank you," Noelle said.

After the two had left but before Noelle could even take off her coat, Dat asked exactly who Holly and Carlos were.

"They have a booth at the market. Well, Holly does. Carlos drops her off and picks her up. Salome knows them."

"But why are they giving you a ride home?"

"They offered," Noelle said. "It saves us money."

"What do you know about them?"

Noelle exhaled. What was Dat getting at? "They live here in Lancaster County. They both go to the community college. Their mother went to help their grandmother."

"So they're unsupervised?"

"They're living on their own." Noelle frowned. "Oh, and they go to a Mennonite church."

Dat harrumphed. "A liberal one, if they go at all."

"Why would they lie about that?"

Dat shuffled toward his chair. "Maybe they want to win your trust."

She wasn't used to challenging Dat, not like some of her sisters had through the years. Instead of saying anything more, even though she longed to, she washed her hands and focused on their supper. She heated up the stew from the night before even though Dat hated leftovers. She couldn't work all day at the market and fix supper too. He'd have to make do.

He didn't complain, but he didn't thank her either. In fact, he didn't speak at all through the entire meal.

After she'd cleaned up the dishes, she opened up the box of chocolates from Holly. They were miniature candles. Noelle offered one to Dat. He popped it in his mouth and then said, "How about another one?"

She smiled, took one for herself, and gave him the box.

The chocolate was good—even better than the Advent calendar chocolates. There were nine in the box, and Holly sold them for six dollars. Noelle couldn't imagine that the ingredients cost much or that making the chocolates took too much time. Jah, the boxes and packaging cost something, but Holly was making good money, especially considering how many she sold.

LuAnne had bought two boxes of chocolates, which was a

significant amount of money for her. If a frugal Amish house-wife would spend twelve dollars on mini chocolates, what would an Englisch woman spend on . . .

Noelle didn't need to do any baking that night, but she would anyway. She had an idea she couldn't ignore.

CHAPTER FOUR

*N*oelle arrived bleary-eyed at the market the next morning. She led the way, carrying a cardboard box, while Pamela trailed behind with more on the dolly. As Noelle turned down the aisle toward her booth, she heard Jesse's laugh before she saw him.

Then Holly's.

She groaned.

The two were at Holly's booth, chatting away.

Once Noelle had all of the product in the booth, she started pulling out the boxes of mini whoopie pies she'd made the night before. Jesse, without saying anything to her, returned to his booth.

But Holly craned her neck and then scurried across the aisle. "What in the world?"

Noelle held up one of the boxes. She'd packed a dozen in a box, visible through the clear lid, and then tied a red ribbon around it.

"Those are so cute," Holly gushed. "What a great idea."

"I got it from you," Noelle admitted.

Holly cocked her head questioningly.

"From your mini chocolates." She lowered her voice. "The ones Englischers are happy to pay top dollar for."

Holly threw back her head and laughed. "Glad my marketing is helping yours."

"Well, we'll have to see how I do."

The bells rang and soon the first of the customers started coming through. Within the first half hour, Noelle had sold three of the boxes of the mini whoopie pies. Soon after that, Steve, the manager, came by. "I thought you might be the purveyor of those little wonders." He nodded toward the whoopie pies as he reached for his wallet.

"I'll give you a box of them," Noelle said.

"Oh no you won't." He pulled out a bill. "If Salome found out, she'd be after me. You giving me that pie was more than you should have." He handed her a ten. "Keep the change."

"Denki," Noelle said. She was selling the mini whoopie pie boxes for eight dollars each, which seemed absurd. If they didn't all sell, she'd lower the price tomorrow.

"I have to say . . ." Steve held the box close. "That apple pie you gave me was delicious. My wife said to tell you thank you."

"I'm glad she liked it."

He held up the mini whoopie pies. "My girls are going to love these too."

Noelle smiled as he continued walking by. He seemed like a nice man, and as if he'd be a good father. And husband.

By noon she'd sold all of the boxes of whoopie pies. After that she sold a few more pies and batches of sticky buns but not much. At quitting time, she counted her money. She'd definitely had her best day yet. She'd go home and make more of the whoopie pies—and maybe some other "mini" items too.

When Holly and Carlos dropped her off, she simply said she could carry the boxes. Perhaps Dat's behavior from the night before had been obvious because Holly stayed in the truck while Carlos helped her carry her boxes, but he left them outside the door. She thanked him and then began moving them inside one at a time.

Dat slept in his chair, his white hair and beard both tousled. She stared at him for a long moment. She knew that men often declined in health after their wives died. Was that happening with Dat? It seemed he was sleeping more and eating less. Except for the chocolate the night before, he hadn't had much of an appetite.

She took off her coat and heated supper before waking him.

"Dat," she said, "time to eat." He stirred but didn't open his eyes. She put a hand on his shoulder. He still didn't open his eyes.

She stared at his chest as she yelled, "Dat!" Again he stirred and his chest rose and fell, just a little. He wasn't dead. But she couldn't wake him either.

She dashed to the front door, grabbed her coat, stepped into her boots, and then rushed out the door, wishing Carlos and Holly were still outside. But of course they weren't. Should she go to Salome's? Or the phone shed? The shed was closer, so she chose it.

She'd never called 9-1-1 before, but Dat had called it for Mamm when she'd had her first stroke. After Noelle dialed and the dispatcher answered, she quickly told the woman on the line what was wrong and what their address was. The dispatcher said an ambulance would be there as soon as possible.

When Noelle hung up, she knew it was likely that summoning EMTs meant Dat would have to go to the hospital, a place to which she'd never wanted to return. She inhaled sharply as she continued on to Salome's. When she arrived, she burst through the front door and quickly explained what happened and that the EMTs were on their way.

"He was fine earlier today," Salome said. "I'll grab the smelling salts. Hopefully he'll revive before they arrive."

Without answering her sister, Noelle hurried back out the door, stumbling as she rushed toward the lane. She caught herself before she fell and continued on in the ruts of refrozen snow along the edge of the lane.

As she reached the new house, red lights fell over the snow, coming from the opposite direction. She left the door open for the EMTs as she rushed into the house. "Dat!" she called out.

Once more he stirred and tried to open his eyes but nothing happened. She hadn't realized her sister was right behind her until Salome said, "Why didn't you close the door? Were you born in a barn?"

"I left it open for the EMTs."

"They might be Englischers, but I'm pretty sure they know how to open a door." Salome's usual cynical humor seemed to Noelle to be rather inappropriate, considering what bad shape Dat was in.

Salome held the smelling salts up to Dat's nose. He jerked away and then opened his eyes as two EMTs came through the door, quickly introducing themselves.

"I'm Jeff," the older one said.

"And I'm Brent," the younger one added. "Tell us about the patient and what's going on," he said as they gathered around Dat and placed their bags on the floor.

Salome held up the smelling salts. "These did the trick."

"How about if we check him out?" Brent asked. "Take his blood pressure. Pulse. That sort of thing."

Noelle nodded.

Jeff knelt down by Dat's chair. "Sir, how are you feeling?"

"Poorly," Dat said. "Been tired all day, and I fell earlier."

"Was anyone with you when that happened?"

Dat shook his head.

Noelle's face grew warm. She shouldn't have left him alone.

Jeff glanced from Salome to Noelle. "Do both of you live here?"

Salome shook her head. "Just my sister. I live down the lane."

"I was working at the Christmas Market all day. I just got home." Noelle's voice shook as she spoke. "I thought Dat was just sleeping in his chair, but when I tried to wake him I couldn't."

Brent took a blood pressure cuff out of his bag while Jeff explained to Dat what they were going to do. After Brent took Dat's blood pressure, he said it was ninety over sixty. "That's low and could explain why you fell. And perhaps why your daughter couldn't wake you."

Brent moved his hand down to Dat's wrist to check his pulse. "Did you hit your head?"

"I do not believe so."

Brent dropped his hand from Dat's wrist and turned to Jeff. "I'm concerned about this irregular heartbeat." He turned back to Dat. "Do you mind if I check for a bump from when you fell?"

"Of course not," Dat answered.

Brent examined Dat's head and then said, "You have a goose egg on the back of your head. We should take you into the hospital and have a doctor examine you."

"I don't think that's necessary," Dat said.

"It is." Noelle touched his arm. "We need to find out what's wrong."

Salome stepped back and brushed her hands together. "You'll need to go with him."

The thought of going with Dat alone worried Noelle. "What about talking with the doctors?"

"You'll manage just fine," Salome said.

"How will we get home?"

Salome shrugged. "Call Pamela, although it might be the middle of the night."

Noelle stepped back beside Salome. "What if Pamela can't get us?"

"I suppose you can take a taxi, but it will be expensive."

Noelle still had the cash from the market in her purse. She'd use that. "What about the market tomorrow? Do you feel up to doing it?"

"Not with my back the way it is."

"What about Moriah?"

Salome shook her head. "She's in no shape to do it either . . ." Her voice trailed off.

"Can you call someone else in the family and see if they can take over for one day?"

Salome wrinkled her nose. "No one else has been involved in the business for years. We can't expect someone to take over just like that. I'll call Steve and tell him our booth will be empty."

Noelle's eyes burned. Salome was right. It wasn't as if any of their sisters or nieces lived in their district or knew anything about the business. She didn't want to lose a day of sales, but she didn't know what else to do. "All right." She headed for the coatrack and grabbed both Dat's coat and hers.

Jeff had left the house but now returned with a gurney. Noelle held the door open for him.

As Salome approached, she sighed and muttered, "I'm sure he can walk."

Noelle didn't respond, but she did grab Dat's cane, grateful for the reminder. He'd need it once he was discharged.

Dat had no signs of a brain injury, so the emergency doctor didn't order a CT scan, but he did order an EKG because Dat's heartbeat was irregular. When the doctor came in again, he said the EKG showed Dat's heart was enlarged. "And you have fluid in your lungs too," he said. "You need to see a cardiologist." He gave Dat a piece of paper with a name and a number on it. "Call on Monday," he said. "And get in as soon as possible."

"Can I go home tonight?" Dat asked.

"We'll see how you do in the next few hours," the doctor replied.

It turned out he was also dehydrated, so the nurse hooked up an IV and also gave Dat a large glass of water with a lid on it. When asked if he was hungry, Dat said he'd eat if it meant he could go home. The nurse laughed and brought him a tray with a bowl of soup, a small salad, and a slice of bread. Thankfully, he ate.

He appeared so vulnerable in the hospital gown. His belly was still round, but his arms and legs were thin. He looked downright fragile. Why hadn't she noticed?

Could his heart be failing him? Had it broken, literally, when Mamm died?

It wasn't until one in the morning that the nurse came in and said the doctor cleared Dat to go home. As the nurse removed the various cords and sensors from Dat, she said to Noelle, "You're a good daughter. You've done a good job caring for your father tonight."

A lump filled Noelle's throat, so she simply smiled at the woman.

The nurse smiled back. "You'll soon be on your way."

"May I use a phone to call a taxi?" Noelle asked.

"Certainly." She nodded toward the door. "But there's a couple of people out here who say they'd like to give you a ride." She pulled back the curtain, revealing Holly and Carlos.

Noelle gasped. "What are you doing here?"

Carlos called out, "Hello, Mr. Schrock."

And then Holly answered Noelle's question. "Steve called me after Salome phoned him. He thought I'd want to know," Holly said. "We've been out in the waiting room."

"All this time?"

She shook her head. "Just for the last couple of hours, after we got our chocolate boxed up. We figured it might take a while here."

"I'll go warm up the truck," Carlos said. "And come around to the exit."

Noelle thanked him. After the nurse gave Noelle a stack of paperwork, got Dat's coat on him, and transferred him to a wheelchair, they all started toward the hall. Holly grabbed Dat's cane from Noelle and walked with it, leaning against it dramatically.

Noelle couldn't help but smile. For being "twins" they were as different as could be.

Dat dozed on the way home, in the passenger seat, as Carlos drove and Holly and Noelle sat in the back seat. Big fluffy snow-flakes began to fall, melting as soon as they hit the windshield.

"You two will be so tired tomorrow," Noelle said.

"You too."

Noelle shook her head. "I'm not going. I'm staying home with Dat."

"So Salome's going?"

"No. Our booth will be empty."

"But it's going to be busy tomorrow. I hate to have you miss out on the big bucks." Holly scrunched her nose. "Give me a crate of your product. I'll sell what I can."

"I didn't get a chance to make more of the whoopie pies."

"Of course not. But give me pies. I'll sell those."

As Noelle thanked her, tears stung her eyes. Holly and Carlos had both been good friends to her. Sharing the Advent calendar. Giving her rides home from the market. Helping with ideas for how to sell more product. Sticking around the hospital until the early morning hours to give her and Dat a ride. Being willing to sell pies for her. She turned her head toward the fields, embarrassed by her emotions.

When they reached the house, Carlos held firmly on to one of Dat's arms while Noelle held on to the other. The first layer of snow was slick, and Noelle held her breath as they propelled Dat to the house. Holly went ahead and opened the door, which Noelle had forgotten to lock.

All three of them got Dat down to his room. He insisted he could change into his pajamas by himself, but Carlos waited at the door in case he got light-headed.

Noelle hurried to the kitchen and filled a box with pies from the refrigerator. "Ten dollars each," she said.

Holly shook her head. "Fifteen. You're not charging enough. I know how long it takes to make one of these things."

Noelle shook her head. "It doesn't take that long."

Holly laughed. "Not for you, but for a normal person it would. You have to think about what you're saving people—not what you put into it."

Noelle had never thought of setting prices that way before.

Carlos came down the hall and said Dat was in bed. Noelle thanked both of her friends and walked them to the front door, thanking Holly again for taking the pies. She was still flabbergasted at their care and generosity. She would expect it from someone in the family, which hadn't happened tonight, but not from near strangers. Except Holly and Carlos didn't feel like strangers.

By the time she checked on Dat, he was asleep. She sat down at the end of his bed and stared at him by the light of his battery-operated lamp. It was much safer for an elderly person than a kerosene one.

What would happen to her if something happened to him? There was no room for her to live with Salome and Ted, especially not with Moriah living there. Paul and LuAnne would let her live with them, but she didn't want that. It would be out of the question for her to stay in the new house. Salome and Ted would rent it out.

Noelle had been so brokenhearted when her Mamm had died that she hadn't even considered that Dat might too. Jah, she knew he'd die someday. But hopefully later rather than sooner.

Why couldn't Salome understand how important it was to have Family Christmas this year? Jah, Mamm had passed on, but Dat still needed all of them. And so did she.

CHAPTER FIVE

everal times during the short night, Noelle checked on Dat, shining her flashlight over him to make sure he was breathing. He was. Finally, at a quarter after seven, the first light seeped through her window, and she arose to another snowy landscape. On most days she would have already been up for a couple of hours with a fire roaring in the woodstove. Instead, a chill hung throughout the house.

After she'd checked on Dat—who was still sleeping peacefully—she stoked the fire. Then she opened her Advent window from the day before and popped the candy in her mouth. If it were up to her, the chocolate would be her breakfast, but hopefully Dat would feel like eating. She read the reference for the verse. Psalm 5:11. She looked it up in her Bible. *But let all those that put their trust in thee rejoice: let them ever shout for joy, because thou defendest them: let them also that love thy name be joyful in thee.*

Rejoice. Shout for joy. Love thy name. It had been a long time since she'd felt any of those things. With Dat's health scare, she was both rejoicing for his life—and fearful of the future. She said a short prayer, asking for God's healing for Dat.

She waited to start breakfast until Dat finally woke just before ten. He'd never slept that late. Dat didn't have much of an appetite either, and he only picked at his dippy eggs. After breakfast, he settled down in his chair. Noelle spent most of the rest of the day experimenting with making mini items. More whoopie pies—mint chocolate chip, peanut butter, marshmallow, and raspberry. Creamsticks. Half-moon pies—cherry, apple, and blackberry. And chocolate. Englischers seemed to like chocolate, more than Noelle had realized.

In the early afternoon, LuAnne stopped by with a chicken and broccoli casserole.

She called out a hello to Dat and then followed Noelle into the kitchen. "Moriah came over this morning and said you took Dawdi to the hospital last night."

Noelle nodded. "He's doing better. I need to make an appointment with a cardiologist though."

As LuAnne put the casserole on the counter, she asked, "Ooh, what all are you baking?"

Noelle explained that she was making smaller items to sell at the Christmas Market. She grabbed a plate and filled it with some mini whoopie pies, creamsticks, and moon pies. She wrapped a towel over the top and handed it to LuAnne.

"Denki. Paul will be thrilled. The kids too." She grinned. "And I already am." Then her expression grew more serious. "It's a great idea," she said. "I think they'll sell really well."

Noelle brushed her hands on her apron. "I hope so."

About an hour after LuAnne left, Salome stopped by. She hovered over Dat for a couple of minutes and was soon satisfied that he was doing better. She joined Noelle in the kitchen.

"LuAnne said you're making new products."

Noelle pointed to a box of peanut butter–filled whoopie pies. "Jah. Aren't they cute?"

Salome rolled her eyes.

"I sold these on Friday—twelve boxes were gone by noon. They were a big hit."

Salome put her hands into the pockets of her coat, which she hadn't bothered to take off. She must not be planning to stay long. "Sales have been down."

Noelle's face warmed. "I think I can get them back up by selling the new items."

Salome shook her head. "We've had a plan—Mamm's plan—and it's worked for years. Maybe it's your selling that has sales down, not the products."

Noelle was sure her face was bright red by now. She turned away from her sister and pulled another sheet of mini whoopie pie cookies from the oven.

"They look like those little French things," Salome said. "Macarons." She imitated a French accent. Noelle had no idea what she was talking about.

"Stick with what we do best," Salome insisted.

"Do you plan to go to the market next week?"

Salome shook her head. "My chiropractor told me to take another week off."

"What about Moriah?"

"She . . ." Salome wrinkled her nose. "Has plans."

"Someone needs to stay with Dat, then, while I'm at the market," Noelle said.

"Really?" Salome turned toward him.

"He's at risk for falling," Noelle explained. "He didn't eat or drink enough yesterday, and the ER doc told him to see a cardiologist."

"That sounds kind of serious." Salome raised her eyebrows. "Maybe he can go over to LuAnne and Paul's while you're at the market. That would be good for Dat—and the kids too."

Noelle pursed her lips to keep herself from saying anything, but she thought a full day over at LuAnne's would wear him out. "Or maybe you, Ted, and Moriah could take turns with Dat here."

Salome sighed. "I'll let you know."

Noelle heated the casserole for supper. As she pulled it out of the oven, a knock fell on the door, meaning it wasn't Salome or Moriah. They'd both walk right in.

She opened it to see Holly's smiling face, holding up a wad of money and an empty crate. "I sold all of your pies."

Noelle ushered her into the house. "Denki."

"And for fifteen dollars apiece."

Noelle took the money. "Wow." Holly *was* a good sales-person, just like Salome.

Holly held up a paper bag. "I also brought you something else. Smaller boxes for your mini whoopie pies. I figure you can sell a half dozen for ten dollars."

Noelle didn't think so, but she was interested in the boxes. She took the bag and pulled a box out. It was a fourth the size of the pie boxes.

"Is that your friend?" Dat called out.

"Jah, Dat. It's Holly."

"Invite her to eat with us."

Noelle glanced at Holly. "Would you?"

"Carlos is out in the truck."

Dat was standing now. "Ask him too."

Holly gave Noelle a questioning look.

"Jah, we'd really like that," Noelle said. "We have plenty."

Both Carlos and Holly yawned several times during sup-per, and Noelle thought again of them going to the hospital the night before and then working a full day at the market. After they ate the casserole, homemade bread, green beans, and applesauce, Noelle served blackberry half-moon pies.

Holly raved over hers. "You're selling these too. Right?"

Noelle shrugged. She hadn't necessarily planned to sell all of the mini items. She wasn't sure at all if she could stand up to Salome and branch out in a new direction. It wasn't as if she would be selling at the market for long. She'd soon be back to solely doing the baking, putting Salome back in charge.

Why was it so hard to stand up to her sister about both the market and the Family Christmas? Why was it so hard for Noelle to stand up to anyone? She'd been taught her entire life to defer to her older sisters, especially Salome. But it was more than that. She'd been cocooned in the safety of Mamm's shadow too, to the point she didn't know what to do when times grew hard.

She felt a wave of helplessness crash over her again, just as she had when Jesse left. When Mamm was sick and then dying. When she couldn't wake Dat.

As Holly and Carlos put their coats on, Dat spoke up from the table. "Do either of you know of a hall that might be available on Christmas? For our family gathering?"

Holly tapped the side of her face. "Have you tried local churches? I know ours does a dinner for the needy on Christmas, but others might be available."

"That's a good idea." Dat turned toward Noelle. "Could you look into that?"

She nodded.

"Oh, I almost forgot. Jesse said to tell you hello." She turned toward Dat. "And he wanted you to know that he's praying for you."

Dat nodded in gratitude. "I always liked that Jesse."

Holly gave Noelle a sly smile and whispered, "Will you ever tell me the story behind all of this?"

Carlos elbowed her.

Noelle patted her friend on the shoulder. "If I ever tell the story, you'll be the first to hear it."

After she'd closed the door behind her friends, Noelle stood for a moment. The truth was, however, that it was a story that ended long ago. There was nothing more to tell.

The next morning, Noelle climbed out of bed to find big fluffy flakes falling in the darkness, piling upon the snow that already covered the ground. Noelle expected to spend another quiet day with Dat, but he said he was feeling much better. After he led the two of them in the closing prayer after breakfast, he said, "How about if we visit Ben and Barbara this afternoon? He invited us last Sunday. They're having a group over for coffee in the early afternoon."

Noelle stood and grabbed their plates. What was Dat doing? Didn't he know she didn't want to see Jesse?

On the other hand, it would be good for Dat to get out of the house—as long as he really did feel up to it.

Dat stood and leaned against his cane. "Noelle? What do you think?"

"Let's see how you feel after dinner."

He seemed to have even more energy after they finished their noon meal, so Noelle bundled up to go out and harness the horse.

Dat stood at the window. "The plows have been by. We need to take the buggy, not the sleigh."

Noelle agreed.

An hour later, when they reached Ben and Barbara's house, Noelle stopped the carriage by the walk to the back door. Ben bounded outside, and Noelle expected him to help Dat up the walkway, but instead he said he'd take care of the horse for her. Grateful, Noelle took Dat's arm and they made their way to the back door. The cold stung her face as she walked, but she found it invigorating. Although she dreaded who she might find inside the house.

Barbara swung the door open and ushered them inside. Noelle quickly scanned the room. Jesse wasn't among the group that gathered.

Relieved, she relaxed a little. After a while, the men drifted into the living room while the women stayed in the kitchen, gathered around the table. Several asked how Salome was doing. Only Barbara knew about Dat's visit to the hospital because, it turned out, Jesse had told them. Noelle shared more about that with all of the women, even though she hated being the center of attention. But it was easier when she was talking about someone else.

A baby's cry interrupted the conversation.

"Oh, the baby's awake." Barbara jumped to her feet. "I'll be right back."

Noelle inhaled sharply. Maybe Jesse wasn't at the house, but his daughter was.

A few minutes later, Barbara returned with the baby in her arms. She headed straight for Noelle. "Would you hold Greta while I heat up a bottle?"

Noelle couldn't say no as Barbara rolled the baby into her arms. *Greta.* It was a beautiful name. Immediately Greta began to cry. Noelle had had so much practice with nieces and nephews that she knew exactly what to do. She stepped to the window and began swaying with the baby. Greta just needed to be distracted until she could eat.

Noelle lifted the baby to her shoulder, aware of Greta's weight against her chest. She felt as if her heart was being crushed and wondered what the other women thought. As she searched their faces, none of them seemed to be aware of the heaviness she felt. Had they all forgotten she and Jesse used to court? Did they assume that she was long over it?

Greta continued to cry, and Noelle patted the baby's back and swayed back and forth until the crying faded away. A few minutes later, Barbara strode across the room, just as the tea-kettle started to whistle. She handed Noelle the bottle and then nodded toward the rocking chair. "Would you?"

Noelle took the bottle and made her way to the chair, hold-ing on to the baby with the other hand. As she sat down, Greta started to cry again. Noelle quickly positioned the nipple into Greta's mouth, and the baby drank voraciously. As she calmed down, her eyes met Noelle's. The baby's were still an inky blue. Maybe they'd lighten up like her father's. Or perhaps her mother had brown eyes and they'd change to that. Greta smiled for a quick moment and then kept sucking.

"You're a natural."

Noelle lifted her head. A woman who was new to the dis-trict had spoken. Noelle simply smiled at her, but a look of confusion passed over Barbara's face as she stood at the stove, watching the scene unfold. Perhaps she hadn't given Noelle the baby on purpose.

Noelle's gaze fell back on Greta. What was it about a baby—any baby—that was so magnetizing? She leaned down and brushed her nose over the top of Greta's head. She smelled of baby shampoo and lotion. Noelle sat up straight again and leaned back against the chair, drawing the baby closer.

When Greta had finished eating, Noelle burped her and then settled her on her lap. The weight of the baby planted her firmly in the present. For the first time since she saw Jesse in the market, her thoughts weren't flitting to the past.

But then Noelle heard footsteps on the back porch. Jesse stepped into the kitchen, his hat in his hand, and froze when his gaze fell on Noelle and Greta.

CHAPTER SIX

When the baby saw Jesse, she giggled and then reached out to him.

"Just a minute, Boppli," he said and then retreated to the mudroom.

Greta began to fuss. As much as Noelle wanted to pass her off to someone else, she didn't want to make a scene. Instead, she began rocking again, which calmed Greta. But when Jesse reentered the kitchen, without his hat and coat, the baby began to cry.

Noelle stood, balancing the baby in her arms as she did, and nodded toward the rocking chair as she met Jesse's gaze. "She wants you."

Jesse smiled as he approached. "Denki for feeding her." He gently scooped the baby, along with her bottle, from Noelle. The sensation of his touch against her arms sent a shiver down Noelle's spine. She ducked her head, but then, as he settled down in the rocker with the baby, her gaze couldn't help but return to him.

He was a natural when it came to the little one. Noelle always knew Jesse King would be a good father.

As Noelle tried not to stare, a group of the men came into

the kitchen, ready to go. Their wives thanked Barbara, and then one by one, the group left.

Dat and Ben, however, stayed in the living room.

Greta was now "standing" on Jesse's lap, tugging on his lower lip. He'd laugh and then she'd giggle. Then she began pulling on his beard.

When Barbara slipped into the living room, Jesse turned the baby around and sat her down on his lap. He splayed his fingers out for her to play with. It was obvious he spent a lot of time with her.

Jesse met Noelle's gaze. "How's your Dat?"

She looked away. "Better." She could feel his eyes on her.

"I've been thinking a lot about our conversation last Sunday."

Noelle held her breath. If she didn't respond, would he stop talking?

Apparently not. "I really did hear you were done with me, that you didn't want me to come home."

"I never said that." Noelle raised her head. "Who would have told you that?"

"Actually," Jesse said as Barbara came back into the room, "Aenti did."

"What did I do?" Barbara stopped in the middle of the kitchen, a smile on her face.

Jesse sighed. "I'm putting you on the spot."

Barbara put her hand on her hip, a smile still on her face. "I don't mind."

"You told me Noelle was done with me," Jesse said, "when I was in Montana."

She nodded her head. "Jah, I did tell you that. Everyone knew it."

Everyone? Noelle's heart nearly stopped. She took a raggedy

breath and looked at Barbara. "Who told you that's what I'd said?"

Barbara tilted her head. "I'm not sure." She shrugged. "It was common knowledge, I think." She continued to the stove, grabbed the coffeepot, and then headed back into the living room.

Noelle struggled to breathe. This so-called common knowledge had ended Noelle's life as she'd known it and changed her future forever.

Jesse, his face pale, leaned toward her. "See?"

Noelle bristled. "If that's what you were told, why didn't you write?"

A pained expression passed over Jesse's face.

"Or call? You had to suspect that what your Aenti said could be gossip."

He shook his head. "I did write."

"I don't believe you," she said.

He shook his head a little. "Well, then it doesn't really matter, does it? You were so mad the last time I saw you before I left that I believed what I was told."

"My Mamm had just had a stroke, and you decided to go to Montana anyway. Of course I was mad."

"Jah, but you didn't do anything to make me think you *wanted* me to come back."

Noelle's head begin to spin. It all made sense now. She'd just assumed that the girls in Montana were a lot more fun than she was. And he used what Barbara had told him to justify going forward with his life—without Noelle.

She managed to stand, make her way into the living room, and quietly tell Dat they needed to go home. She couldn't spend another minute with Jesse King.

More snow fell Sunday night, and on Monday, after break-fast, Noelle had to shovel her way to the phone shed to call the cardiologist, a Dr. Chris Morrison. She was able to get an appointment for Dat the next Tuesday, so she called Pamela and arranged for a ride. Then she did the laundry in the old wringer washer they'd brought from the Dawdi Haus and hung it out on the line that ran on a pulley from the back porch to the pole in the yard.

When Dat settled down for a nap, Noelle headed toward Sa-lome's with the casserole pan for LuAnne and the money from the Christmas Market sales from the week before, including what Holly had given her. Salome did all of the bookkeeping and would need to make the deposits, then she'd pay Noelle her percentage from the business.

When Noelle arrived at the Dawdi Haus, her heart swelled a little. Would it always feel like home to her? It was where she'd grown up. Where Jesse had courted her. Where she'd nursed her own broken heart. There were so many memories wrapped up here.

Was the end of their relationship truly due to gossip going around their district? Something Barbara had heard and relayed to Jesse? Noelle felt ill at the thought.

She knocked again, and Salome finally answered the door but didn't invite Noelle inside, which seemed odd. Noelle handed her the envelope of money and then asked if she could speak to Moriah.

"She's not available," Salome said, which wasn't a phrase she normally used either.

"Would you ask her if she would help me bake tomorrow?"

Salome pursed her lips. "Are you going to follow Mamm's plan about the products?"

"Am I working at the market on Thursday?"

Salome nodded.

"I think, perhaps . . ." Noelle's voice was so low *she* could barely hear it. She cleared her throat. "I believe I will be selling some of the mini items again."

"The business will be ruined by the time my back is healed." Salome shook her head and then closed the door.

Stunned, Noelle headed toward the farmhouse. What was going on with Salome? She didn't want to celebrate Family Christmas. She wanted to be completely in charge of the baking business. She was ignoring Dat's condition. She'd practically just slammed her door in Noelle's face. And she was being secretive about something.

Tears threatened to flow as Noelle took a deep breath and pushed through the back gate of the farmhouse. She'd come the closest she ever had to standing up to Salome, only to be shut down. She traipsed through the snow up to the porch and knocked softly. Perhaps LuAnne was napping while the little ones did.

However, after a couple of minutes, she came to the door with her two-year-old, Willy, on her hip. Noelle followed her inside, thanking her for the casserole and putting the pan on the counter.

The farmhouse was over a century old with the original hardwood floors, molding, and fireplace. Ted and Salome had put in new kitchen cabinets and a new woodstove, which still barely kept the drafty place warm. The Dawdi Haus and now the new house were both much better insulated. But LuAnne loved the old house and Noelle loved that about her.

"I was wondering if you'd heard anything about using the school for Family Christmas?" Noelle asked.

"I asked when I dropped the kids off," LuAnne said. "It's already been claimed for Christmas Day by another family."

Noelle's heart fell. "Any other ideas?"

LuAnne shook her head. "You could call some of the nearby churches. Like the Mennonite one that's close by. Maybe they could help us out."

Noelle nodded, thinking of what Holly had suggested. She hated making phone calls, but she'd force herself to do it.

"I have another question to ask you." She explained about how Dat couldn't be left alone, at least not for long, and she needed to work at the market this week.

"I'll work it out with Salome and Moriah," LuAnne promised. "I'll take responsibility to make sure someone is with him."

Noelle thanked her. That was a big worry off her shoulders.

She stopped by the phone shed on the way back and pulled out the phone book, going through the Mennonite church listings. Finally she found the one closest to them. She took a deep breath and dialed the number, then managed to explain her request to the woman who answered.

"I'm sorry," the woman said. "Another family is having their gathering at the church that day."

Noelle thanked the woman and hung up the phone. She called the other two nearby churches and got the same answer.

She arrived at the market on Thursday morning with her boxes of mini whoopie pies, half-moon pies, and creamsticks, along with an assortment of regular-sized pies. Holly wasn't in her booth; instead, Carlos was setting everything up.

"Where's my twin?" Noelle asked, surprising herself with how light and cheery she sounded.

Carlos grinned. "She's taking her last final."

Noelle didn't know what else to say. She knew a "final" was an exam, but she had no idea how difficult it was or what it really meant.

"She's going to take the bus later."

Noelle wished she could just watch their booth so Carlos could pick Holly up, but she knew it would be hard to manage if it got busy. And hopefully it would.

At first it wasn't, and the morning dragged along. Carlos stepped back to Jesse's booth. The two must have joked about something because soon they were both laughing. The sound of Jesse's laughter was like a stab to her heart. She'd missed it.

On Sunday, on her way home from Ben and Barbara's with Dat, after the revealing conversation with Jesse, Noelle wondered if Jesse had been out courting someone that day. Once again, he'd find someone he'd have more fun with, someone more outgoing than she was. He'd probably had dinner at some girl's house or, if she was in a different district, attended church with her. He wouldn't stay single for long, which would be a blessing. The sooner he was married again, the better—for all of them.

It was almost noon by the time Holly showed up. First she *oohed* and *aahed* over Noelle's new products. And then she claimed to be good luck because business actually picked up.

One customer bought three boxes of Noelle's mini whoopie pies. Then a man bought ten of the half-moon pies, saying he was taking them back to his co-workers. He grinned. "They'll owe me big-time."

Another customer came specifically for a pie and asked Noelle if she could make five more for Christmas. Noelle said she could, as long as the woman could pick them up on Christmas Eve. Noelle wrote down the woman's order and then gave her the address of the new house. Then she smiled at the woman and said, "Merry Christmas!"

The woman smiled back and thanked her profusely.

Noelle wouldn't tell Salome about the special order. She'd only be critical of another new business idea.

"What was that about?" Holly asked from across the aisle.

"Pies for Christmas."

"Ooh, you're branching out."

Noelle gave her a sassy smile.

"And enjoying it. Your customer service has really improved, ya know?"

Noelle ducked her head at the compliment, but Holly was right. She'd made the new sale without a second thought. And she liked the customer. She was beginning to like all of the customers, to her surprise.

Jesse walked by her booth in the midafternoon. Noelle was afraid he might stop and talk with her, but he went across the aisle and started chatting with Carlos.

"Dude," Carlos said. "Have you still not sold anything?"

"You mean besides that hope chest that just got hauled out of here?" Jesse responded.

He'd made one for Noelle all those years ago. She turned her head away from the two, trying to stop the memory, and prayed for a customer.

"Maybe you should make something smaller—like Christmas ornaments," Carlos joked.

That actually wasn't a bad idea. Although it would be a waste of Jesse's skills to do that. She turned toward them. "How about little rocking chairs and chests? For kids?"

Jesse took a step backward while Holly turned toward her, even though she'd been talking to a customer. "Did you just say something? To Jesse?"

Noelle swallowed hard, trying to think of something witty to say. Nothing came, but thankfully Jesse found his voice. "That's a great idea. In fact, I just finished a rocking chair for Greta. I'll try to sell it and make her another one."

With Holly back in the booth, Carlos spent most of his time

hanging out with Jesse or running errands for Holly. Getting her food from the kitchen area. A glass of water. Bringing another plastic crate of chocolates from the truck.

By late afternoon, Noelle had sold almost all of the whoopie pies and half-moon pies and most of the creamsticks. She still had five more large pies to sell. When Steve walked by, she handed him a berry one.

"Yours are the best pies," he said in a whisper as he pulled a ten and a five from his wallet.

She shook her head. "Let me give it to you."

He grinned. "I insist on paying. My family is going to be ecstatic." He balanced the pie in one hand and turned his baseball cap around with the other. That seemed to be the sign that he was ready to close up the market for the day.

A half hour later, Noelle crated the remaining three pies, four boxes of creamsticks, and the two half-moon pies that were left. As she worked, Holly's phone rang. The girl pushed a button, held it up to her ear, and said, "Hi, Mama! How are you?"

Then she listened.

Then she started speaking in Spanish. Finally she said, in English, "I'll talk to Carlos. TTYS. Love you!"

A stab of jealousy speared Noelle's heart. If only she had her mother to talk to now. To tell her about Salome not wanting to do Family Christmas. To confide in her about Jesse coming back. To worry with her about Dat's possible health problems.

Shame filled her. It wasn't right to be jealous. But there had been so many times she had been. Jealous when Moriah married. Jealous of the girl who dated Jesse. Jealous of so many things. She'd been consumed with it.

Noelle's heart hurt. Was she going to be that person? One consumed with jealousy? With ill will for others?

Holly hadn't packed her candles yet. They still sat on the

counter—the four purple ones with the white one in the middle. Hope, joy, peace, faith. And Jesus.

Jealousy was the opposite of all of those.

LuAnne was true to her word and coordinated Dat's care. Paul went over in the mornings, and then after LuAnne had taken her older kids to school, she and the toddler and pre-schooler spent mornings with Dat. After she fixed his dinner and they'd all eaten, she made sure he was down for a nap and then took the little ones home for theirs.

Midafternoon, Ted came over and sat with Dat, staying until Noelle returned home from the market. She wasn't sure why Salome and Moriah weren't taking turns, but she didn't ask.

Thursday sales at the market were good, but Fridays and Saturdays were even better. And she had repeat customers coming back each day for more. Each day Noelle was nearly out of product and went home to bake more during the evening and late into the night. By Saturday, she was yawning. But it was all worth it when she handed the money over to Salome after Holly and Carlos dropped her off. This time her sister did invite her in.

"You're doing better," Salome said as she shuffled through the bills. It was as close to a compliment as she would get from her oldest sister. Noelle didn't respond.

"Is Moriah around?" she asked instead. "I'm hoping she can help with the baking on Wednesday."

Salome pursed her lips, and then a rustling down the hall caught Noelle's attention.

Moriah appeared in her robe.

"Are you ill?" Noelle asked.

"Jah," Moriah said. "I haven't felt well for a few days. If I'm feeling better on Wednesday, I'll come over."

Dat didn't feel up to going to church the next morning. Thankful that the appointment with the cardiologist was only two days away, Noelle tried not to worry about him. He had a cough that was new, and he seemed to be short of breath as he walked from the table to his chair. But at least he hadn't fallen anymore.

In the early afternoon, just before Noelle was ready to walk with Dat down the hall to his room, a knock fell on the door.

Noelle opened it to find Barbara, Ben, Jesse, and Greta on the stoop, bearing soup, bread, and peanut butter spread from church.

"We figured you could use a break, considering everything you're doing," Barbara said. Noelle, determined to be hospitable even though it was difficult seeing Jesse, invited them in, took their coats, and then started a pot of coffee as the men, along with Greta, gathered in the living room. Dat perked up at having visitors and insisted he didn't need a nap after all.

"I have pie," Noelle said to Barbara.

"Of course you do." The woman smiled. "The best pie in the county."

As Noelle cut into a blueberry one, Barbara said, "I feel so bad about last Sunday, when I realized I'd repeated gossip to Jesse. . . . After you left, we talked about it more, but I can't, for the life of me, remember who said it."

"Don't worry about it." Noelle took a stack of plates from the cupboard. "It was a long time ago."

"No. I feel awful," she said. "You two were perfect together. I felt so bad for Jesse when you called it off—or when I thought you called it off. I wanted to console him. . . ."

Noelle blinked as she scooted a piece of pie onto the first plate. She wished Barbara would stop talking. Perhaps she sensed Noelle's discomfort because she at least changed the topic. "I stopped by and saw Salome on Friday. It's a shame about her back."

Noelle nodded.

"I think probably the stress of caring for your Mamm finally caught up with her."

Noelle cocked her head.

"And, of course, the stress of Moriah's loss. And now that the one-year anniversary is here, I think they're all having a hard time."

Noelle agreed.

"Salome said how fortunate you are to be young. To have a strong back. To only have yourself to think of, instead of a family too."

Noelle froze. She had Dat to think of. True, there was only one of him, but it wasn't as if she was carefree.

"Salome didn't say this, but I gathered she's feeling the weight of your entire family on her shoulders. Your Mamm was so good at keeping everyone connected."

Noelle felt a wave of sympathy for Salome. Perhaps being the oldest sister was harder for Salome than Noelle realized.

Barbara jumped topics again. "I'll really miss that sweet baby if they go back to Montana."

Confused, Noelle froze, the coffeepot in midair. "What?"

"You didn't know?" The woman continued on before Noelle could respond. "Greta's grandparents in Montana are hoping he'll go back."

Noelle looked past Barbara at Jesse and the baby, who were sitting together on the sofa. While Dat and Ben talked, Jesse made funny faces at the little girl. Why did Noelle feel sad at the thought of Jesse leaving again? Wasn't that what she wanted?

On Monday evening, Noelle traipsed through the snow to Salome's house and asked if she wanted to go to the cardiologist appointment the next morning. Salome assured her she didn't. "You can handle this," she said. "My back still isn't doing well."

"Does that mean I'll be doing the market again?"

"Jah. It's just three more days."

Noelle turned to go but then stopped and faced her sister again. "We haven't found a place to have Family Christmas. How about if we just have it in the shed? We can get the church wagon benches and put them around in a big circle."

"The Beyers are using the benches for their gathering," Salome said. "Besides, if we did that, I'd end up doing all the work."

Noelle didn't bother to say that she'd do everything. Cook the turkeys and hams. Set up. Clean up. All of it, if she needed to. "Aren't our sisters and their families planning on getting together?"

Salome shook her head. "They've all left messages on my machine, and I've called everyone back to tell them we're not doing it."

Noelle's heart sank. "But what about Dat? He wants us to get together. He'll be disappointed."

Salome sighed. "I don't think he will. He told me he doesn't feel up to much these days. You're right—he's worse than I'd realized. I think it will be a relief for him too."

Flabbergasted, Noelle stuttered, "That's not what he's said."

"Nothing lasts forever. There are seasons in life and this one has ended." Salome crossed her arms. "You'd better go check with LuAnne about who's looking after Dat the next three days. I think Paul will be gone for most of Thursday. I'm not sure the same schedule will work."

Deflated, Noelle said, "I'll go talk to LuAnne." As she left

Salome's, she realized she was looking forward to working at the market on Thursday. She wanted to see if she could sell even more products than she had the week before. And she wanted to see Holly and Carlos. And, even though it was hard to admit it, there was a part of her that wanted to see Jesse too.

CHAPTER SEVEN

$\mathcal{T}$uesday morning, Pamela picked up Dat and Noelle for the cardiologist's appointment. The office was a block from the hospital in Lancaster. Again, Noelle felt anxious. After a long wait, Dat was finally called back to the exam room. Noelle held his arm as he shuffled along, his cane dragging along the carpet.

Dr. Morrison turned out to be a middle-aged woman with straight, shoulder-length gray hair. She chatted with Dat, putting him at ease, and then took his medical history. She then asked him about his family medical history.

Dat acknowledged that his father had died of a heart attack in his late sixties. "And all of his brothers died in their sixties or seventies, probably from heart problems," he said. "But I am not certain. They were spread all over Pennsylvania."

The doctor asked him to describe how far he could walk without getting winded, and he answered, "By the time I walk from my bed to my chair, I am ready to sit down."

The doctor listened to his lungs, commenting that there were signs of congestion. Then she listened to his heart. When she finished she said, "I'm picking up abnormal heart sounds that indicate heart failure. And your EKG from your hospital visit indicates an enlarged heart." The doctor smiled at him kindly. "Many people with heart failure have high blood pressure, which you don't presently have. We'll monitor that. But I will prescribe an angiotensin-converting enzyme inhibitor, which will help open up your narrowed blood vessels."

"I am not afraid to die," Dat said.

The doctor nodded. "I guessed that about you. But I don't want you to have any unnecessary discomfort or pain either." She looked from Dat to Noelle and back to Dat. "You have class IV congestive heart failure. You should do what you enjoy doing and spend as much time with loved ones as possible. Most people with this condition live a year or so after being diagnosed."

Noelle's hand flew to her chest. She *was* going to lose Dat too. Forcing her hand back to her lap, she exhaled. It wouldn't do any good for Dat to see her alarmed.

The doctor said to pick up the medication at the pharmacy attached to the clinic, and then that she wanted to see Dat again in a month. "Call me if you have any questions." She looked at Noelle. "Don't hesitate to call 9-1-1, like you did before, if your Dat worsens."

Dr. Morrison leaned toward Dat. "This is tough news. I know you're brave, but are you doing all right?"

He nodded. "I lost my wife three months ago. I would like to stay around longer for Noelle—she's my youngest daughter— but like I said, I am not afraid to die." His gaze met Noelle's. "And this should give me time to figure out things for her."

The doctor nodded at Dat. "I admire your fortitude." Then she smiled at Noelle. "And yours too."

Noelle wanted to protest about hers, but she wouldn't make things worse for Dat.

As they sat in the pharmacy waiting room, Dat, grasping

his cane, leaned toward her and said, "I'm going to spend the day at LuAnne's on Thursday. She came over while you were taking the wash off the line yesterday."

"Why didn't she talk to me?"

"I think she was afraid you wouldn't approve, but I am fine with it. I enjoy being around the children. You can have Pamela drop me off when she takes you, to spare me from walking over."

Noelle agreed.

He turned toward her, his pale eyes shining. "Let's not tell the others about my condition until after Christmas. I will call and tell them then." He smiled a little. "Let's have one last Family Christmas, our first with your Mamm gone and perhaps our last before I go, with no extra sadness or fussing over me."

Noelle inhaled and then swallowed hard, feeling as if she couldn't speak. She stared down at her snow boots as she exhaled. "Salome doesn't think we should have it this year."

"Well, we should." Dat tugged on his nearly white beard. "This is my family. I want us to be together."

"But we don't have anywhere to meet together. LuAnne and I both tried to figure something out and haven't been able to."

"Let's both ask the Lord to provide a place, then. And wait and see what happens."

Pray? Jah. But wait? Noelle wasn't sure if that was the best thing to do anymore. Perhaps she'd waited long enough for too many things already. But she had no idea what else she could do.

Wednesday morning, when it was obvious Moriah wasn't coming to help, Noelle walked over to Salome's again. This time it was not to try to solve the Family Christmas dilemma—jah, she was praying *and* trying to figure out what she could do—but to beg Moriah one more time to help her.

This time Ted answered the door. Moriah sat at the table, a mug in her hand. Thankfully she was dressed. That seemed to be a good sign.

Noelle stomped the snow from her boots and asked Moriah again for assistance. "I can't do this alone," she said.

Moriah stared for a moment.

"Are you doing anything else today?" Noelle asked.

Her niece shook her head.

"I think I can do really well with sales, if I have enough product. And I can't come home on Thursday and Friday and mix up enough to bake and then sell the next day. Mixing up the dough and fillings today will give me a good head start, so tomorrow all I will have to do is bake. I need help."

Moriah wrinkled her nose.

Ted nodded. "Noelle is right. She's bringing in the money, but we can't expect her to do it all by herself."

Noelle wasn't sure he'd defend her if Salome was in the room, but she was thankful for him speaking up. "And the truth is, I'm lonely baking by myself. It isn't nearly as enjoyable as it would be with you. I miss you." Working in the Kicha alone paled in comparison to baking with someone she loved.

Moriah sighed and then finally said, "I'll come over when I'm done with breakfast."

Noelle thanked her and left. She'd confess her jealousy to Moriah as soon as she arrived. It had been a long time coming.

Even though Noelle had been determined to speak with Moriah, she found herself full of fear. The kitchen was filled with the aroma of the first batch of half-moon pies already baking, the savory scent of the crusts mixing with the sweetness of the apples. As Noelle continued to try to work up her courage, Moriah said, "Thank you for insisting I come over today. I feel better working with you."

"What do you mean?"

"I've been—depressed. Much worse than after Eugene died even. This first-year anniversary has hit me really hard." Moriah dumped vanilla into the sugar and butter mixture in the bowl for the creamstick filling and then began to mix it with a wooden spoon.

Noelle's heart skipped a beat. Moriah had been under a lot of stress, but Noelle hadn't been empathetic. Not at all. She reached for her niece's hand and squeezed it. "I'm so sorry."

Moriah's eyes misted over. "Denki. I hope I can shake this."

Noelle wanted to say "You will," but she couldn't know. "Come over whenever you can. And I'll check in with you more."

As she rolled the dough for more half-moon pies, her grip tightened on the handles of the rolling pin that had been worn smooth by years of use by Mamm. Noelle cleared her throat. "I need to speak with you about something, to apologize."

Moriah gave her a questioning look.

Noelle put the rolling pin down and wiped her hands on her apron. "After Jesse left, when you and Eugene married, I was jealous. Really jealous. It wasn't that I wasn't happy for you. I was. But at the same time I was full of self-pity." Noelle met her niece's gaze. "I'm sorry."

Moriah nodded curtly. "I knew you were." She drug the back of her hand across her forehead. "And then, when Eugene died, were you happy? Relieved I wouldn't have a husband after all?"

Noelle gasped. "No. Of course not. Why would you think that?"

Moriah shrugged. "Because you were so jealous before."

Noelle feared she might dissolve into tears. "No wonder you've been so cold to me."

"Jah. At first I was just numb. But as the first anniversary approaches, it all hit me again. And I felt so disconnected from you."

Noelle had heard once that sin separates. She could see that. Her jealousy had put a wedge between her and Moriah. And that had led Moriah to believe that Noelle could actually find relief in Eugene's death. "I'm so sorry." Noelle grasped Mamm's old rolling pin again as she spoke, as if she could find strength in it. "I found no joy in Eugene dying. My jealousy was from my own grief." The thought made her ill. "Actually, from my own hurt pride that Jesse didn't come back and embarrassment that I wouldn't be marrying."

"But you didn't want him to come back."

Noelle's heart sank. "Barbara said she heard that too, but she couldn't remember who told her. But I know I didn't tell anyone that."

"Mamm told me. She said you were done with Jesse. She told me and a few other women."

"Like whom?"

"Well, Barbara . . . like you said." Moriah's face grew red. "Mamm said you were so mad at him you didn't care if he ever returned."

Noelle grasped the rolling pin again, bracing herself against the hollowness growing inside of her. "I don't remember saying that. . . . It's certainly not the way I felt." Had she said something similar? Something that Salome could have misconstrued? She had been mad at Jesse for leaving—especially when she felt she needed him most.

A wave of nausea swept through Noelle. To think Salome told others Noelle didn't care if Jesse ever returned—*before* he started dating the Englisch girl.

Noelle released the rolling pin and rubbed her hands on her apron. "I can't remember what exactly I said about Jesse, but when he left, even though we'd fought over him leaving at all, I expected he would come home. I still expected we'd marry. That I'd spend the rest of my life with him."

Moriah wiped her hands on her apron. "I'm so surprised to hear that. It's not what people were talking about, not at all."

It all made sense now. Noelle must have said something out of frustration, and Salome had misinterpreted it. She'd gossiped about what she didn't understand. What a horrible combination, like a bad batch of yeast that caused the dough to fall flat and useless instead of rise.

Another wave of nausea swept through her. "I'll be right back," she said to Moriah and then hurried down the hall to the bathroom. After locking the door behind her, she couldn't stop the tears as she sat on the edge of the tub. A sob shook her and then another.

Moriah knocked on the door. "Are you all right?"

"Jah," Noelle managed to gasp. "I'll be out in a minute." Nothing was as she thought it was. Jesse hadn't come back because *he* felt rejected, *not* because he'd rejected *her*. Not because he'd found someone who was more fun, more outgoing. But simply due to Salome's gossip. Another round of sobs shook her.

But she had to take responsibility too. She shouldn't have said anything to anyone, especially not Salome—she knew better. And she should have written Jesse a letter or, better yet, called him. She knew his wounds and his fears of being abandoned after his father died and his Mamm left.

She thought of him, alone in Montana. Feeling rejected. She couldn't help but ache for him, for that young man from three years ago. If only she could reach out to him and tell him so.

Finally she composed herself and washed her face.

When she returned to the kitchen, Moriah shot her a concerned look. Noelle ducked her head and, with a heavy heart, grasped the rolling pin again and went to work on the pie dough.

It was her careless words that had done Jesse harm. Now she needed to apologize to him too.

Thursday morning as Noelle rode with Pamela to the market, they passed a windmill with its blades spinning wildly. Although there was now only a dusting of snow on the ground, it was bitter cold outside. And windy. Noelle felt as icy on the inside as the weather was on the outside.

She'd all but given up on Family Christmas. Jah, she and Dat had prayed, and she'd been determined to do what she could to find something. But nothing had come from their prayers. Or from her hopes.

The Advent verse she'd read that morning was Psalm 29:11. *The Lord will give strength unto his people; the Lord will bless his people with peace.* She didn't feel peace about not having Family Christmas. Nor about Jesse. Could she feel joy if she felt no peace? Did she have enough faith that she'd be able to experience either?

When Noelle arrived at the market, Holly and Carlos helped carry in boxes while she wheeled the rest on the dolly. "Are you ready for a crazy day?" Holly asked.

"Jah." If only she could do well enough to convince Salome that her new ideas could succeed.

As Noelle unpacked and placed her baked goods on the shelves, she snuck a glance at Jesse's booth. But he wasn't there. The man she'd seen the first day she'd worked at the market, the carpenter who'd hired Jesse, was setting up the merchandise.

Noelle's heart lurched. Perhaps Jesse and Greta had returned to Montana already. Perhaps she'd missed her chance to apologize to him. If so, she'd need to write him a letter.

"Where's Jesse?" Holly asked.

Noelle shrugged.

"Why don't you go ask that guy?"

"Good idea." She grabbed an apple half-moon pie—there wasn't an Amish man in the world who wouldn't eat one in the morning with his coffee—and headed toward the carpenter.

"*Guder Mariye.*" She handed him the pie. "How are you doing?"

He grinned. "*Gut.*" Taking the pie, he added, "Denki."

"I'm a friend of Jesse's," Noelle said. "And thought I'd check up on him."

"Jah, well, someone needs to," the man teased as he unwrapped the pie.

Noelle didn't want to ask if Jesse had returned to Montana. She scrambled for a moment, not sure how to phrase her question. Finally she asked, "Is he ill?"

The man shook his head as he took a bite of the pie. Once he'd swallowed he said, "Delicious. I'll be coming by your booth before the day is over." The man took another bite.

All she wanted to know was why Jesse wasn't at the market. "Is everything all right?"

The man nodded and took another bite. When he swallowed again he said, "His little girl is sick. He's taking her to the doctor. He said she's been out of sorts the last few days, and he's worried because of some condition she has."

Noelle thanked the man for the information. No one had said anything about Greta having a "condition." She returned to her booth, told Holly what was up with Jesse, and then sold her mini selections and pies for the next nine hours. Thankfully Carlos returned to the market midmorning and relieved

Holly and Noelle, so they could take a couple of breaks and eat their lunches.

At quitting time, Noelle only had a couple of regular-sized pies left and a few boxes of creamsticks. All of the whoopie pies had sold, along with the half-moon pies. When Steve walked by, she offered him a whole pie again, saying, "I've had a really good day. I'd like you to take it."

"Denki," he said, a smile on his face. He took the box and then asked about placing an order with her. "My wife was going to make pies for Christmas Day, but then she asked if we could buy them from you. She says yours are much better." He lowered his voice. "I would never tell her this, but she's right."

Noelle wasn't sure either one of them was right, but she knew how much work it was to put together a holiday meal. It would be much easier for his wife to order the pies.

"We're having a large group. I think we'll need five pies." He grinned. "So there will be leftovers."

"No problem," Noelle said. "But can you pick them up on Christmas Eve? I can't deliver them."

"That works." They arranged the details and then Steve put his baseball cap on backward, picked up the pie, and continued on through the market.

Salome had never taken orders for Christmas pies before, and here Noelle had taken two. She wouldn't put out a sign, advertising the service—not this year, anyway. And she doubted Salome would be in favor of it for next year. But Noelle was pretty sure it was a service worth looking into, especially if she was going to continue doing the baking and the selling. As for the extra money from the Christmas pies this year, she'd put it toward Dat's new medicines. And pray that he would live long enough to enjoy another Family Christmas.

CHAPTER EIGHT

On Friday morning, Noelle's heart raced when she arrived at the market. Jesse was back, along with five little rocking chairs, two tiny chests, and a child-sized bookcase. She intended to speak with him. She really did. But she didn't manage to. Part of the reason was she lost her courage. Her other excuse was that she was swamped.

In the early afternoon, Carlos gave Jesse a break. Again, Noelle lost her nerve in telling him she needed to speak with him. But when he stopped by her booth, she did ask how Greta was doing.

"Better," he said. "She gave us quite a scare though. I'm grateful I have Aenti Barbara to help me through all of this."

Noelle gave him a questioning look, hoping he'd continue. When he didn't, she couldn't stop her curiosity. "What's going on?"

"She has a disease. It's worse than what we'd thought." His expression grew forlorn.

"I'm sorry," Noelle said. "How long have you known she had it?"

He swallowed hard and then, when he spoke, his voice was faint. "Since soon after she was born . . ."

She didn't press him any further. He seemed so sad. Instead, she gave him a box of creamsticks.

"Denki," he said. "These are my favorite."

She remembered.

He held the box in both hands. "And I'm grateful for the idea to sell *Kinder*-sized items too." He nodded toward his booth. "I've already sold four of the rocking chairs and one of the chests. And I have a buyer interested in the bookcase."

"*Wunderbar*," Noelle said. "Too bad it takes so long to make them."

He shrugged. "They're not too hard. I have two more chairs I'll finish up tonight. And a bookcase."

He held up the box of creamsticks. "Anyway, it's been good working at the market with you. If I don't see you before closing, I'll see you tomorrow." As he turned to go, a wave of sadness washed over Noelle. Once he returned to Montana, that would be it. Tomorrow was all she had.

On Saturday morning, the last day of the Christmas Market, Noelle had almost worked up the courage to venture back to Jesse's booth when Holly called across the aisle, "Can you believe this is it?"

Noelle shook her head.

"I'm really going to miss you, Twin." Holly grinned.

"I'm going to miss you too." Noelle's voice quavered, and she couldn't manage even the smallest smile.

Holly took two big steps across the aisle and wrapped Noelle up in her arms. "Ahh," she said. "It's been such a gift from God to spend time with you this last month."

Noelle hugged her friend back. Behind Holly, three of her five candles of Advent glowed. *Hope, joy, peace.* Tomorrow was *faith*, the last Sunday of Advent. She was thankful for her friend and what she'd taught her. She'd gradually realized throughout the month that the verses she read each day had touched her soul. The friendship, the scripture, the encouragement—all of it had helped lift her out of her grief. How odd that even with Jesse close by, she'd grown stronger.

"I have something to tell you." Holly pulled away. "But later. When we have a few minutes."

"All right." Noelle didn't expect it was anything serious. Hopefully, Holly would suggest they get together sometime in the next couple of weeks. Noelle would like that.

"Hey!" Holly let go of Noelle. "Did you find a place for your Family Christmas?"

Noelle shook her head. "I don't think we're going to have it."

"Oh, that's horrible. Why not?"

"I couldn't find a place big enough. The school was already booked and the churches near us as well. The church wagon has already been claimed, so we wouldn't have enough seating if we used the shed. It just didn't work out."

Holly tilted her head. "What about here?"

Noelle wrinkled her nose.

"In the dining room. You could use the kitchen too."

"Does Steve rent it out?"

"I don't know, but you should ask him. He likes your pies so much. Maybe you could—"

"Make his Christmas pies for free? And offer him an extra one every week for the next year."

"Not that many." Holly laughed. "But it's a good idea. How about one a month though instead of one a week?"

Noelle pondered the idea.

"But you have to actually ask him." Holly glanced back toward Jesse's booth. "You seem to have a habit of wanting to talk to someone but then not actually doing anything."

"Is it that obvious?" Noelle whispered.

Holly crossed her arms as a sassy expression landed on her face. "Actually, it is."

Before Noelle could protest, the first group of customers entered the market. They kept coming—wave after wave after wave. Over and over, Noelle was grateful that Moriah had helped her mix up batter and fillings on Wednesday so all Noelle had to do was bake on Thursday evening and Friday evening too. She could barely restock and wait on customers.

She'd realized, over the last couple of days, that she'd finally gotten a handle on sales. With each request for a pie, Noelle asked if the customer would be interested in a box of mini whoopie pies too. "They're one of a kind." She would smile. "Minis are the new big thing."

Box after box sold.

Then, when young customers asked for a box of the minis, Noelle would suggest they pick up a pie for their mothers, saying, "It's the best gift you can give her."

She even found herself joking with customers. But mostly she found herself smiling more and more and saying, "Have a wonderful Christmas." And she meant it. She'd learned to care about the Englischers.

All of her positive interactions had increased sales.

For the first time, Noelle could imagine Salome at the market. Maybe she spoke cynically about the Englisch at home, but Noelle guessed at the market that she had to be outgoing and personable to sell as much product as she did. Maybe there was a side to Salome that Noelle didn't know. Maybe she gossiped about others because she didn't feel that positive about herself. For the first time, her heart ached for her sister, instead of just for herself.

Carlos floated between Holly's booth and Noelle's, and a couple of times he went to check on Jesse. Noelle noticed some people carrying the small rocking chairs and one man carrying a small chest. Another man carried a large rocking chair. It seemed that even Jesse was doing well.

The day passed in a blur. At one point, Carlos managed the chocolate booth and Holly came over to restock Noelle's products while she waited on customers. When they had a lull, Holly said, "You've really gotten the hang of selling."

Noelle agreed. "And I'm actually enjoying it," she whispered to Holly, who laughed. Noelle would miss the market and wondered if, when it opened again in March, she might continue doing the selling. Perhaps if Noelle offered to do it, her sister would welcome being done with it. But before she had a chance to ask Holly if she'd be back in the spring, another wave of customers appeared at the booth.

Around five, Steve came by with his baseball cap already turned around. Holly quickly scooted over to Noelle's booth and squeaked, "It's now or never."

Noelle took a deep breath and then said, "Steve, I have something to ask you."

He smiled. "If it's to take a pie off your hands, the answer is I'll buy one."

"Actually, it is." She handed him a peach one. "But I won't take your money because I'm hoping to bribe you. Do you ever rent out—or barter for—the kitchen and dining area?"

"When?"

She grimaced, imagining what his reply would be. "Christmas Day."

He threw back his head and laughed. "Honestly, no one's ever asked. But it's definitely available."

She quickly explained the trade she had in mind. When she finished and he didn't answer right away, she wished she'd offered him one a week.

But then he said, "I think we can work that out. I'll give you the key when I pick up the pies on Christmas Eve. I'll give you the security code then too." He went on to explain that the oven in the kitchen was gas, and that there was a checklist to close up the kitchen and dining hall. "I'll give you my phone number in case you need it," he said. He grimaced. "Oops, you probably don't have a cell phone, right?"

"Oh, I have plenty of nieces and nephews who haven't joined the church who do," she said. "We'll be fine."

As Steve walked away, joy flowed through her. She'd been bold enough to ask for something she needed—because she'd developed a relationship with Steve.

Grateful for Holly's prodding, Noelle gave her friend a thumbs-up.

They had a place for Family Christmas! She couldn't wait to tell Dat.

At six, the melodic ringing of the bells signaling the end of the day—and the end of the Christmas Market—brought tears to Noelle's eyes. She'd miss Holly most of all, but also the vibrancy of the market, including the customers. Jah, something had definitely changed inside of her. She enjoyed the chaos, the masses of different people, and the unique creativity that each vendor brought.

It took another half hour before all of the customers finally made their way out. Noelle didn't have much product left, so she decided she'd give the rest to Holly as a happy birthday gift. Although she'd save one pie for Jesse as a goodwill gesture before she talked with him. If she actually could. Perhaps she'd waited too long.

He passed her, pushing two large rocking chairs, a hope chest, and a bookcase on a cart to load in his wagon. She held up the pie, trying to get his attention, and then waved with her free hand. But he didn't see her.

She set them down and crossed the aisle with two other pies and a box of creamsticks for Holly. "Happy birthday, Twin."

Holly's hand went to her chest. "Denki." She took the baked goods and placed them in one of her crates. "I have something for you too."

She handed Noelle a box marked *Advent wreath*.

Confused, Noelle shook her head. "I can't take this."

Holly bit her lip. "Do you mean you can't have it in your house? That it's too Englisch?"

Noelle shook her head. "No. It's yours. It means so much to you."

"That's why I'm giving it to you. Because I want you to have it." The girl licked her lips and then said, "Now is when I need to tell you our news."

Noelle clutched the box of candles, dreading what Holly might have to say.

"We're leaving tonight for Mexico."

Noelle gasped.

"Our grandmother isn't doing well. We've tried to get her a visa to come here, but we haven't been able to. That's why my mother went down there. But now we need to go also."

How had Noelle missed that her mother had gone to Mexico? She lowered her voice. "Can you come back?"

"Of course. We're US citizens. So is our mother. Mama got her green card through our dad, and then became a citizen."

Noelle finally felt bold enough to ask more. "Where's your father now?"

"He passed away a few years ago. He worked construction and was suffocated when a ditch collapsed."

Noelle gasped again. "How horrible." She realized that was most likely why Carlos and Holly had come up to the hospital to be with her when Dat was in the ER. They knew her fear. Again, she felt remiss that she didn't previously have that important piece of information about Holly's life.

A sad expression fell over Holly's face as she continued speaking. "Our Mennonite church sponsored us after he died so Carlos and I could take classes and Mama could build up her business." She tried to smile. "But now we need to go be with our family."

Noelle agreed. "Will you come back?"

"Of course." Holly sighed. "Maybe not here though. I'll let you know." She handed Noelle a piece of paper. "This is my grandmother's address and my cell phone number. I'd love to stay in touch."

Noelle took the paper, put the box of candles in one of her empty crates, and pulled a scrap of paper and a pen from her purse. She quickly wrote down the phone shed number and her address too.

As Holly took it, she said, "There's one more thing. Our truck is stuffed and ready to go, which means we can't give you a ride."

"Oh." Noelle wasn't sure how she'd get home then, but she figured she'd start by calling Pamela. "May I borrow your phone?"

"No," Holly said. "I already arranged a ride for you."

"What?"

Holly grinned. "Jesse said he'd take you home."

Noelle walked out of the market with Holly, bundled up in her coat, bonnet, scarf, and gloves. The two hugged good-bye and promised to keep in touch as Noelle held Jesse's pie in one hand and Jesse and Carlos loaded Noelle's empty crates into the back of the wagon and then covered them with a tarp. The two draft horses that would pull the wagon snorted in the cold.

Noelle reached up and put the boxed pie on the wagon bench and then Jesse helped her up. There was a wool blanket waiting for her to spread over her legs. Three years ago, she would have sat close to him to keep warm. Instead, she spread the blanket over her lap and then pulled it up to her chin, holding it with her hands.

Once Jesse was on his side of the wagon, he turned on his battery-operated lantern and hung it from the hook. The wagon also had the required orange triangle on the back and a string of LED lights too.

"I thought I'd take the back roads," Jesse said. "To avoid traffic." He glanced over at her. "I just wanted to let you know."

She nodded. Jesse might have broken her heart—for a reason she now understood—but she wasn't afraid of him.

"Denki for giving me a ride." She nudged the pie closer to him. "This is for you to take home."

"I appreciate it," he said. "I've never had a pie better than yours. . . ." His voice trailed off and they rode in silence.

The wagon bounced along, slower and rougher than a buggy. The light from the lantern bounced along the ribbon of a shoulder and off the snow. A cradle moon rose over the trees at the edge of the field. Noelle couldn't help but smile at the beauty of the landscape.

Finally Jesse spoke. "Holly said you had something you needed to speak with me about."

Noelle cleared her throat as the wagon bumped along and managed to croak, "She did?"

He nodded.

There was a reason Noelle needed a friend like Holly. God had brought the girl into her life at exactly the right time. Still, she could pretend she didn't know what Jesse was talking about . . . or she could do the right thing. The choice was hers.

She cleared her throat again and then said, "Jah, I do have something I want to say. I've been putting it off the last few days." She tightened her fists around the edge of the blanket, determined to communicate what she needed to. "For the last three years, I thought you'd rejected me. And then I thought you were lying to me about it when you returned to Lancaster. But after you told me what Barbara had said, I found out it was true. Someone did say I didn't want you to come home." She exhaled. "It was Salome."

He glanced at her, his face pale in the lantern light.

"Jah, I was mad that you left," she explained. "But I fully expected you'd come back, that we'd patch things up. But then I heard you were dating an Englisch girl."

He quickly interjected, "Only because you were done with me."

She nodded. "I must have said something to Salome that she interpreted that way, but it's not how I felt. I can see now how hurt you must have been when you believed I'd rejected you, especially after all you'd been through."

They rode on in silence, but then Jesse pulled his hand down over his mouth and tugged on his beard. Finally he said, "I did write you a letter because I wanted to hear it from you, in writing, that you no longer cared about me. Honestly. I sent it but never heard back." He turned toward her, and for a moment she could see his kind, clear eyes.

"I never received it. I promise." Her heart sank. All the mail for both the Dawdi Haus and the big house went to the box on the highway. Salome was the one who usually collected it. Had she not given Noelle a letter from Jesse on purpose?

They reached the covered bridge. The light dimmed as the beat of the horses' hooves grew louder on the bare wood. "I'm sorry," he said, "that you never received it."

She nodded. She was sorry too.

"Instead," he said, "I went out with the Englisch girl a few times, which was enough to know that wasn't what I wanted."

"I thought maybe you went out with her because she was more fun than I was. More outgoing."

Jesse turned toward Noelle, his eyes appearing as if they were stinging in the cold. "But I always had so much fun with you. . . ."

Noelle stared straight ahead, not sure whether to believe him or not. "What happened after you dated the Englischer?"

"I met Alana."

Noelle continued to stare straight ahead as they came out of the bridge. Of course his wife had a name. It stung for half a moment—until she recognized her jealousy. The woman was Greta's mother. Jesse's wife.

"I admit," he said, " that Alana and I probably married too soon. I was hurt. She needed someone to help her. I needed to pour myself into someone, something."

"Was something wrong with her?"

Jesse frowned. "She had the same thing Greta does."

"Oh no," Noelle said.

He nodded. "But we didn't realize how dangerous it was until she hemorrhaged after the birth."

"Oh, Jesse." All of her jealousy dissolved in an instant. "I can see why you're going back."

"Going back?"

"To Montana. With Greta. You want to be closer to Alana's family."

"Who told you that?"

"Barbara."

He smiled wryly. "Nothing has changed in Lancaster County, has it?"

"What do you mean?"

"Assumptions. Gossip."

"You aren't going back?"

He shrugged. "Jah, I'll go back to visit. I want Greta to know her grandparents and all of that, but Barbara misunderstood. I want Greta to have better care than Alana had."

"What do you mean?"

"She inherited Alana's disease. It's called Von Willebrand, a blood disease, and it's somewhat common among the Amish," he said. "I plan to do everything I can to make sure my daughter gets all the care she can, close to the doctors who know what she needs. Noelle, I'm staying in Lancaster County."

CHAPTER NINE

*D*at beamed when Noelle opened the door and he saw Jesse carrying her empty crates.

"Come in," Dat called out. "Can you sit for a while? Maybe have supper with us?"

Jesse thanked Dat for the invitation but said he needed to get home, joking, "I don't want Greta to forget who I am."

Dat nodded sympathetically. "She has a good father."

Noelle thanked Jesse and walked him to the door. He gestured outside, and she followed him out onto the stoop. "I have a gift for you too." He pulled a six-inch rectangle-shaped box wrapped in white paper from the pocket of his coat and handed it to her.

"Denki," she said, surprised he would give her anything. "Should I open it now?"

He nodded.

She unwrapped it, opened the top flap of the box, and saw it was a red vase. Exactly like the one he'd given her before.

"Your Dat said the other one broke."

"Jah." She swallowed the lump in her throat, not sure if she was more surprised that Dat remembered the vase was from

Jesse, that Dat had mentioned it to Jesse, or that Jesse had found another one just like it for her.

She looked up from the vase and met his eyes.

He smiled. "Merry Christmas."

"To you and Greta too."

"And happy birthday." He smiled again.

"Denki," she said.

As Jesse headed out to the wagon, Noelle stepped back into the house, fighting back her tears. Jesse King was a good man. If only she hadn't doubted that three years ago.

She took off her coat, took a deep breath, and then turned toward Dat. "I have good news. At least I hope so." She hung up her coat and explained that they could use the market kitchen and dining room for their Family Christmas. "I hope it's not too late to notify everyone—and everyone can still make it."

Dat grinned and grabbed his cane. "We need to call your sisters."

"I was thinking I'd make the calls tomorrow."

"No, tonight." He took a step toward her. "First we should go speak with Salome and get her on board."

"Ach." Noelle hurried to Dat's side. "Are you sure that's a good idea?"

Dat nodded.

"All right." Noelle wasn't so sure, but she'd do it for Dat. "I'll go harness the horse."

"I think I can walk," he said. "I have to go nearly that far to get to the phone shed."

"I can make the calls," Noelle said.

He shook his head. "I'd rather."

After they'd bundled up, they started out into the night. Noelle shone a flashlight with one hand and hung on to Dat with the other. Thankfully it hadn't snowed any more that day, so the path was clear.

Dat talked about his day with LuAnne and her brood. "I am a little sad you are done with the market," he said. "It has been good to spend time with the little ones."

They stopped at the phone shanty so Dat could catch his breath. He literally leaned against it. "We could go ahead and make the calls," Noelle said. "And then I can go over to Salome's and tell her."

"Nee." Dat's voice shook a little. "We need to keep going."

They stopped one more time, at the gate to Paul and LuAnne's backyard. While she waited for Dat, Noelle turned her attention toward the house. LuAnne stood at the kitchen window as Paul came up behind her. He wrapped his arms around her growing middle and nuzzled her neck. LuAnne leaned back against him.

Noelle quickly glanced away, but the image stayed with her—as did both the longing and the ache in her heart.

When they reached the Dawdi Haus, Noelle knocked while Dat struggled to catch his breath. "Dat," she whispered, "are you all right?"

He nodded but couldn't speak and still couldn't when Salome opened the door. "Dat," she said, "is everything all right?"

He nodded.

"What's the matter?"

"He needs to talk with you is all." Noelle tightened her grip on Dat's arm. The truth was, she needed to speak with her sister too. "May we come in?"

Salome, wearing a thick sweater over her dress and apron, swung the door open, and Dat toddled in, with Noelle holding firmly to him. Moriah sat curled up on the sofa in her robe with a scarf on her head, reading *The Budget Newspaper*. She looked as if she'd been crying.

"Are you all right?" Noelle asked. Clearly her talking the other day hadn't cured her of her grief, but of course it would take more time.

Her niece nodded, put the newspaper down, and scurried off the couch and toward the hall.

"Is she ill?" Dat asked.

In a chilly voice, Salome said, "You could say that." Then she asked Dat for his coat.

He shook his head but then sat down on the sofa. "We can't stay long. I just need to give you an update."

"On?"

"Family Christmas."

"Oh, that. We're not having it this year."

"No, we are," Dat said. "Noelle found a place. The dining hall at the market."

Salome crossed her arms. "What an odd place to meet."

"I think it is perfect," Dat said. Noelle guessed it had been years since he'd been there, and it looked totally different now, but she appreciated his support.

"I'm going to call the other girls," he said. "And tell them."

"I still don't think it's a good idea."

Dat glanced from Noelle to Salome. "I was going to wait to tell you this, but my health isn't well. This could be my last Christmas—"

Salome waved her hand toward him. "I know you've grown weaker, but are you serious about your health being bad?"

"Jah," Dat answered. "The doctor said my heart is failing."

Salome wrinkled her brow. "I'm sorry to hear that." Concern washed over her face. "But maybe everyone should visit you in small groups over Christmas." She nodded toward the hall. "Moriah is having a hard time with it being a year since Eugene died and all." Salome continued, her voice still low. "It's a hard anniversary. We've been really worried about her."

"Mamm!" Moriah appeared in the doorway to the hall, sounding more like herself than she had in over a year. "Stop trying to protect me. Jah, I'm going through a rough time, but that doesn't mean I don't want all of us to get together. That doesn't make any sense."

"But you don't want to be around all those couples. And babies. You told me it was hard for you."

"Jah, it's difficult. But it's harder not to be."

Salome bit her lower lip and then asked, "What do you mean?"

"You don't listen to me. You guessed at what I meant and then jumped to a decision."

Noelle couldn't help but think that Salome had done the same thing to her all those years ago. But at the same time she could see that Salome was trying to protect Moriah. Had she been trying to protect Noelle in some way too?

Moriah continued. "If you'd asked me about whether or not to have the Family Christmas, I would have said I wanted it." She crossed her arms, in exactly the same stance as her mother. "I thought *you* didn't want it because of your back and how much work it is."

"Well, my back is still sore, but you've been so sad, so—"

"Depressed?"

Salome nodded.

"Well," Moriah said, "I'll be a lot more depressed on Christmas Day sitting around here than being with our family."

Our.

Family.

The two words rang like the Christmas Market bells in Noelle's head.

"We need to all be together," Noelle said to Salome, thinking of Family Christmas a year ago, right after Eugene died. Moriah was surrounded with care and love. "We need to be together because we need each other."

And in a family, it was important to speak the truth. It was time for Noelle to stand up to Salome about something that really mattered. She cleared her throat. "But like Moriah, I need you not to make assumptions about me and not to speak about me to others."

Salome's expression hardened. "What are you talking about?"

"Jesse. Word got back to Montana that I wanted nothing to do with him, when, in fact, I still thought I'd spend the rest of my life with him."

Salome's face reddened. "Marrying him and going with him when Mamm was so sick would have broken your heart. He left you when you needed him most." She paused for a moment and then said, "You never say anything critical about anyone, but even you said how hurt you were. He didn't deserve you, Noelle."

After reaching for Dat to steady herself, Noelle finally responded, her voice shaky. "We were in a rough patch was all. I shouldn't have said anything to you, but you shouldn't have said anything to anyone else, especially not Barbara. And I need to know this: Did a letter from him come for me?"

Salome lifted her hands. "I was only trying to protect you."

A sob rose from Noelle's chest and she gasped. "You had no right."

Salome rubbed her forehead with the tips of her fingers and was silent for a long, long moment. Finally, she said, "All right—you've said your piece." She turned toward Moriah. "You too." Then back toward Noelle. "I'll try to do better, for both of you."

Noelle exhaled. "Denki." It was probably as close to an apology as she would get from Salome.

Moriah's heavy eyes met her mother's. "I'm glad we'll have Family Christmas this year."

Salome responded with a quick nod.

After a long pause, Dat said, "We had better go." He turned toward Salome. "Merry Christmas. We will see you on Wednesday." He turned to Noelle as she helped him stand. "What time?"

Her voice still shook as she spoke. "Our usual—four o'clock." That gave everyone time to travel.

Moriah still stood in the doorway to the hallway. She called out to Noelle and then said, "Denki."

Noelle smiled slightly. "Would you come bake with me on Monday?" Her voice was still unsteady. "I have orders to fill. I'd love to spend more time with you in the kitchen."

"I'd like that. I'll see you then."

Thankfully Salome didn't ask about the orders. Noelle would tell her later.

Once they were in the phone shed, Dat patted Noelle's shoulder and sat on the stool inside. "I am sorry about the miscommunication concerning Jesse." He wouldn't call it gossip, but it was clear he understood what had happened.

Noelle smiled at him, grateful for his care.

He went ahead and made the phone calls. Noelle was surprised that he knew the phone numbers of all of her sisters from memory. She thought that was something only Mamm kept track of. He left the same message on each machine—that he wasn't well, that he wanted one last Family Christmas, and that it was scheduled for four on Christmas Day at the market.

After he made the last call and hung up, he said, "I need to make one more call, but the number is escaping me."

"Who, Dat?"

"I want to leave a message for Jesse, to invite him and Greta."

"Ach, are you sure?"

110

"Jah." Dat looked up at her with his pale blue eyes. "If you don't mind."

Noelle smiled, just a little. "Actually, I'd like that."

On Christmas Eve, both Steve and the woman who'd ordered pies stopped by to pick them up. Noelle was thankful for Moriah's help making them and was sure she could expand that part of the business for next year. Perhaps for Thanksgiving too.

That evening, Dat sang "Happy Birthday" to her and gave her a card from the collection Mamm had always kept on hand. It was a sweet moment, which she was grateful for. Her eyes teared at the thought of him not being around much longer.

"How are your friends?" Dat asked. "Did they make it to Mexico?"

"I hope so." Noelle tucked the card back into the envelope. Carlos had said it was over two thousand miles to where they were going. "I'm going to call Holly after I'm done with the dishes."

"Go call her now," Dat said. "I'll clean up."

Obviously, Noelle didn't hide her shocked expression because Dat chuckled and said, "Happy birthday."

She slipped into her coat and boots and hurried out to the phone shed. The big house was all lit up, and she imagined the fun the children were having.

Holly answered after the first ring. "Noelle? Is that you?"

Noelle laughed. "It's me."

Then they both said, "Happy birthday" at the same time, followed by laughter all around.

"Are you at your grandmother's?" Noelle asked.

"Well, we would be if someone hadn't gotten lost."

"Who was navigating?" Carlos called out. "Or who was supposed to be?"

"True." Holly laughed again. "We're about an hour away."

They talked some more about Holly and Carlos's travels, and then about their time together in the market. "Call me on Thursday," Holly said. "And let me know how your Family Christmas was."

"And you can tell me about yours too," Noelle answered. She was sorry Holly had left Lancaster County but glad she'd be with her mother and grandmother. There was nothing like family.

After they said their good-byes, Noelle started back to the house. As big fluffy snowflakes began to fall, she turned her head up to the inky sky. A single star shone between the clouds. *Therefore the Lord himself shall give you a sign. . . .* She couldn't help but smile in gratitude.

On Christmas afternoon, Noelle checked her purse to make sure she had the key Steve had given her. Then she and Moriah helped Dat out to the buggy that they'd already loaded with supplies and food for the Family Christmas meal.

As Noelle spread a blanket over Dat's lap, he looked her in the eye. "Denki," he said, "for making all of this possible."

She nodded in return and then smiled as he patted her hand. Hope, joy, peace, and faith. She'd found elements of each this Christmas. She prayed she could carry them into Family Christmas.

She took the back roads to the market. When they arrived, she turned on the lights and the heat first and got Dat settled in a chair, wrapping a blanket around his legs. As she and Moriah unloaded the buggy, Paul and LuAnne and their kids arrived and, surprisingly, Salome and Ted too. Noelle hadan't expected them until later.

The stove in the kitchen was new and easy to use, the counter space was ample, and everything was sparkling clean. Noelle, Moriah, LuAnne, and Salome chatted away as they got to work putting the turkey, hams, and pans of mashed potatoes in the ovens to heat, starting the gravy, and opening jars of applesauce. Thankfully, Salome wasn't gossiping. But what Salome said next completely caught her off guard.

"We had our best year ever at the Christmas Market." Salome kept her head down as she sliced a loaf of bread. "Even with missing one day."

"Wow." Moriah turned toward Noelle. "Great job."

Noelle's face grew warm.

Salome put the knife down and met Noelle's gaze. "In fact, I think you should take over the business. I could use a break, frankly. And your ideas really paid off."

Noelle stammered, "I'll need help."

"I'll help," Moriah said. "It would be my pleasure."

Noelle smiled and simply said, "Denki." Her mind whirled with ideas. They could try new recipes and research more packaging before March. She looked forward to working with her niece and rebuilding their relationship.

Soon, Englisch nieces and nephews, who'd never joined the church and had driven to the market, arrived. Many gave their parents rides. Other family members who had joined the church arrived in buggies, all bundled against the biting cold. Of course there were lots of children and babies and starry-eyed newlyweds.

For the first time in three years, Noelle wasn't jealous. And she realized that by taking charge and planning the celebration, she was thinking about others more than herself. That truly brought her joy.

Noelle kept an eye on Moriah as they moved to the dining area and spread plastic tablecloths over the tables. She seemed to be doing all right. She seemed to be smiling more than Noelle had seen in the last year.

As Noelle greeted a niece who hadn't joined the Amish, along with her husband and their new baby girl, who was Greta's age, she thought of Jesse. He hadn't returned Dat's message. Would he and Greta come? Or would they stay far away from her?

When it was finally time to eat, they all gathered around in a circle. Dat cleared his throat and said, "I'm so glad all of you were able to come on such short notice. A Family Christmas is just what this old man needs."

Moriah called out, "It's what we all need."

Several people laughed while others murmured in agreement.

Dat smiled and said, "On this day, we are thankful for our Lord Jesus coming to earth as our savior. Our faith in Him gives us hope. Today we are especially thankful for the peace and joy that only He can bring." He bowed his head. "Let's pray."

As Dat started the silent prayer, the dining hall door creaked open, and Jesse, holding a sleeping Greta, slipped inside. Noelle met his gaze and he smiled shyly. He made his way around the circle, and she stepped to the right to make room for him.

Jesse shifted Greta to one arm and, as Noelle bowed her head to pray with her family, he reached for her hand. Noelle knew he wouldn't hold it for long, not in front of her family, but she was certain he would reach for her again. And when he did, she'd call Holly and tell her the story of Noelle and Jesse.

Of how God was bringing healing and a new hope to both of their lives.

Baked Creamsticks

(RECIPE COURTESY OF AMISH365.COM)

Creamsticks

1 cup	shortening
1¼ cup	mashed potatoes
1 quart	milk, scalded
1 cup	sugar
1 tablespoon	salt
½ cup	warm water
3 packages	yeast
1 tablespoon	sugar
6	eggs, beaten
11–12 cups	flour

Put shortening, potatoes, milk, sugar, and salt in a large bowl. Stir until shortening and sugar are dissolved. Put warm water, yeast, and 1 tablespoon sugar in a small bowl. Add eggs and yeast to first mixture. Stir in enough flour until dough is not sticky. Cover and let rise until double. Roll out dough. Cut in 1x3 inch strips. Let rise until double. Bake at 350 degrees for 15–20 minutes. Let set until they are cold. Cut a slit on top and put in filling. Then top with favorite icing.

Filling

2 cups	milk
6 tablespoons	clear jel*
Pinch	salt
2 teaspoons	vanilla
2 cups	sugar
1½ cups	Crisco

Combine milk, clear jel, and salt in saucepan. Cook until thick. Add vanilla and cool. Cream together sugar and Crisco. Mix with cold cooked mixture and mix well.

Caramel Icing

½ cup	butter
1 cup	brown sugar
¼ cup	milk
2 cups	powdered sugar

Melt butter, add brown sugar, and cook over low heat for 2 minutes, stirring. Add milk and stir until it boils. Cool. Add powdered sugar.

*Clear jel is a thickener that can be found in most bulk food stores. If you don't have access to clear jel, cornstarch is an appropriate substitute.

AN
AMISH
Christmas
RECIPE
BOX

JAN DREXLER

To the memory of Ruth Ann

Soli Deo Gloria

CHAPTER ONE

Ada Weaver eyed the frozen puddle in front of the door of Heritage Amish Furniture, a stack of boxed baked goods balanced in one hand, her key to the store in the other. To open the door, she would have to lean over that ice without dropping the six boxes full of cupcakes. Her sister Rose had left the house ten minutes ago, but she usually entered the store through the workshop, leaving Ada to unlock the customers' entrance.

"Rose!" Ada leaned as far over the ice as she could to peer in the window. Rose was nowhere in sight.

She reached out with her toe to knock on the door but nearly lost her balance.

"Let me help you."

The voice came from behind as a gloved hand took her key, reached past her, and unlocked the door. As he turned the doorknob, Ada looked up into the face of *Dat*'s newest employee.

"*Denki*," she said, stretching one foot over the ice and onto the threshold. "We'll have to put ice melt out right away, before any customers show up."

The young man grinned, his glasses steaming in the warm room. He wore a black knit cap and a black coat, just like all the Amish men in the Shipshewana area wore in the winter. His brown eyes didn't meet hers but looked around the store as he took off his gloves.

"I haven't been in the shop before." He fingered a display of wooden Christmas tree ornaments. "You sell more than just furniture in here."

"For sure, we do." Ada unwrapped her shawl and hung it on the wooden hook next to the door. "Dat says folks don't make a large purchase like furniture very often, but you never know what they'll walk out with when they come in to browse."

He walked along the counter until he reached the glass cases where the baked goods were displayed. Ada took the boxes behind the counter and stacked them on top of the first display case, opening one and setting the cupcakes she had baked that morning on a tray. The cookies Rose had brought over from the house were still in their boxes on top of the second case. While she worked, she searched her mind for the young man's name. She remembered that he had moved to Wisconsin several years ago when they had both finished their schooling, but the family had moved back to Indiana last week.

"Who makes the cookies and cupcakes?" He straightened up, still not looking at her.

"I do. Rose and I work in the store together, but she doesn't like to bake. So, she takes care of dusting the display furniture and ordering the other items we sell." She glanced at him. "Rose is my sister, and I'm Ada."

He grinned again. "I remember you from school. I'm Matthias Yoder. Your Dat hired me yesterday to work in the factory."

She nodded, glad that he had taken the hint and she didn't have to ask his name outright. "He told us about you last night at supper. He said you have a lot of experience working with wood."

Just then Ada saw movement through the window on the far wall, the one that looked out into the parking lot. Amos Hertzler coasted to the bike rack and inserted the front wheel of his bicycle between the bars. She waited as he entered the door to the furniture factory, but he didn't turn toward the window. Amos never turned toward her.

Ever since Amos started working for Dat a year ago, soon after moving to Shipshewana from Nappanee, Ada had waited for him to notice her. It was hard since they didn't belong to the same church district, but someday he would turn and look toward the store on the way into the workshop. Then she would wave to him. He would stop, then a slow smile would appear. He would start walking toward her—

"Who made these?" Matthias asked. He had walked over to the display of floor clocks on the far wall and run his hand over the wooden case of the tallest one.

"Dat makes all the clocks." Ada pulled her thoughts back as she worked to keep a note of pride from her voice. She started transferring the cookies to the display case. "People come from as far as Missouri to buy them."

"This is fine craftsmanship." Matthias came back to the counter. "That's one reason why I wanted to work here. My Dat worked with Leroy before we moved to Wisconsin, so I knew I had to look him up when we came back."

"I remember him. Ervin Yoder was one of Dat's best wood-workers, and customers still ask about his work. He'll have to come in and say hello. I'm sure Dat will be happy to see him again."

"Dat passed on in the spring." Matthias kept his gaze somewhere around his toes.

"I'm sorry to hear that."

"Denki."

As Ada slid the spatula under the last cookie on the tray, it broke before she could put it in the case. She sighed as she picked up the two halves.

"I guess this one won't make it to any of our customers." She glanced at Matthias. "Would you like it?"

The grin came back. "Are you sure?"

She laughed. "I certainly don't need to eat any more cookies." She tugged at the apron that always seemed to get twisted, but Matthias didn't seem to notice. He had taken a bite of the soft sugar cookie and was chewing it with his eyes closed.

"Delicious. Just like the ones *Grossmutti* made when I was a boy."

"I'm glad you like it."

He finished the cookie and leaned over to look into the display case again. Besides the sugar cookies, there were chocolate chip cookies and oatmeal raisin, as well as chocolate cupcakes decorated with orange and red frosting leaves.

"You must have folks who stop by here just for the baked goods."

Ada nodded, her face growing warm from his praise. "The tourists pass the word on to their friends. And plenty of the local folks stop by, too. I have several orders for pies for Thanksgiving this Thursday."

Matthias glanced at the clocks as one wheezed, getting ready to strike eight o'clock.

"I had better get to work. It's almost time, and I don't want to be late on my first day."

"There's a door to the workshop back there." Ada pointed past the clocks to a hallway. "You can go that way."

As Matthias disappeared down the hall, Rose came into the shop from the showroom. Most of the furniture was displayed in the large building attached to the shop.

"Who was that?" Rose hung the feather duster next to the cash register and flipped the light switch. The lights on the cash register display blinked as the power turned on.

"Dat's new employee in the workshop, Matthias Yoder. He opened the door for me when you were nowhere to be seen."

"I was dusting. But if you needed help, why didn't you come in the back way?"

Ada shrugged. "I always come in this way."

Rose straightened a Christmas ornament on the display. "You just want to be able to watch Amos come to work."

"What's wrong with that?" Ada checked the supply of bakery bags and dry-wax tissues to handle the baked goods.

"If you came in through the workshop, perhaps you would actually be able to talk to him."

Her face burned at the thought. "That would be too forward. I could never do that."

"You'll never get his attention sitting in the store all day."

Ada scooped some ice melt from the container under the cash register and opened the front door. Rose was right. But how did a girl make a boy pay attention to her? She watched the white crystals bounce on the ice, making sure she scattered them evenly. She would never be as bold as some of the girls. Some of them would actually drive their pony carts past a boy's home in the summer, hoping to attract his attention. She scattered the last of the ice melt and went back inside.

"How did you get Johnny to notice you?" she asked as she replaced the scoop.

Her sister shrugged as she leafed through the receipts from yesterday's business. "He just came over to talk to me at the Singing one night."

Ada leaned on the bakery case, her chin in her hand. Rose was pretty, and her dresses were never too tight. She never slipped on the ice, or spilled her drink at McDonald's, or even said something she wished she could take back. No wonder Johnny had snatched her up as soon as he saw her. They had been going steady for nearly six months now, and Ada was sure they would be getting married next fall. Then Ada would be the only one of the four sisters still left at home.

She sighed. The way things looked, she would always be the sister living at home.

When Matthias reached the house he shared with *Mamm* on the north side of Shipshewana, he coasted into the driveway on his bicycle, his chin buried in his coat collar. Leroy's other employees, Amos and Vernon, had both said they would be driving their buggies tomorrow. Snow was in the forecast, and it was time to put the bicycles away for the year. But Matthias would have to continue to rely on his.

He opened the door to the small barn and wheeled the bicycle in. The cow had already come in from the pasture, and Matthias didn't blame her. It was cold out there this evening. He worked his stiff fingers to get some feeling back into them, then poured some feed into the cow's manger.

The cow was older, but still a good milker. His brother-in-law Simon had loaned her to Mamm when he bought this place for her last week. Simon's family had a dairy farm, a big sprawling place down near Millersburg. When he had married Sally, Matthias's oldest sister, twelve years ago, Dat had been happy that she would always be well provided for. Matthias's other sisters, Marian and Elizabeth, had also married well.

A year after Elizabeth's wedding, Dat had decided to move to Wisconsin in search of more opportunities for Matthias.

Matthias stripped the last drops of milk from the cow's

126

udder, pushing away the regrets. Thinking of the what-ifs was Mamm's favorite pastime, but he was determined not to fall into that same rut. He had a good job now, and things would slowly improve. Although Mamm had already stated that they wouldn't be buying another horse and buggy. Not after what had happened in Wisconsin.

The kitchen window shone with a welcome glow as Matthias fastened the barn door and headed toward the house with the pail of fresh milk. Clouds filled the sky, blocking the after-sunset glow, and flakes of snow danced in a gust of wind—big clumping flakes that clung to the tree branches. Matthias opened the kitchen door.

Mamm stood at the stove, stirring green beans in a pan. She turned when the door opened.

"Don't forget to shut the door tight behind you," she said.

She took the pail of milk as Matthias removed his coat and gloves. He hung his hat on the hook over his coat.

"It's getting cold out there, and snow is in the air."

"I'm thankful we have this nice warm house." Mamm took a casserole from the oven and set it on the table. "The days are short, and the wind blows cold, but we're snug in our little home."

Matthias paused, wondering which poem the phrase had come from this time. Mamm loved her poems, and even wrote them. Twice, her poems had been published in the *Budget*, the Amish newspaper.

"How was your first day at work?"

"It was fine." Matthias washed up at the sink. "The other two men helped me learn my way around, and Leroy gave me some easy tasks to do."

"Your Dat always liked working for Leroy." Mamm set a plate on the table piled with slices of fresh bread. "He said

Leroy Weaver was the fairest boss he had ever known." She turned to stir the green beans. "Did you meet anyone else?"

"I talked to one of Leroy's daughters."

Matthias dipped into the pail of milk and filled a glass. He set it at his place at the table as Mamm beamed at him.

"If I remember right, the Weavers have four daughters. Which one was she?"

"Ada." He took a long drink of the milk. It had been hours since the sandwich he had downed at lunch. "We were in school together, but I don't think she remembered me."

Mamm frowned as she set the beans on the table and took her seat. "Ada?" She thought for a minute, tapping her forefinger on the table. "She must be the youngest one."

Matthias smiled. "She is certainly a good baker. She gave me a cookie, and it was just like Dat's Mamm used to make."

Mamm raised her eyebrows. "That is a good quality to look for in a wife, when the time comes."

"The time has already come. I'm twenty-one years old."

Mamm laid her hand on his. "I know, son, I know. It seems like you're getting older, but you've only just begun your life. Don't be in too much of a hurry to grow up."

Matthias suppressed a sigh as Mamm bowed her head for the silent prayer. Most of his friends in Wisconsin had married by the time they were twenty and were living their lives. Raising their families. Working on their own farms. And yet Mamm continued to treat him like a boy.

Mamm passed the dish of green beans to him, signaling the end of the prayer before Matthias even started praying. But that didn't mean he couldn't thank the Lord for his food.

Thank you, Lord, for this food. He put half the beans on his plate and handed the dish to Mamm. *And for granting me safety on the way home.* He held his plate close to the casserole dish as Mamm spooned a generous serving of lasagna onto his plate next to the beans. *Help Mamm to realize that I should be the man of the house, now that Dat is gone.* Last of all, he helped himself to a thick slice of homemade bread. *And thank you for my job.*

"Elizabeth stopped by this afternoon," Mamm said as she spread butter on her bread. "She was happy to hear that you found a job so soon."

"I'm glad, too." Matthias cut into the lasagna with the side of his fork.

"She brought little Ann with her." Mamm stared toward the window. "I don't think you know how difficult it was for me to move to Wisconsin and leave the girls behind."

Matthias watched a tear slide down Mamm's cheek. "I know the move was Dat's idea. But he was right. He could afford to buy a farm there, while the price of land is too high here."

Another tear followed the first one. Matthias set his fork down and moved his chair next to Mamm's. As soon as he sat next to her, she leaned her head on his shoulder. He put an arm around her, holding her tight.

"I wish we had never moved. If only your father had been content with what the Good Lord had given us here, instead of trying to have something more."

Matthias had heard Mamm's complaints before, but he let her talk.

"If only we hadn't moved, your father would still be with us today. We wouldn't have lost everything. We would still be living in our home instead of . . ."

Her voice trailed off, but Matthias knew what she was thinking. After selling the farm in Wisconsin and paying off the loan, and then paying for their train tickets home to Indiana, Mamm had only had enough money left to buy this little house on the outskirts of Shipshewana. Hardly three acres, the property would keep a cow and a horse and allow Mamm to have a garden. This drafty little one-bedroom house with its old asphalt siding was their only home.

He stared at the window over the sink, barely noticing the fat, wet snowflakes that splatted against the dark pane. This wasn't a house he could ever ask a wife to share with him. He couldn't expect any woman to be happy sharing this little place with her mother-in-law and sleeping in the attic. Marriage, even if he met the right girl, would have to wait until things got better.

Matthias pulled his plate across the table and continued eating, one arm still around Mamm's shoulders, and pushed away that thought. He would just have to learn to be content with the way things were. He had no guarantee that their lives would ever improve enough that he could think of a home and family of his own.

The morning before Thanksgiving, Ada leaned over the kitchen sink to gaze out the window. The lamplight streaming from the kitchen into the early morning darkness made the snow look like sugar frosting on the tree branches. The breeze swirled flakes through the air, turning the yard into one of those snow globes the *Englischers* liked so much. A gust of wind toppled the line of snow on the branch closest to the window, and the entire length drifted to the ground. A squirrel, intent on gathering as many acorns as it could, ignored the fresh fall. It tunneled its nose along the ground, only its tail bobbing in the air behind it, making Ada laugh.

"*Ach*, look at that!" Mamm said, peering through the window next to her. "Not only an early snow, but it's still coming. I hope it stops soon."

"I like the snow," Ada said.

"You won't like it if it keeps customers away today." Mamm took a breakfast casserole out of the oven. "Did you get all of the pies baked?"

Ada turned from the window to finish placing the pie shields on the two pecan pies that were set to go into the oven.

"I only have these two left." She adjusted the oven temperature, then started setting the table for breakfast.

"Will they be done in time?"

"That won't be a problem. Mrs. Cunningham told me her husband would pick them up on his way home from work this evening."

Mamm opened a jar of canned peaches. "After those pies go into the oven, would you have time to bake a couple pumpkin pies for our dinner tomorrow?"

Ada glanced at the clock above the sink. "For sure. It's only six-thirty, and I've already made the crusts."

"The crusts for what?" Rose breezed into the kitchen, tying on her apron. She was late, as usual, but still looked as fresh and unhurried as Mamm always did.

"Tomorrow's pies," Mamm said. "You're just in time to finish setting the table. Dat will be in soon."

"Will both Carolyn and Malinda be able to come for dinner tomorrow?" Rose asked, taking four plates from the cabinet.

"They'll be here for the whole day." Mamm's smile was bright. "Both families will come after breakfast and stay until just before it gets dark. Wilmer and Henry are planning to help Dat fix the saw in the workshop, so we girls will have plenty of time to chat. It will be just like old times."

"Except for the babies."

Rose made a face that Ada couldn't understand. How could someone not like babies? Both of her older sisters had little girls, both less than a year old. Ada never tired of caring for her nieces, but Rose was always quick to pass them back to their mothers as soon as they got fussy.

Mamm chuckled. "The babies are the best part."

After breakfast, Dat went out to the workshop, but Mamm refilled their coffee cups.

"While we have a minute, I want to go over tomorrow's tasks with you girls."

Rose spooned some sugar into her coffee and exchanged her usual "here we go again" look with Ada. Ada pressed her lips together to keep from grinning. Mamm never started a day without penciling her to-do list on the back of an old envelope, and a big meal like tomorrow's meant that she had jobs for each of them.

"Ada, you'll make the rolls, won't you?" Mamm tapped her list with her pencil, frowning at it.

"For sure. I'll make potato rolls. They're easy, and everyone likes them."

"And Rose, I'll need you to make the green bean casserole." She added an item to her list. "And we'll need to peel the potatoes."

"I'll do that in the morning," Ada said. "I need a potato for the rolls, so I might as well peel all of them."

Mamm patted Ada's hand. "What would I do without my Ada? I'm so happy that you don't have a beau. I can count on you being at home to help with many Thanksgiving dinners to come."

Rose set her coffee cup down. "What if Ada does find a beau?"

Ada's face was hot. "I'll still help Mamm in the kitchen, you know that."

Mamm gave her a bright smile, then went on through her list, assigning more tasks to each of them.

"That will do it. After dinner, we'll be able to relax for the rest of the day."

"I noticed you didn't put Malinda's or Carolyn's names on your list," Rose said, finishing her coffee.

"They'll be busy enough with their families. And they're each bringing something to share."

"All the more reason for me to get married," Rose said, laughing.

Mamm gave her a mock frown. "The sooner, the better."

While Ada and Rose washed the breakfast dishes, Mamm went to finish the morning chores in the rest of the house. As soon as she left the kitchen, Rose leaned close to Ada.

"I had an idea," she said as she dried a plate. "I thought of it last night."

Ada frowned. Rose's ideas rarely turned out well. "What is it?"

"You want to attract Amos's attention, don't you?"

Swirling the dishcloth around in the casserole dish, Ada eyed her sister. "What do you have in mind?"

Rose's face lit up. "Don't worry. You'll love it!" She leaned even closer and whispered, "I call it the *Great Cookie Campaign*."

Ada shook her head. "I'm not going to push myself at any man."

"You don't have to. That's the best part." Rose started drying the silverware in the dish drainer. "All you need to do is to make a batch of cookies for the guys in the workshop. No one will know you are targeting Amos. You know you bake the best cookies around, and he'll be sure to notice you."

Ada looked out the window. The snow had stopped, and the sky was gray as the sun came up somewhere behind the clouds.

"Do you really think it would work?"

"How could it fail?"

Ada grinned at Rose. "You know that most of your schemes fail."

"Name one."

"What about the time when you thought Dat should buy some goats to mow the grass for us?" Before Rose could answer, Ada continued, "Or the time when you tried to attach a pulley for the clothesline to the attic eave."

"It isn't my fault that the wood had rotted. Dat even thanked me for finding it so he could fix it."

"But the only way we found out was when the pulley gave way and all the clean laundry fell into the barnyard."

Rose dried the next two plates in silence. Then she said, "This plan is a good one. It won't backfire. The worst that can happen is that Amos still doesn't notice you."

Ada wrung out the dishcloth in the sink, then pulled the plug, letting the soapy water drain away. Rose was wrong. The worst that could happen would be if Amos laughed at her. But maybe Rose was right, and no one would know she was trying to attract his attention.

"All right. Tell me how it would work."

Rose grinned and leaned her elbows on the kitchen counter.

"After this week, we have three weeks before Christmas is here. Choose four of your favorite cookie recipes. Special ones that you don't usually make for the store. Then bake a different recipe each week between now and Christmas and save the best one for Christmas Eve. You know Vernon and that new boy will appreciate the cookies, too."

"I suppose that sounds like it might work."

Rose grabbed her hand. "I know it will. Let's think about which recipes you can make."

"I have to get these pies out of the oven first and make pumpkin ones for our dinner tomorrow." Ada opened the oven door.

The pecan pies that had been baking during breakfast were done perfectly. She set them on top of the stove.

"We can talk while you work." Rose opened the far drawer and rummaged through it until she found a scrap of paper and a pencil.

Ada took her mixing bowl out of the cupboard and opened the refrigerator door to find the rest of the pureed pumpkin she had made for pies.

"What kinds of cookies do you suggest?" she asked as she grabbed the bowl of eggs, too.

"Remember when you made molasses crinkles last summer? Those were good."

"They were good, weren't they?" Ada cracked the first egg into the mixing bowl. "And I haven't made oatmeal chocolate chip cookies for a long time. Most of the customers at the store would rather have oatmeal raisin."

"Wonderful! We have two already." Rose wrote them down on the paper. "What else?"

As Ada whisked the eggs in the bowl, she thought through all the cookie recipes she had in her file.

"Everyone likes decorated cookies. In the recipe cards that Grossmutti gave me, there is a recipe for icing flavored with anise and I've been wanting to try it on gingerbread cookies. I think they would look very pretty with blue sugar sprinkles."

Rose added to her list. "We only need one more. Something special for Christmas Eve."

Ada set the timer as she thought. "It should be something very special, shouldn't it?"

"Maybe a heart-shaped cookie. He'd be sure to get the message then."

Her stomach a bit queasy at the thought, Ada shook her head. "I don't want to be so obvious."

Rose laughed. "I suppose that is too much. You don't have to worry about that, not with the delicious cookies you make. You know that they say the way to a man's heart is through his stomach."

Ada checked the pies she had taken out of the oven. She had glazed the pecan halves before placing them in a swirling pattern on top of the pies, and they glowed in the early morning light. Mrs. Cunningham would be pleased with such beautiful pies to serve her guests. If anything would get Amos to notice her, it would be her baking. She couldn't do any less than go into this project wholeheartedly.

She pulled her recipe box close and started thumbing through the cookie section. "Here are those almond crescents Mamm likes so well."

"Those are good, but you want something that shows how much you love Amos, don't you?"

"But I don't love him. At least, not yet." Ada pulled a recipe card out. She hadn't noticed this one from Grossmutti before.

"What is that?" Rose peered over her shoulder and read the note Grossmutti had written across the top of the card. "'Thumbprint Cookies. My Ben's Favorite.'"

Ada's eyes grew misty as Rose's voice brought back the memory of her grandparents. They had been so close, even after years together. Their marriage was the kind Ada wanted, with a man who loved her through all the ups and downs of life.

"This is the one," she said. "I'll make them with red jam in the thumbprint. They'll look wonderful for Christmas Eve."

And maybe, she thought, *they will become Amos's favorite cookie, too.*

CHAPTER TWO

While Matthias milked the cow on Thanksgiving morning, he considered the day ahead.

His three sisters and their families were coming to spend the day, but he had no idea how they would all fit into the house. Mamm was determined that the family should all be together if possible, and Matthias knew it was to help fill the empty spot Dat had left behind. But this first Thanksgiving without him wasn't going to be fixed by crowding the family into their tiny kitchen and front room. His oldest sister, Sally, had volunteered their big, welcoming house for the gathering, but Mamm had refused.

Taking the milk into the kitchen, Matthias drew a deep breath. Mamm had been up and working even before Matthias this morning, and the kitchen was filled with scents of the good things to come. He peeled off his gloves, closing his eyes as he waited for his steamed-over glasses to clear. Turkey. Potatoes. Onions and sage. Bread dough rising. When he opened his eyes, the first thing he saw was Mamm's face, pink from the oven's heat and smiling as she washed a mixing bowl.

"Breakfast is ready for you," she said. "Leave the milk on the porch, and I'll take care of it later."

"When did you have time to fix breakfast?" Matthias asked as he sat in his chair.

"It was no trouble."

Mamm was right. It had been no trouble. She set a bowl of cold cereal in front of him and a pitcher of last night's milk.

"You go ahead and eat."

"When will you have your breakfast?" Matthias poured the milk over his corn flakes.

She waved his concern away as she opened a large pot on the stove and peered inside. "I had a slice of bread as I was making the stuffing." Taking a fork, she poked it into the rising steam.

Matthias crunched his corn flakes, watching her. Dinner would be a feast, as it always was on Thanksgiving. It would more than make up for his light breakfast.

When he finished, he took his bowl to the sink and washed it in the waiting water. Then he caught sight of Mamm struggling to lift the heavy pot.

"Let me do that." He grasped the handles. "Where do you want it?"

She peered at him, worry creasing her brow. "Are you sure that isn't too heavy for you?"

"I can handle it easier than you can. Where do you want it?" He couldn't believe Mamm thought she could carry this pot full of potatoes and water by herself.

Mamm placed the strainer in the empty side of the sink. "Pour it in here."

As Matthias tipped the pot, the water and potatoes fell into the strainer, filling it. He pulled it back and looked inside. There were still plenty of potatoes in the water.

"How many potatoes did you make?"

"Only ten pounds," Mamm said as she dumped the first potatoes into her largest mixing bowl, then stood back as Matthias emptied the pot. "Do you think it will be enough?"

"We'll have plenty. Didn't Elizabeth say she was bringing potatoes?"

"We don't want to run out."

"There's no danger of that." Matthias set the empty pot on the counter. "What else needs to be done?"

"We need to set up the extra tables in the front room. I thought the older children could eat in the kitchen, and the adults and the littlest ones will be in the front room."

"I'll get the tables down from the attic."

"Don't forget the chairs, too," Mamm said as he started up the steps.

By the time the folding tables and chairs were set up, the front room had no extra space. When the families started to arrive, the house was crowded. Like usual, as soon as Simon and Sally arrived with their five children, Simon took over.

"Let's get these tables in order," he said, his voice booming over the girls' chatter. "Eli, fold up those chairs for now."

He directed his ten-year-old son to put the chairs against the wall, then moved the two folding tables together into one long one. Matthias had separated the tables so they would seat more people, but he knew better than to argue with Simon. Now that Dat was gone, Simon was the oldest man when the family gathered together, and he stepped into the role as if it was his right.

When it was time to sit down for the meal, Matthias went to find a seat in the living room with his sisters and their husbands, but all the chairs were taken except the one closest to the kitchen. Matthias couldn't take Mamm's seat.

She passed him as he stood in the doorway, her hands filled with bowls of mashed potatoes to set on the table. "What is wrong, Matthias?"

"There isn't a spot for me to sit at the table."

"You're in the kitchen today." She paused and looked at him, her eyes bright with the joy of having the family together. "The children love it when you spend time with them."

Matthias took his seat at the kitchen table with his nieces and nephews. All of them, from Eli down to his two-year-old nephew Charles, stared at him. Eight children crowded on the benches on either side of the table. Matthias sighed. From his seat, he could see into the living room, where his brothers-in-law were laughing at a comment Simon had made. A comment Matthias hadn't heard.

He tapped one finger against his knee, waiting for Simon to start the prayer. He tried to push away the growing irritation. He was twenty-one years old and should be the man of the house. But Mamm still treated him like one of the children.

Four-year-old Yost poked his five-year-old cousin Susie, and Matthias glared at him. He should be sitting in the living room with the other adults, not in the kitchen babysitting these youngsters he barely knew. When would Mamm stop treating him like a boy?

The week after Thanksgiving, Ada prepared for the first phase of the Great Cookie Campaign. On Thursday night, Ada had mixed the batter for the molasses crinkle cookies and set the bowl in the propane refrigerator to cool. Early on Friday morning, she shaped the cookies while she preheated the oven.

Just like Dat had tools specially made for working with wood, Ada had collected the tools that made her baking easier. For cookies, she had purchased a dough scoop that measured each cookie to a uniform two-ounce size. She rolled the first scoop between her floured palms to make a perfect ball and placed it on the parchment-lined cookie sheet. When the cookie sheets were filled, she washed the flour off her hands, then rolled each ball in a bowl of sugar. She slid the two cookie sheets into the large oven and set the timer.

As the spicy molasses fragrance filled the quiet kitchen, she washed the bowl and utensils, then started measuring the ingredients for the first batch of cookies for the store. By the time the molasses cookies were baked and cooling on the racks, she slid two cookie sheets filled with oatmeal raisin cookies into the oven. Next would be the sugar cookies, made with the dough that had been in the refrigerator overnight with the molasses cookies.

Long ago, Ada had worked out her baking routine so that she would be finished using the oven by the time the rest of the family woke up. She loved working in the kitchen this early, with the house quiet and no one around to interrupt her. After the cookies were done, she would frost the cupcakes she had baked yesterday afternoon.

As she was mixing the frosting, Mamm came into the kitchen, tying her apron. She peered out the window over the sink.

"The sky is beginning to lighten up, and it looks like the clouds have scattered away. A sunny and frosty morning for the first week of December." She patted Ada's arm as she reached around her for her mixing bowl. "You made extra cookies this morning, I see. Are you trying something new in the store?"

Ada felt her face heat. She and Rose could laugh about the Great Cookie Campaign, but she knew Mamm wouldn't approve.

"They are for the workers in the shop. I thought it would be a nice gesture for them, with Christmas coming and all."

Mamm cracked eggs into her bowl. "That is thoughtful.

Vernon lives alone, so I'm sure he doesn't get such a treat very often."

Ada held her bowl close, whipping the frosting. Vernon was a bachelor and close to Dat's age, but everyone knew he would never marry. He might be an adult, but his mind was a child's. Mamm was right. He would appreciate the homemade cookies.

Just then, Rose came into the kitchen. She grabbed the egg basket from the counter and tossed her shawl around her shoulders.

"Sorry I'm late. I slept in again."

Mamm frowned. "You're making a habit out of these late-night hours. Isn't it a bit chilly to spend so many evenings driving through the country with Johnny?"

"But it's fun," Rose said. "I'll be back in time to help with breakfast."

Mamm shook her head as Rose slammed the door. "Those two had better get married soon. Their courting is wearing me out." Then she smiled at Ada. "Thank goodness you don't have a beau, Ada. You are content to stay here at home with me, aren't you?"

"For sure," Ada said, stirring the frosting slowly. The texture was just right. "But I might have a beau one day."

Mamm gave her shoulders a squeeze. "Not my Ada. I don't know what I'd do without you."

Ada didn't say anything and instead started frosting the cupcakes. She swirled each one with white icing, then sprinkled red and green sugar over the top, holding her mouth in a tight line. If she opened it, she might say something that would disappoint Mamm, but if she didn't, the tears welling up inside her might spill out. How could Mamm think she would be happy living at home for the rest of her life?

At the same time, Mamm was right. Pretty girls won beaus.

Slim girls who giggled together at fellowship dinners after church had beaus. Not the girls whose apron strings were always a bit too tight.

After breakfast was done and the dishes cleaned up, Ada took the boxes of cookies and cupcakes to the store. The sun had warmed the ice to slush, even though the wind was still brisk.

As she filled the glass cases with her baked goods, Vernon's buggy went past the store window, followed by Amos's buggy. She smoothed her apron, trying to still the butterflies in her stomach. Rose came into the front of the store just as Ada took a deep breath and picked up the plate of molasses crinkles.

"Is Amos here already?" she asked, putting away her duster and switching on the lights.

"He drove his buggy, so he arrived earlier than usual." Ada tugged on her skirt to straighten it.

"You look fine."

Ada gave her sister a smile of thanks, then saw the new worker, Matthias, ride past the window on his bicycle. She took another deep breath as Rose gave her shoulder a little push.

Matthias hung his coat on the hook next to Amos's and Vernon's, then unwound the wool scarf from his neck. As he hung his hat on the hook with his coat, the door leading to the store opened and Ada came into the workshop with a plate of cookies in her hands.

Her cheeks were bright red as she let the door close behind her. Matthias smiled, waiting for her to look his way. When they had been in school together, he had been convinced she didn't like him at all. Unlike some of the other girls who huddled in groups and giggled whenever he looked their way, Ada spent their recess and lunch times sitting with a book, engrossed in whatever story she was reading. The longest conversation he ever had with her was last week, when he talked with her in the furniture store.

Ada didn't look his way but shifted from one foot to the other as she stared at Amos and Vernon. The two men were sitting at the lunch table, drinking coffee before the clock struck eight. They didn't notice as she stood there, her eyebrows peaked and her lip pulled between her teeth. The rosy cheeks had faded. She took a step back toward the door. The plate tilted to one side and the cookies slid toward the edge.

Matthias crossed the space between them in two strides and tipped the plate up until it was level again.

He grinned when she gave him a startled look. "I didn't want you to spill the cookies. They look delicious."

She laughed, the sound tight and strained, and tightened her grip on the plate. "Would you like a molasses crinkle?"

"I was hoping you'd offer me one."

"Ada! What do you have there?" Amos's voice echoed in the quiet workshop. "Cookies? Are they for me?"

Matthias eyed the cookies, ready to choose one when Ada spun around to look toward Amos, pulling the plate out of his reach.

"I made them for you and everyone in the workshop." She walked to the table, nearly tripping over a rough spot in the cement floor.

Amos sat up and reached for the plate, a grin on his face.

"Denki." He grabbed a cookie and shoved it into his mouth, then handed the plate to Vernon.

By the time Matthias reached the table, Amos had grabbed two more. Ada's face was red again as she watched Amos. "Do you like them?"

"Sure." Amos shrugged and pushed another cookie into his mouth. He glanced at the clock as he stood up, putting a fourth cookie into his work apron pocket. "Got to get to work."

"I'll leave the rest here on the table," Ada said as Amos and Vernon walked toward their workbenches. "You can have more later."

Matthias took a cookie from the plate as Ada's voice faded. She stared after Amos and Vernon, but they paid no attention to her.

"It was nice of you to bring the cookies." Matthias bit into the treat, the sugary outside giving way to the tender molasses cookie. "This is delicious. I think I like this one better than the sugar cookie I had before."

The corners of her mouth quivered a little as she rubbed her palms on her apron. "They're only molasses cookies." Her long dark eyelashes glistened as they brushed her cheeks. "Nothing special." She walked back to the door that led to the store, her shoulders rounded.

Matthias watched her through the door's window until she disappeared into the furniture store. After growing up with three sisters, he knew girls could be moody sometimes, but he didn't remember Ada ever being upset about anything. Even during math, if she had made a mistake on a problem she was working on the chalkboard, she would only laugh it off and try again. He took a second cookie, then made his way to his workbench just as Leroy came into the shop.

The older man clapped his hand on Matthias's shoulder. "How are things going, Matthias? You seem to be settling into the job."

"*Jah*, for sure." Matthias turned to Leroy. "I appreciate you giving me this opportunity to work."

"You're a skilled wood-crafter, just like your father was. I have a proposition for you." He led the way to a different work-station where the bench was filled with carving tools. "Many of our customers like special touches on their furniture. Things like this."

Leroy handed a table leg to Matthias. It was made of oak with dark mahogany inlaid in a narrow band that followed the grain of the oak from the foot to the top, where the leg would be fastened to the table. Matthias couldn't resist running his finger along the dark stripe. The inlay was flawless. The mahogany and the oak were wedded together as if they had grown that way.

"This is beautiful." He handed the leg back to Leroy. "Who crafted this?"

"Your father." Leroy stroked the smooth wood. "He did this one as a sample, and we had many orders based on it. But after your family moved to Wisconsin, I had to take it off the sales floor. I couldn't find anyone else who was interested in trying to duplicate it."

Matthias glanced across the workshop. Amos and Vernon had turned on their power saws and were cutting lengths of wood to the specified sizes for the furniture, just as Matthias had spent the last week doing. His hands ached to do finer work. Hand work. "I would like to try, if that's all right."

Leroy chuckled. "That's what I hoped you would say." He gestured toward the tools on the bench. "Try it out. See what you can do."

"I can't promise I'll finish anything today."

"I don't expect you to. This is an experiment. If you can do it and like it, we'll both be happy. If not, you can always join Amos and Vernon again."

Nodding his thanks as Leroy went to his office, he turned to the workbench and picked up a chisel. The wooden handle was smooth to his touch, worn by hours of use. His Dat had used and loved these tools and had crafted beautiful furniture with them. Matthias had learned to appreciate woodcarving from him and spent every spare minute with his knife and a block of wood in his hands. His heart thudded as he examined the table leg. Could he hope to duplicate Dat's skill?

He rummaged through the scrap bin until he found what he was looking for, a nice piece of oak and a sliver of mahogany. Taking it back to the workbench, he spent the rest of the morning experimenting with the tools, seeking the best way to work with the wood to make it yield to the vision he had in his mind.

The time passed unnoticed until Amos and Vernon turned off their power saws, signaling that it was noon and time for lunch. His stomach growled, reminding him that it had been hours since he had eaten Ada's cookies, and he reluctantly left his work. He rolled his shoulders as he walked to the table in the corner of the building with his lunch box. After the break, he would have to remember to sit on the stool Leroy had provided for him.

Amos and Vernon sat at the table already, their lunches laid on the table, the last of the molasses cookies in Amos's hand.

"Those cookies were pretty good," Vernon said. He unwrapped his sandwich.

"Better than any you could make." Amos popped the last of the cookie in his mouth and unwrapped his sandwich. "You should think of giving up the bachelor life, Vernon. Marry a girl like Ada and you'd be eating well for the rest of your life."

Vernon blushed, glancing at the door. Leroy's office was empty, and Matthias figured the boss had gone to his house across the driveway for his dinner.

"Ada's too young for me. You know that." Vernon took a bite of his sandwich. "Besides"—he spoke around his mouthful of bread and peanut butter—"I'm too old to get married."

Matthias took his sandwich from its wax-paper wrapping. Turkey and mayonnaise on white bread. He took a bite as he listened to Amos and Vernon.

"What about you?" Vernon asked, giving Amos a soft punch on his shoulder. "You should marry Ada."

Amos shook his head. "No way," he said, using the Englisch phrase. "I don't want to be saddled with a tub like her."

As Vernon answered with a snorting laugh, Matthias squirmed in his chair. He hardly knew either of his co-workers, but he couldn't let Amos's comment slide by. "Ada's a nice girl."

Amos laughed. "A nice girl? Nice and plump. She would eat her husband out of house and home."

"Is that all you think is important in a girl?" Matthias worked to keep his voice even and pleasant. "A girl like Ada would make a fine wife for anyone."

"What do you know about it?" Amos laughed even harder. "Guys like you and Vernon couldn't even get a prettier girl to talk to you."

Matthias took another bite of his sandwich, working to ignore the other men. Ada's lovely face came to his mind, her pink cheeks glowing from the cold air on that first morning he came to work. He couldn't think of a prettier girl than Ada.

CHAPTER THREE

On the second Friday of the Great Cookie Campaign, Rose reached around Ada's shoulder and grabbed a cookie off the cooling rack.

"No more of that!" Ada said, shoving Rose aside with her hip. "These cookies are for the guys in the workshop."

"You mean they're for Amos," Rose said, giving Ada a playful shove in return.

"Shh!" Ada frowned at her sister. "No one is supposed to know about that."

"You mean the Great Cookie Campaign? Don't worry. Mamm is upstairs and Dat is still in the barn doing his chores." She took a bite of the cookie. "Mmm. You haven't made oatmeal chocolate chip cookies in a long time. These are delicious. Do you think Amos will like them?"

Ada sighed. Last week had been disappointing, with Amos devouring the cookies and ignoring her. "I hope so. He seemed to like the molasses crinkles, but he still didn't act as if he knew I was there."

"Did you talk to him?"

"Of course I did. I even asked if he liked them."

"What did he do?"

"He ate another cookie and went off to work."

Rose leaned against the sink, watching her mix up another batch of gingerbread. "He'll have to notice you today. Just smile and be nice to him."

The dull headache that had plagued Ada all week started up again. She put her mixing spoon down and looked at Rose. "Do you really think he will? You don't think I'm going to be an old maid?"

Rose shook her head. "You won't be an old maid. Not with the way you bake."

"But Amos never looks at me. I don't think he even notices anything I do or say."

"Maybe he isn't the one for you. Maybe the Good Lord has someone else in mind to be your husband."

Ada pressed her lips together. If the Good Lord had someone else for her, he would have shown up by now, for sure.

"*Nee*, it can't be. Amos is the only one for me."

"What about the new boy? Matthias?"

"I've known him forever." Ada went back to her mixing. "We were in school together before he moved to Wisconsin."

"So what's wrong with him?"

"Nothing." Ada paused, picturing Matthias in her mind. His smile was the thing that struck her the most. His smile was friendly, and she never got the feeling he was making fun of her. "Nothing is wrong with him. He just isn't Amos."

"And Amos is perfect."

Ada almost agreed, then she saw the teasing look on Rose's face. "All right, he isn't perfect. But he is so good-looking, he must be nice. I just want to get to know him so I can see what he's like for myself."

"As long as you're sure, then I'm on your side." She snatched another cookie, then grabbed her shawl from the hook. "I'm going out to gather the eggs. Let me know what Amos says when you deliver those cookies."

"I will," Ada said, pouring the gingerbread batter into the cake pan.

But later, at the end of the noon break when she took the plate of cookies into the workshop, Amos wasn't there.

"He telephoned the office this morning," Dat said, helping himself to a cookie. "He said he was sick today."

"I hope it isn't anything serious."

"Nothing the weekend won't cure." Dat went into his office, a frown on his face.

Matthias smiled at her as he took a cookie from the plate. "I wouldn't worry about Amos. He'll be fine on Monday."

"Oh." Ada looked at the plate in her hand. So much for getting Amos to notice her today.

Vernon patted the table. "Set that plate down here, Ada. I'll eat Amos's share." He chuckled, sounding more like a cackling hen than anything else.

Ada set the plate on the table, next to a toy horse. When she looked at the horse again, she saw that it wasn't a simple toy. Picking it up, she ran her fingers along the horse's mane, the curves making it look like the horse was facing into the wind.

"Who made this?"

Matthias took it from her, turning it in his hand, rubbing a rough spot on the horse's flank.

"I did." He set it back on the table, where it balanced perfectly.

"It looks just like a horse."

He grinned. "I hope it does. I'm making it for my nephew's Christmas present."

"You have several nephews, don't you?"

"Five, if you count the baby."

"Are you making horses for all of them?"

He opened his lunch box and set a cow on the table next to the horse. "Not just horses, but cows and pigs, too. My Dat made barns for the boys last year, so I had the idea of making animals to go in the barns."

Ada picked up the cow. It was about four inches high and held its tail along the side of its flank, as if it was swishing a fly.

"They are very realistic. I've never seen such fine work."

"It's just a toy." Matthias shrugged. "I make them in my spare time."

"What else do you make?"

He glanced at the clock. "We have time before I need to start working again. I'll show you what Leroy asked me to work on."

He led her to a workbench. A vise held a piece of wood on top of the bench. In the center of the wood was a long groove.

"I'm inlaying mahogany into this piece of oak." He leaned over the bench and brushed a piece of curled wood away. "The hardest part was figuring out which tools to use to make the groove. I remember watching Dat do it, but that was years ago."

Matthias picked up a narrow piece of darker wood and pressed it into the groove.

"That's going to be beautiful," Ada said. She leaned closer. The dark band was striking in contrast to the lighter oak.

"I hope the customers think so." He looked at her, his dark brown eyes glowing. "I'm just glad I was able to get it to work."

She noticed a finished table leg lying on the workbench. "Will it look like that when it's done?"

Matthias nodded, picking it up. "Dat made this one, and Leroy wanted me to see if I could replicate it."

"I remember when we used to sell these tables in the store. The customers have been asking if we have more." Ada ran her finger along the mahogany inlay Matthias had just inserted until a sharp prick stopped her.

"Ouch." A splinter had embedded itself deep under her skin.

"That's what you get for fooling around with my work." Matthias grinned at her as he grabbed her hand and pulled it under his work light. He flicked the light on and examined her finger, holding her arm under his elbow, pinning her against him. Ada tugged at her arm, feeling a bit foolish, but Matthias gripped it tightly.

"Hold still. This won't take a minute." He took a pair of tweezers from his bench and bent his head over her hand.

Gritting her teeth, Ada waited for the sharp pain she knew would come when he drew out the splinter, but before she felt anything, he released her.

"You got it out already?" she asked, looking at her finger.

"It isn't difficult if you get to the splinter right away. But if you let it sit in there for a day, or even a few hours, then it's painful to get out."

"Jah, for sure. I've had my share of splinters."

Matthias took a small tool and eased the inlay out of the groove.

"Why are you taking it out? It was perfect."

"Now that I know it fits, I need to glue it in."

He picked up a bottle of wood glue and started dropping beads of the white liquid in the narrow groove with a steady hand. Ada leaned her elbow on the workbench, watching until he reached the end of the groove. Then he picked up the inlay again and set it in place. Once he pressed it into its spot, he wiped away the excess glue with a cloth.

"I don't know how you do it," Ada said. "My hands would have been shaking so much that I'd never get that in there on the first try."

He grinned at her. "And I don't know how you bake such delicious things. If I tried baking, it would come out burned or lopsided."

She shrugged, feeling her cheeks warm. "I just pay attention to the details."

"That's the same thing I do."

The clock by the lunch table struck one.

Ada glanced at Matthias's project one more time and sighed. "I had better get back to the store. It's Rose's turn to take her lunch break."

"Be sure to wash your finger and put a bandage on it. You don't want it to get infected."

He turned back to his work, rubbing away another bead of glue as Ada walked to the door that separated the workshop from the store. She sent Rose to lunch and was taking her place behind the counter before she remembered that today's Great Cookie Campaign had been a failure. Amos wasn't at work. How could she have forgotten about that?

After Ada left, Matthias gave his project one last wipe with a damp cloth, then picked up the small scraping plane. He had sharpened the blade and cleaned the tool, and now applied it to the wood using short, light strokes. He worked quickly, only smoothing the seam between the inlay and the wood, not shaping the leg. As the curls of wood fell from the plane in fine lacy spirals, his mind wandered to Ada.

He liked her. He had liked her when they had been in school together, even though she had ignored him. But that had been all right. He had never been one of those boys who did crazy stunts during recess to get the girls' attention. That kind of fooling around was more for guys like Amos. Matthias had never been that bold.

Blowing the wood spirals away, Matthias stooped to look across the inlay, then applied the scraper to a section that still looked uneven.

The workshop was quieter today with Amos gone. Vernon was using the band saw on the other side of the big room, but without the shouting banter he and Amos usually exchanged during the day. The frown on Leroy's face earlier made it clear that the boss wasn't happy that Amos had called in. Matthias had heard of workers who would call in sick on Friday so they could have a long weekend, but only the Englisch would resort to lying to their bosses that way, wouldn't they?

Matthias moved the plane to another rough place and continued the short strokes.

Amos was a puzzle. He looked Amish in his dress and the way he lived, but he acted like an unbroken colt fighting the harness. Matthias's mind went back to the hurtful comments he had heard Amos and Vernon make about Ada last week. Leroy would never allow talk like that in the workshop when he was around, and Matthias didn't like it, either. Talking about someone like that was uncalled for. He just hoped Ada never heard comments like those.

He ran his finger along the inlaid wood. No splinters remained.

"How is it coming?"

Leroy had walked up to the workbench while Matthias had been engrossed in his work.

"I think this one is working out so far." Matthias stepped back so Leroy could examine his progress.

"Beautiful," Leroy said. "Your Dat couldn't have done a better job on the inlay. But it isn't a table leg yet."

"I thought I'd try doing the inlay first, and then shape the table leg. I tried shaping the leg before doing the inlay and just couldn't get it to work. The curve in the leg's shape made it too difficult to get it to look right."

Matthias took the piece of wood out of its clamps and handed it to Leroy. His boss looked at it from all angles.

"The inlay is nice and deep. It looks like your method might work."

"I'll let the glue dry over the weekend and work on the shaping on Monday."

Leroy passed his thumb across the grain with a smile of satisfaction that eased Matthias's worries. If Leroy was pleased with his work, then he knew he had done the inlay correctly.

"How is your mother doing?" Leroy said, leaning back against the workbench. "She has gone through quite a bit, with the move back to Shipshewana and all."

Matthias shrugged. "I think she's getting along fine. She likes being back here where we're close to the girls."

"But?" Leroy's gaze didn't waver.

"She regrets moving to Wisconsin. I think she believes things would have turned out differently if we had stayed here."

"Jah." Leroy crossed his arms. "I have gotten that feeling from what my wife has told me. Franny thinks that Essie is holding on too dearly to the past."

Matthias took a rag and started wiping his tools and putting them away. "Are you asking as a friend or as a deacon?"

Leroy chuckled. "I guess a little of both. As a deacon, I'm concerned about all the members of the *G'may*. We're a family, and if one is suffering, we're all suffering."

"I think Mamm is beginning to adjust. Dat's passing was sudden." Matthias swallowed. He didn't trust his voice to speak normally.

"Did you get Ervin's investment back when you sold the farm in Wisconsin?"

Matthias shook his head. "Dat had taken out a mortgage to buy it. After the funeral, Simon took the first offer that came along, but it was only enough to pay off the loan. He sold the livestock to buy our place here and to pay for the expenses of moving back to Indiana."

"Your horse and buggy?"

Matthias's throat closed. "We lost them in the accident."

Leroy stroked his beard while Matthias put the chisels back into their case.

"If you were in need, you would tell me, wouldn't you?"

Matthias hesitated. "Dat wasn't one to ask for help. I don't know how Mamm feels about it."

"It's a prideful man who considers himself above the rest of the community. The church supports all its members."

"Simon gave us a cow to use, and the girls all made sure the cellar is full. We have plenty to eat."

"But you ride your bicycle to work, even when it's snowy and the days are short. You're riding to and from work in the dark."

Matthias closed the chisel case and put it in the drawer. He didn't have an answer for Leroy. The old house on the other side of town was small and crowded. Mamm spent money to hire a driver rather than buy a new buggy and horse. And at night . . . Mamm sat in her chair through the long evenings, staring out the dark window.

Leroy leaned closer. "We're here to help, Matthias. There is money in the deacon fund to provide your family with a driving horse and a buggy. We will make sure you have enough propane to last the winter. I also know that the Fishers butchered an extra steer this week. They'll send some of the meat to your house."

With a sigh, Matthias turned to Leroy. "I don't know what Mamm will say about it, but I can only give you my thanks."

Leroy put a hand on Matthias's shoulder. "Don't worry about Essie. I'll see if Franny can go over this afternoon and talk to her about it." He grinned. "And now, speaking as a friend and your boss, I want to make sure you know you have a job here as long as you want it. Consider yourself one of the family."

"I want to earn my job. Don't keep me on if I don't fit here."

The older man chuckled. "Never worry about that, son. Your work speaks for itself. You have a knack for working with wood, and your skills are valuable to us."

Matthias took a rag and wiped the newly inlaid wood one last time. "I wish today wasn't Friday. By tomorrow, the glue will be dry, and I could start working on shaping the table leg."

"You could come in, if you'd like. Franny and I will be in Middlebury, visiting her sister for the day, but Ada and Rose will be working in the store. Just let yourself in and work as long as you want to."

"I would like that, if you don't mind."

"Not at all. Folks have been asking for fine woodworking in the store, but there aren't enough hours in the day for me to work on both furniture and the clocks. The sooner we can put one of your pieces in the showroom, the sooner we'll be able to start selling them."

"You're that certain? I've only done one inlay. This is a long way from being a piece of furniture."

"I've watched you work. You have your father's skill and attention to detail. I'm sure your pieces will sell just as well as his did."

Matthias smiled as he took a deep breath of the comfortable scent of wood and sawdust, feeling more at home than he had for years.

By the time Rose returned from her dinner break, Ada was ready for her help. The sun had emerged from the gray clouds and turned the afternoon into a sparkling wonderland of snow. Shoppers, eager to find something special for Christmas, filled the little shop. Ada kept busy ringing up purchases on the cash register and serving cups of hot cider, while Rose took orders for furniture.

One couple, their last customers of the afternoon, purchased Ada's favorite clock. She loved the stained-glass panels Dat had inserted into the tall case, depicting a pair of red cardinals.

"Cardinals mate for life," said the *Englisch* woman, Mrs. Wilson. "I've always thought of them as a symbol of a long and happy marriage."

Mr. Wilson winked at Ada as he handed Rose a card with their address on it. "Until I met Mary, I thought a marriage could either be long or happy, but not both. She proved me wrong." He put an arm around his wife's shoulders and gave her a gentle hug. "Guess how long we've been married."

"Oh, Bert. It isn't fair to put these girls on the spot like that." Mrs. Wilson laughed as she gave her husband a loving look.

"I'll guess," said Rose. She grinned at the couple as she handed the receipt to Mr. Wilson. "I think you've been married for forty-five years."

Mr. Wilson turned to Ada. "Now it's your turn. What do you think?"

Ada concentrated, noting the comfortable way Mrs. Wilson laid her hand on her husband's shoulder and the soft look in Mr. Wilson's eyes.

"I think you've been married longer. Maybe fifty years?"

The couple looked at each other. "You're both wrong," said Mr. Wilson. "Our wedding was fifty-five years ago today."

"You must have been very young," Rose said.

Mrs. Wilson giggled. "We were. Bert joined the army before he graduated from high school, and we wanted to get married so I could go with him when he finished boot camp. He was eighteen and I was sixteen."

"I was stationed all around the world. Germany, Iceland, Korea—"

"And I followed him all the way." Mrs. Wilson's eyes grew misty. "Until he was sent to Vietnam. Then I stayed behind, worrying and praying for two years before he came home."

Ada couldn't imagine living in a different country or having a husband who was fighting in a war. "Do you have children?" she asked.

Mrs. Wilson shook her head. "The Lord never blessed us with little ones, but he gave us each other." She gave her husband another loving look. "This clock is very special. We first saw it in your shop here last summer and decided to save our money until we could buy it."

"I hope you enjoy it for a long time," Rose said as Mrs. Wilson buttoned her coat in preparation to leave.

The older woman didn't answer, but a tear trickled down her cheek.

"Now, none of that," Mr. Wilson scolded as he took her hand. "We promised each other there would be no tears today." He looked at Rose and Ada, his own eyes glistening. "This is our last anniversary together, and our last Christmas until we meet in heaven. I won't be here next year, according to the doctors, so this clock will have to keep Mary company until she joins me."

Ada's own eyes grew damp. "Keep in touch, won't you? Stop

by the store whenever you want to and let us know how you're doing."

"Do you hear that, Mary?" Bert kissed her cheek. "I'm not leaving you alone. You have friends wherever you go."

The couple waved their farewells and Rose locked the door after them, turning the Closed sign to face out the window.

"They were nice people, weren't they?"

Ada wiped her eyes, then started boxing up the few remaining cookies from the bakery case. "Such a sad story, though. She will miss him so much when he passes on."

"But she has a lot to be thankful for," Rose said as she took money and papers out of the cash drawer and put them in the deposit bag to carry to the house. "They've had a long life together and have many memories to look back on."

Ada finished with the cookies and started walking through the store, straightening merchandise as she went. When she passed the cardinal clock, she stopped and ran her finger over the red bird on the front. The bandage on her finger made her think of Matthias and her cookie delivery that day.

"I forgot to tell you," she said, giving the beautiful clock one last look before moving on to the next display. "Amos didn't come to work today, so he wasn't there for his cookies."

"What did you do with them?"

"I gave them to Vernon and Matthias. Even if Amos wasn't there, at least someone could enjoy them."

"Did Dat say where Amos was?"

"He called in sick, but Dat said it in a funny way, like he didn't believe that Amos had told him the truth." Ada turned an ornament on the little display tree so that it faced the front. "Amos wouldn't lie, though. Would he?"

Rose closed the cash drawer with a thump. "I don't know him that well. He's your beau."

"He isn't my beau." Ada took her shawl from the hook. "I just want him to be."

"You don't if he is untruthful. If he lies to his boss, he'll lie to his wife, too." Rose tossed her shawl around her shoulders and flipped off the light switch. "I already locked the door. We'll go out through the workshop."

Ada started down the dark hall. "But I don't know if Amos lied. What if he's really sick?"

"You'll have to wait until Monday and ask him."

Rose pulled the workshop door open. The big room was dark except for a light over Matthias's workbench and a lantern shining from Dat's office in the far corner.

As Rose crossed the open area to Dat's office, Ada walked over to Matthias's workbench. He was bent over another piece of oak, inserting another inlay. Three finished blocks were on the bench next to his work area.

"You've gotten a lot done this afternoon."

Matthias grinned at her but didn't stop his careful, methodical work. "I wanted to get all four legs this far along, so the glue can dry overnight. Leroy said I can come in and work on them tomorrow."

"Did you know it's after six o'clock?"

A line appearing between his eyebrows was the only sign that he had heard her.

"Vernon must have gone home an hour ago."

Matthias straightened, wiping the new inlay with a rag, then he stared at her. "It isn't really six o'clock already, is it?"

When she nodded, he glanced out the dark window, then at the work on his bench.

"I was supposed to milk the cow at five." He rubbed the back of his neck. "But at least all four legs are inlaid."

While Matthias switched off his work light and took his coat from the hook next to the workshop door, Ada got her plate from the lunch table. She wrapped the three remaining cookies in a napkin and handed them to Matthias.

"You should take these with you."

He grinned as he put the cookies in his coat pocket. "Denki. I might even eat them on the way home."

"Did you ride your bicycle again today?"

Matthias nodded as he fastened his coat.

Ada glanced at the window. The sun had already set. "It's dark outside, and cold. Why didn't you drive to work this morning?"

He pulled his knit cap over his ears. "We don't have a buggy yet." He grinned at her. "Don't worry about me. I'll be careful riding home."

Wintry air swept into the workshop as Matthias left, making Ada shiver. She hoped he didn't live too far away.

CHAPTER FOUR

*M*atthias wished he could start work earlier on Saturday morning, but with Leroy and his wife gone for the day, he would have to wait until Ada and Rose arrived at the store at eight o'clock before he could go to the workshop. So, he spent extra time cleaning the cow's stall and putting down fresh bedding.

He was eating breakfast when he heard a buggy in the driveway.

"Who could that be?" Mamm asked, peering out the window. "It looks like Deacon Weaver."

Matthias joined Mamm at the window. She was right. Leroy stopped a strange horse at the rail at the end of the sidewalk. The Weavers' buggy, driven by Franny Weaver, stopped beside him.

"I told Franny not to bother with a horse and buggy for us." Mamm turned away from the window and stomped back to the sink. "She said we needed one, but I told her I didn't want one. We're getting along fine without it."

"And I told Leroy we would be happy to have it." Matthias cleared the table before Leroy and Franny came to the door.

"We need better transportation for the winter. My bicycle won't go on the roads when the snow gets deep."

Mamm looked at him, her eyebrows raised. "It wasn't your place to tell them such a thing. You're only a boy."

"I am a man, with a man's job and a man's responsibilities." Matthias's stomach quivered as he faced his mother. "It's my decision to make, for the good of our family."

Mamm turned back to the sink full of dishes. "We don't have a family. Not anymore."

Matthias had no answer to that comment. He crossed the room to let Leroy and Franny in.

"I didn't expect you to come by today," Matthias said.

Leroy glanced at Mamm, still standing at the sink with her back to them. "One of the older couples from the church are heading down to Pinecraft for the winter. They usually leave their horse with their son while they're gone, but they agreed that you could take care of her just as well. She's yours until spring."

"We don't need a horse and buggy," Mamm said, turning around and drying her hands on a dish towel. "I told Franny yesterday. We don't want it."

"Matthias needs a way to get to work," Leroy said. "He can't ride his bicycle all through the winter."

Mamm sank into a chair at the table. "I promised myself that he would never drive a buggy. Not after what happened to Ervin."

Leroy pulled out one of the chairs and sat across from Mamm. "Ervin was in an accident. The horse isn't to blame, or the buggy. A careless driver, a rainy night, and a slippery road were all factors. But that is in the past."

"I'm not going to let my boy drive a buggy."

Franny sat down next to Leroy. "But, Essie, he has to be able to go to work."

Mamm's lower lip trembled. "He can call a driver or ride his bicycle."

Matthias sat next to Mamm and took her hand in his. "We need a buggy, and Leroy has arranged for one. We're going to accept it with gratitude and humility."

Mamm clung to his hand. "I won't have you driving after dark."

"That isn't possible." Matthias kept his voice gentle, remembering how dark it had been on that terrible night last spring. "It will be after sunset when I come home from work this winter. But I will follow the laws and use the safety precautions allowed by the church."

Mamm's mouth trembled.

"Essie," Leroy said, "this is up to Matthias. He's the one who needs to make the decision."

"He's a boy. It's my place to decide for our family."

Franny shook her head. "He is a man, Essie. Not your little boy anymore. He needs to take his father's place."

"I don't want him to have to grow up too fast." Mamm laid her hands in her lap, twisting them together. "I'll ask Sally's Simon. He'll know what to do."

Matthias resisted the urge to argue with Mamm. Simon had stepped into Dat's role as soon as he heard about the accident. He was the one who had advised Mamm to sell the farm in Wisconsin and come back to Indiana. He was the one who had found this house for them. But was Mamm right to depend on him so much?

Leroy leaned over the table. "Simon has his own family. He's responsible for his family's dairy and his position as deacon in his own G'may. He shouldn't also be expected to be the head of his wife's family, not when you have a grown son to help you. Matthias is old enough and mature enough to take on whatever responsibilities he needs to. I wouldn't have hired him if I didn't think so."

Mamm didn't look at any of them. Leroy signaled for Matthias to follow him outside.

"We'll let Franny talk to her," he said as he stepped off the porch.

"Have I done something wrong?" Matthias asked, following Leroy as he walked over to the borrowed horse and buggy. "Should I have been making the decisions all along instead of letting Simon take over?"

Leroy adjusted the horse's blanket as Matthias stood close, letting the mare take in his scent.

"It's a difficult situation, especially since your Mamm still considers you to be too young to take on your family responsibilities. Simon is quite a bit older than you, isn't he?"

"He's almost fourteen years older."

Leroy nodded. "On top of that, he's one of those fellows who takes charge whenever there's a need." He patted the horse's neck again. "That isn't a bad quality, but it's time for you to step up and take care of your Mamm. It's a hard thing to do, I know. I was the oldest of thirteen children when my Dat passed on. At eighteen, I needed to take care of the farm and my younger siblings. My mother was overwhelmed. I know you can understand that."

Matthias nodded.

"Do you agree with the decisions Simon made?"

"I would have bought a bigger place and farther from town." Matthias said, looking at the small frame house. "This is fine for the two of us, and it's what we could afford. But I don't think Simon was considering that I might marry one day."

"It only has two bedrooms?"

"One. I sleep in the attic while Mamm has the bedroom."

"And it would be hard to bring a wife home, let alone try to raise young ones here."

The thought of Ada's smile startled Matthias. A girl like Ada would make a wonderful wife.

He grinned at Leroy. "If I ever find the right girl to marry, we'll have to sort that out."

The older man chuckled as Franny came out the door. "I'm sure you'll come up with a solution. We need to get going. I told the girls you'd be coming to work in the shop this morning."

"I'll leave soon. I want to make sure Mamm is all right before I go."

"By the way," Leroy said as he picked up the reins, "the mare's name is Nellie Belle."

Matthias waved as Leroy and Franny left. Nellie Belle? That was a different name for a horse.

But then, almost everything was different since they moved back to Shipshewana. Leroy was right. Mamm would get used to him being the man of the family eventually, but it would be a long time before it felt right to him.

The store was busy on Saturday morning from the moment Ada flipped the sign to Open. The bell above the door tinkled constantly as customers entered and left, most of them carrying their purchases of Christmas ornaments or other goods from the store. In addition, nearly all of them purchased a cupcake or two, or a dozen cookies. Rose kept busy in the showroom, taking orders for furniture.

The weather was warm and sunny, so Ada propped the door open at the end of the hall leading to the workshop. Matthias was at his workbench, but he was concentrating on his task and didn't look up when she waved.

When the morning rush was over, Rose came back from the showroom and collapsed into the rocking chair they kept for customers. "You know I love it when the store is busy, but I don't think I've ever seen this many people at once."

"It's getting close to Christmas." Ada was replenishing the bakery display while she had a chance. "Vernon and Amos will have a lot of deliveries to make on Monday."

"That will make Dat happy," Rose said. She yawned.

"Were you out late again last night?"

"Johnny and I spent the evening at his brother's house, playing games with his family. We had a lot of fun."

"That wouldn't keep you out late."

Rose smiled. "We took the long way home." She sighed. "There's nothing like having a beau to make the days wonderful."

"I think you're in love." Ada leaned on the counter, enjoying her sister's happiness. If only Amos would ask to take her home from next week's Singing or come by this evening to spend some time with her, if he wasn't still sick. No matter what Rose had said, Ada trusted Amos. If he had told Dat he was ill, then he was.

The line of grandfather clocks started chiming the hour.

"It's noon already?" Rose asked. "We should take our lunch break while the store is quiet. You go first. But eat in the workshop so I can call you if we get busy again."

Ada grabbed her paper lunch bag and walked down the hall to the workshop. Sunlight streamed in the windows at both ends of the big room. She set her lunch on the break table and walked over to Matthias's workbench.

"I'm taking a few minutes to eat my lunch, now that the morning rush is done. Are you ready for a break? You can join me."

Matthias released the clamps from the table leg he was working on. "That's a good idea, although I hate to stop working."

She sat at the table and took her sandwich from the bag. "Everyone needs to take a short rest once in a while." Ada took out an apple and put it next to her sandwich. "Bring your lunch over and we'll keep each other company."

When Matthias opened his lunch box, a small round piece of wood was on top of his lunch.

"What is that? Another farm animal for your nephews?"

"Not this one." He handed it to her. "This is a present for my Mamm."

The bird was shaped, but only partly carved. Ada turned it in her hands. It was about four inches long and looked as if the little creature was struggling to emerge from the wood like a chick from its egg.

"What kind of bird will it be?"

"A chickadee. Mamm had a bird feeder outside the kitchen window in Wisconsin and loved to watch the chickadees that came to the feeder all winter long. Another present for her will be a new bird feeder, since we left the old one behind."

"Will you paint the bird? Or leave the wood plain?"

"I like to use an oil-based stain on the birds I carve. It gives the feathers color without covering up the beauty of the wood grain." Matthias took a bite of his sandwich.

"How do you make the feathers?" Ada asked.

"I'll show you."

Matthias pulled out a small knife from his pocket and took the bird from her. He used the narrow blade to cut fine lines into the head, working while Ada finished her sandwich. Then he handed it back to her. He had given the bird a beak, with tiny feathers surrounding it. The feathers continued down the bird's neck and toward the hint of a shoulder emerging from the wood.

"This is going to be beautiful. Your Mamm will love it."

"I hope she does." He finished his sandwich and reached in his lunch box for an orange. "Do you like birds?"

Ada felt her face heat up. No boy had ever asked her what she liked.

"Jah, I do. We have a bird feeder outside our kitchen window, too. My favorites are the cardinals." She held her apple in her hand, forgotten. "Did you know that cardinal pairs stay together for life? I just learned that yesterday."

"I didn't know that. How did you find out?"

Ada hesitated. Would he laugh if she told him about the Wilsons?

"There was an older couple in the store yesterday. They bought a clock to celebrate their anniversary. They have been married fifty-five years."

Matthias sat back in his chair, his face thoughtful. "Fifty-five years is a long time. I hope my marriage lasts as long."

A sinking feeling settled in the pit of Ada's stomach. "You're getting married?"

He turned bright red and started clearing away his lunch with jerky motions. "I mean, when I do get married. I don't have any—" He glanced at her and looked away. "I mean, there isn't anybody." He threw his wrappings in the trash. "I mean, I haven't met—" Matthias stopped himself with a sigh. "Nee. I'm not getting married. But I want to. Someday."

Ada watched him as he sat down again and drummed his fingers on the table. Most boys she knew didn't talk about getting married. Some of them acted as if dating was a game and you only got married if you lost.

"Why?" She felt her face heat again. "I know why I'd like to get married someday, but you're a man. Why do you want to?"

"It's good to marry and raise a family." He looked at her. "We have a godly heritage. All Christians do, but especially we Amish. We need to teach our faith and heritage to the next generation. It's the most important thing we can do with our lives."

Ada stared at him. He had spoken her own thoughts out loud. If only Amos—

"Ada!" Rose's voice echoed down the hall from the store. "I need your help!"

She stood and tossed her napkin in the trash, folding her paper bag to reuse another time. "I have to go back to work."

Matthias got up from his chair, too. "So do I."

"I enjoyed our lunch together."

He smiled at her, his face growing red again. "I did, too. We'll have to do it again sometime."

Ada went back to the store and her customers. If only Amos were more like Matthias.

Matthias arrived at work early on Monday morning, eager to start his day. By the time Amos and Vernon arrived, he had already started sanding the table legs, taking short, quick strokes with the coarsest sandpaper. Leroy had a power sander he could use, but Matthias preferred to feel the wood under his fingers. Dat had taught him that quality furniture shouldn't be rushed.

After his co-workers arrived, they sat at the lunch table, waiting for eight o'clock and the official start to the workday. Vernon's laughter echoed in the big room. Matthias drained the mug of coffee he had brought with him from home, then headed to the coffee urn Leroy kept in the break area.

"I wasn't really sick," Amos was saying as Matthias passed the table. "Susie wanted to visit her sister's family in Centreville, Michigan, for the week, so I drove her up there." He leaned over the table. "But Leroy doesn't need to know I took the day off for that. I have five sick days left, and I plan to use them before the end of the year."

Matthias stopped by the table as he stirred creamer into his coffee. It had been hard to make friends with Amos and Vernon, but chatting for a few minutes might help him get to know them better. "Who is Susie?"

Amos glanced at him. "She's a girl I know."

Vernon laughed again, his voice cackling. "I'd say you know her." He winked at Matthias. "She's trying to get him to marry her."

"She's trying to trick me into it, you mean." Amos frowned. "But if I marry anyone, it might as well be Susie."

"She must be a girl from your G'may," Matthias said. "The only Susie around here is old enough to be my grandmother."

"Amos has dated girls from all over," Vernon said. His voice was colored with a mixture of pride and envy. "I wish I had half the girlfriends he does. He had four girls at once one time."

Amos shrugged. "You just need to know how to handle them, and don't let them have any idea that the others exist."

"You mean, each girl thought she was the only one you liked?"

"It would have been a disaster if they had found out. I would never have gotten a date again."

Matthias stared at the other man. He would never think of living the way Amos talked about, lying to his boss and dangling girls on a string as if they were fish.

With another cackle, Vernon said, "There's always Ada the Cow. She'd be happy to date you no matter what you did."

Amos joined in Vernon's joke. "She's that desperate, isn't she? I might just do that."

"That's cruel," Matthias said. "Ada isn't anything like that."

"You don't think so?" Amos grinned. "Then why does she bring in special cookies for us? You've seen her stumbling over her own big feet, that sappy smile on her face."

Matthias's heart pounded. "Maybe she's just trying to be nice."

"Nice?" Amos drained his cup and threw it in the trash. "Maybe I'll ask her on a date. Just for a lark before Susie comes home. She would say yes so fast that you would think I offered her a pile of gold."

Leroy came in the door that led to the driveway, stomping snow off his feet. "Good morning, boys. Are we ready to get to work? We have deliveries to make today, and we got several new orders over the weekend to start on."

As Amos stood, he leaned close to Matthias. "I'm right about Ada. If I get around to asking her out, she'll jump at the chance."

Leroy walked over and handed a sheaf of papers to Amos. "Here are the deliveries. One of them is the clock with the stained-glass cardinals, so be careful handling that one. I don't want it broken." He turned to Matthias. "Amos and Vernon can handle the deliveries. I want you to start on the orders. How are you doing on the table you've been working on?"

Matthias led him over to his workbench and showed him the progress he had made on Saturday. "They are all shaped, and I started sanding them this morning."

Picking up one of the legs, Leroy looked closely at the curved shape and the inlay. "That's fine work. I hate to interrupt your progress, but these new orders need to be done in time for Christmas, and that's only a little more than a week away. I have them in my office."

By the time Leroy had gone over the new orders, Matthias knew his time would be filled. There were several orders for the Lazy Susans folks liked to use in the center of their dining tables. There were also a few requests for what Leroy called "TV trays," although Matthias had no idea why someone would want a special tray for their television.

"You'll have to ask Rose or Ada to show you the sample we have in the showroom," Leroy said. "We try to keep several on hand, but they all sold on Saturday. The display sample is the last one left."

Matthias went into the store first, glad for an opportunity to warn Ada about Amos's idea to ask her out. As he walked down the short hallway, he tried to figure out how to approach the subject. How did you tell someone that if the guy did ask her out, it was only to prove how desperate he thought she was?

Ada was at the bakery display, filling the trays with cookies.

"Any broken cookies today?" He grinned, feeling a little foolish. He always felt foolish when he didn't know what to say.

She gave him one of her beautiful smiles. "For sure." She picked up a frosted sugar cookie shaped like a wreath and handed it to him. "It isn't broken, but it's a bit crooked. It turned out as an oval instead of a circle."

He took a bite of the cookie, delaying what he had to say as long as possible.

"Leroy sent me in to look at something he called a TV tray. Do you know what he means?"

"We have one in the showroom. I'll show it to you as soon as I'm done here."

Ada finished filling the cookie tray, then led the way through the opening to the other building. Furniture filled the space, separated into different sections. She walked past the dining tables and hutches to an area filled with desks, chairs, and smaller tables for use in a living room.

"This is it," she said, stopping at a little table shaped like the letter C. "It's for folks to use while they're sitting in a recliner or other living room chair. The base slides under the edge of the chair so that the top can be over their lap." She carried it to a mission-style chair and ottoman. "Try it out."

Matthias sat in the chair and Ada pushed the little table close. He ran his hand over the top. It was small. Hardly bigger than a magazine or newspaper.

"What do you put on it? You couldn't work on it or use it to put a puzzle together."

Ada giggled. "Englischers like to eat while they watch television. They say the tables are perfect to hold their cup of coffee or a plate."

Matthias got up from the chair and picked the little thing up. Leroy had handed him order sheets for eight of these, but as he looked at the simple construction, he knew he could easily make twenty by next Saturday while working on his other projects at the same time.

From the far end of the building, he could hear Rose humming a tune. If he was going to talk to Ada about Amos, he needed to do it now.

He cleared his throat. "Can I take this sample back to the workshop?"

Ada nodded. "You'll need it for a pattern."

"Leroy gave me the plans with all the measurements, but I want to make sure I put it together correctly."

He glanced toward the end of the showroom where Rose was dusting bedroom sets. "I need to tell you something about Amos."

Ada turned pink. "What about him? He isn't still sick, is he?"

Matthias shook his head. "He told me he might ask you out,

but—" He stopped speaking. Ada's face was a mixture of pain and happiness, and the pink had turned to bright red.

"When?" Her breath came in gasps. "Did he say when?"

"Soon. But, Ada, don't go out with him."

"Why not?" She checked her *Kapp* with one hand while she straightened her apron with the other.

"If he asks you, it's only to prove you would go with him. But he isn't a nice man. He'll only try to make you look foolish."

Ada acted like she hadn't heard him. "I knew he would notice me eventually."

Rose came toward them, her feather duster dangling from one hand. "What is going on? Are you all right, Ada?"

Ada pushed past Matthias and grasped her sister's hands. "Amos is going to ask me out. The Great Cookie Campaign worked!"

"The Great Cookie Campaign?" Matthias looked from Ada to Rose. "What's that?"

Rose giggled. "It's a secret."

"We can tell him now." Ada was smiling wider than he had ever seen. "Rose had the idea for me to take cookies to the workshop on Fridays to get Amos to notice me, and it worked."

"Wait a minute—"

Ada interrupted him. "And Amos was only there for one of the Fridays."

"Ada, listen to me. Amos isn't going to ask you out because he wants to spend time with you. He and Vernon were laughing about you and calling you—" Matthias stopped. "Well, calling you names. If he asks you out, turn him down. Please."

She turned toward him, frowning. "You don't even know Amos. I've been waiting for this too long to let you spoil it. I think you're just jealous because you didn't think to ask me out first."

As Ada hurried toward the entrance to the store, almost running, Matthias looked to Rose for help.

"Tell her I was only trying to warn her. She shouldn't go out with Amos. He already has a girl."

Rose looked at him, her eyes narrowed. "Maybe Ada is right. Maybe you are jealous. Don't ruin this for her. She's been working too hard for it."

She left him standing alone in the showroom, the little table dangling from one hand. Was he jealous? He didn't think so. All he wanted to do was protect Ada from being hurt.

CHAPTER FIVE

By Friday, Ada was beginning to think that she heard Matthias wrong. Every time Amos came into the store with Vernon to carry something out to the delivery wagon, she waited for him to look at her.

She had imagined the scene over and over. He would watch her until she looked up, surprised to see him. Then that slow smile would appear on his face as he walked over to her. He would lean across the bakery display case and reach one finger to touch the end of her nose. Then he would say—

"Ada?" Rose's voice broke into her daydream. "You're doing it again. The telephone was ringing, and you didn't even hear it. I had to answer it in the showroom. What are you thinking about?"

"I was just wondering when Amos was planning to ask me to go out with him. It's already Friday."

"Did you take the gingerbread cookies in to the workshop? They smelled wonderful when they were baking this morning."

"I'm going to take them at noon." Ada glanced at the row of grandfather clocks; the place where the cardinal clock had stood still looked empty. "It's a quarter to right now." She straightened her apron. "Will you mind the store while I take the plate of cookies in?"

"Are you going to take them now?"

Ada pulled her lower lip between her teeth. If she took them now, Amos would be working and might not see her come in. But if she waited until just after noon, all three of the workers would be eating their lunches, including Matthias. She hadn't spoken to him since Monday, when he tried to tell her not to go out with Amos.

"I'll wait until twelve o'clock. Amos hasn't asked me out yet, and if he's eating lunch when I go in, that will give him a chance to talk to me."

Rose leaned on the display case, right where Ada had imagined Amos would be when he finally talked to her. "If he asks you out, what will you say?"

"Do you really think I would turn him down?" Ada brought the box of frosted gingerbread cookies out from under the counter along with the wooden tray she would put them on.

"Sometimes it's better if you don't act too eager."

"I'm not taking any chances that he might change his mind."

Ada opened the box, taking a deep breath. The anise flavoring in the frosting mingled with the light spiciness of the gingerbread. She had tasted one of the cookies this morning and thought they were delicious.

Rose leaned over, taking in the fragrance. "Does Amos like licorice?"

"I don't know." Ada placed a dozen cookies on the tray. "The anise isn't too strong."

"But you know it's there."

"It's only a little spicy. I think it tastes wonderful combined with the ginger and molasses."

Ada covered the tray with a cloth napkin and glanced at the clocks. "Five more minutes."

"You aren't nervous, are you?" Rose giggled. "This could be the conclusion to the Great Cookie Campaign."

"I hope it is." She looked at the clocks again. Four minutes until noon. "What if he doesn't ask me out, though? What if Matthias was wrong?"

Rose shrugged. "Then you keep on baking."

Three minutes.

"It is only a few days until Christmas Eve. Are you still planning to make the jam thumbprint cookies?"

The first clock whirred in preparation to strike twelve. Ada hiccupped. It wasn't noon yet. Dat had set the clocks to chime one after the other, from a minute before noon to a few minutes after. Some customers often stopped by the store just to hear them.

Ada nodded in answer to Rose's question and picked up the tray of gingerbread cookies. She took a deep breath, then started for the workshop.

As she opened the door, she saw that her timing was perfect. Vernon had already sat at the table, while Amos was walking toward it with his lunch box in his hand. Matthias wasn't anywhere that she could see.

She tried to keep a smile on her face as she walked across the room to the lunch table, but her hands were shaking, and she felt hot, then cold. What if she dropped the tray? What if she tripped over that rough spot on the floor?

Ada stopped and looked down at her feet. There was the spot. She stepped across it, then continued toward the table.

"Cookies again?" Amos said, grabbing one. He winked at her. "You're spoiling us, Ada."

She couldn't speak. Her mouth gaped open as she pushed out, "Jah."

At the same time, Amos held the soft, frosted cookie inches away from his nose. He sniffed, then dropped it onto the tray of cookies.

"That smells awful." He glared at Ada, wiping his nose on his sleeve. "What did you put in those?"

"I thought you'd like them." Ada swallowed, fighting to hold back her tears. "The frosting has anise in it—"

"Anise?" He pushed the tray toward her as he sat in a chair. "What's that? Poison?"

"It's a flavoring . . ." Ada let her voice fade as Amos took a long drink from his thermos. "I can bring you a different kind from the store."

He nodded, taking a bite of his sandwich. "Make sure they're good."

Ada took the tray and started for the hallway to the store, stumbling over the rough place in the floor. Vernon's cackling laughter followed her.

The tears were flowing by the time she reached the store. She breathed a sigh of thanks when she saw that Rose was alone.

"What happened?"

Ada shook her head and hiccupped again. "He didn't like them." She put the tray on the bakery case and filled a box with a dozen frosted star-shaped cookies that glistened with white sugar crystals.

"What did he do?"

"He didn't like how they smelled. He didn't even try them. But I promised I'd bring him a different kind of cookie." She closed the box and started for the workshop again.

"Wait," Rose said. "Are you sure you want to give him something else after he refused the ones you made?" She pointed toward the gingerbread cookies.

"I need to make it up to him. I want him to see that I can make him happy."

Ada hurried toward the workshop, ignoring Rose's voice calling after her.

Matthias had been looking forward to his lunch break and Ada's weekly delivery of cookies, but then Leroy had asked him to come along to a customer's house. When Amos and Vernon had delivered the cardinal clock earlier in the week, the case had been damaged.

"I want you to see how I handle customer problems like these," Leroy said as he drove toward Middlebury. "The Wilsons were understanding about the damage when they called, but I want to make sure they're happy before we leave today."

The Wilsons were an older couple who lived in a duplex on the far edge of Middlebury. Matthias remembered that Ada had mentioned them, and that they had celebrated their fifty-fifth wedding anniversary recently. When Mrs. Wilson answered the door, Mr. Wilson waved at them. He looked frail and rested in a chair the entire time he and Leroy were there.

Mrs. Wilson showed Leroy the damaged case. "I hate to complain, but Bert said you would want to know what happened."

"He was right," Leroy said. "Whatever goes wrong, we want an opportunity to make it right." He motioned for Matthias to examine the case. "What do you think?"

Matthias knelt down. The skirting along the front edge of the clock was splintered. He felt along the back of the splintered area. The skirting was a separate piece of wood from the main case.

"It will be a simple job to replace the splintered part with a new piece of wood. We only need to find one that will match it."

Leroy knelt beside him, then rummaged in the bottom of his tool chest and pulled out a finished skirting that matched the splintered one.

He winked at Matthias. "Don't look so surprised. When Mr. Wilson called and described the damage, I went ahead and made a replacement."

Matthias grinned back at him. "I suppose you only brought me along to hand you the tools you need."

"Nope. I need you to hold the clock steady so I can work."

As Matthias held the clock securely, careful not to put any pressure on the stained-glass inserts, Leroy visited with the Wilsons while he worked. "Are you looking forward to spending Christmas with your family?"

"We are spending Christmas Eve with our church family. Other than that, there are only the two of us." Mrs. Wilson sat in a chair next to Mr. Wilson's and took his hand. "We'll spend a quiet day remembering our Savior's birth."

Leroy knocked out the broken wood with his hammer. "That's the same way we'll spend Christmas Day. We plan to spend Little Christmas with our married daughters and their families on January sixth. We'll exchange presents with them then."

Mrs. Wilson nodded. "On Epiphany. We celebrate then, too, remembering the wise men who visited Jesus."

Leroy checked the fit of the new wooden skirt, then applied glue to it and pressed it into place.

"How many children do you have?" Mr. Wilson asked, his voice sounding strained and tired.

"We have four daughters," Leroy said as he and Matthias eased the clock back into place. "Two are married, and we still have two at home. You probably met Rose and Ada when you came to the store to buy the clock."

"Oh yes, we did. Such nice girls. You are very blessed, Mr. Weaver. And this must be your son," Mrs. Wilson said, smiling at Matthias.

"We are blessed," Leroy said, then patted Matthias's shoulder. "But Matthias isn't our son. He's a fine employee, though."

Mr. Wilson leaned forward in his chair and winked at Matthias. "Then you should snatch up one of those girls for yourself, young man. Don't let another day go by without finding a good wife." He looked at Mrs. Wilson. "Life is too short as it is. Don't wait to take hold of God's blessings."

Matthias felt his face burn, but Leroy turned the conversation away from him as he made sure the Wilsons were satisfied with the repair to the clock.

"Don't hesitate to call if you notice anything else that needs to be fixed," Leroy said as they left the couple's house.

Mrs. Wilson walked them to the door. "Thank you so much for coming," she said, almost whispering so that Mr. Wilson wouldn't hear her. "I didn't think it was anything to worry about, but Bert insisted that it had to be perfect."

"I understand wanting our loved ones to have the best." Leroy bent his head so he was level with Mrs. Wilson. "Is he very ill?"

"It's cancer." The older woman's eyes filled. "Some days he seems quite healthy, but on days like today the pain is terrible."

"I will remember to ask the Good Lord to sustain both of you through this time."

"Bless you." Mrs. Wilson squeezed his arm, then waved to Matthias to come close. She tugged at his arm until he bent down next to her, and then she gave his cheek a quick kiss. "Both of you. God bless you."

"Have a wonderful Christmas," Leroy said, opening the door.

"We will." Mrs. Wilson stood in the doorway, waving as they walked to the buggy. "We will."

As they drove away, Matthias realized his eyes were misty. "They were a nice couple."

Leroy nodded. "They have a hard few months ahead of them, but their faith will help."

"We could have taken the clock back to the workshop to fix it." Matthias watched the fields as the horse trotted along.

"We could have. But I heard something in Mr. Wilson's voice when he called this morning. Maybe it was his illness, or maybe it was loneliness. I felt like they needed us to make a house call."

When they reached the state highway, Leroy turned right instead of left.

"This isn't the way to Shipshewana," Matthias said.

"It's time for lunch, and one of my favorite restaurants is down here in Topeka."

Matthias grinned. "Do you mean Tiffany's?"

"It's the place to go for pie, and their salad bar is the best around." Leroy jabbed him with his elbow. "And I'm buying."

The restaurant was busy since it was a favorite eating spot for both the Plain people and the Englisch, but Leroy and Matthias were able to find a seat at one of the long center tables. After they filled their plates at the salad bar and had taken a moment for a silent prayer, Matthias started in on his selections, taking a bite of the pickled beets.

"I wanted to talk to you about something," Leroy said, slicing his red-beet egg. "The Wilsons brought up a subject that Franny and I have been discussing. You know we don't have any sons, but I want our furniture business to continue after I'm too old to run it."

"Aren't either of your daughters' husbands interested?"

Leroy shook his head as he spread some tuna salad on a cracker. "They both work on their families' farms. The young man Rose is interested in has a factory job, but I don't think he has what it takes to run a business." He rested his forearms on the edge of the table and looked at Matthias. "Working in a business and running one are two different things. I'm sure you've noticed that."

Matthias nodded, taking the last bite of his salad as the waitress brought their meals. He turned to his plate of roast beef and mashed potatoes and waited for Leroy to get to the point.

"Neither Vernon or Amos are capable of managing a business, either. You can tell a lot about a man's character by watching him work. They do their tasks well, most of the time. I'm disappointed by their carelessness with that clock, and they'll be reprimanded for it."

"You won't fire them, will you?"

Leroy sighed, staring at his plate. "Amos is the one who is responsible. Vernon just follows along with whatever others are doing. And it's the first time Amos has been this careless. I'll talk to him but give him another chance." He looked at Matthias again. "I don't think he'll last much longer at the shop, though. His heart isn't in the business. He doesn't have a love for woodworking the way you do." Leroy breathed in the aroma of his chicken and noodles. "I don't want my opinion of them to go beyond this conversation." He raised his eyebrows.

"I wouldn't think of saying anything you don't want me to."

Leroy paused, staring at him as if he was sizing him up, or waiting for a signal before going ahead.

"I want to offer you a partnership in Heritage Amish Furniture."

Matthias choked, then took a drink of water. "What? Me? I'm your newest employee. I don't have the skills you need, or the experience."

"I can teach you how to run a business. But I can't teach anyone how to connect with customers the way you did with the Wilsons today, or how to handle wood with that special touch. You have skills that our business needs."

Matthias stirred the gravy into his mashed potatoes, his thoughts whirling. "You aren't doing this because you, well, feel sorry for me and Mamm, are you?"

Leroy grinned. "Not at all. I'm doing this because I've been looking for a partner for a few years now. I would have offered it to your Dat, but I didn't think of it until your family had already moved to Wisconsin. You've shown that you have the same skills as Ervin, and not only in woodworking."

"Can I have some time to think about it?"

Leroy nodded. "Take all the time you need."

Saturday morning was even busier than the previous week had been. While Ada helped the customers who were waiting to purchase items in the store, Rose took two more orders for furniture. When the last of the current group of customers left the store, Rose grabbed her lunch bag from under the counter.

"I'm going to eat my lunch before anyone else comes. Call if you need me."

As Rose disappeared down the hall to the workshop, Ada went around the store, straightening displays. She was replenishing the ornaments when Rose came rushing back, her face bright with excitement.

"Did Matthias show you the bird he is making for his Mamm?"

"For sure, he did. It's going to be beautiful when he finishes it."

Rose nodded. "That is exactly what I thought. Our customers would love to buy carvings like that." Her enthusiasm was contagious.

"You're right," Ada said. "But could he make enough to keep the store stocked?"

"I asked him about that. He said he would have to think about it." Rose smiled. "You should convince him to do it."

"Why me?" Ada put another ornament on the display rack.

"Because you're his friend. I hardly know him."

Ada turned the rack to another spot that was nearly empty. Were she and Matthias friends? They got along all right, but she wasn't sure he would consider her a friend. She hadn't spoken to him for almost a week. Besides, what would Amos do if he thought she was friends with another boy?

"Did he seem willing?"

Rose shrugged. "Sure. He didn't want it to interfere with his job, but he said he can carve a bird in just a few days once he's done with the Christmas presents he's making for his family."

"What would Dat say?"

"I'm certain he'll love the idea. He might even let Matthias work on the carvings in between projects in the shop."

"You might be right, but you still need to tell Dat about the idea before making any arrangements with Matthias."

Rose sighed. "You're always so practical." Then she grinned again. "But I know Dat will love this idea."

As her sister went back to the workshop to finish her lunch, Ada heard a buggy drive into the parking lot. She moved to the counter so she could be available if they had questions, then froze as she glanced out the door's window. The customer was Amos, and he was with a girl.

The couple came in the door, the girl looking at Amos with the kind of look Ada longed to give him.

"Why did you bring me here?" she asked.

Amos grinned at her, oblivious to Ada's presence. "I want to show you the furniture I make. You're going to like it."

He guided the girl through the doorway to the furniture showroom, his hand resting on her back in a protective gesture.

"It must be his sister or a cousin." Ada whispered the words to herself, ignoring the pounding in her head.

She looked into the showroom. Amos was showing the girl a chest of drawers, demonstrating how easily the drawers glided. Their heads were close together as they examined the piece. As much as Ada wanted him to, he never treated her like he was treating this girl. Even when she had taken the fresh cookie stars to him yesterday, he hadn't even glanced her way as he ate them two at a time.

The bell over the door tinkled and Ada was forced to turn her attention to the next customer.

"I'm looking for a wooden rolling pin," the Englisch woman said. "My daughter wants one for Christmas, although I don't know why. She doesn't bake." She gave a little laugh. "Maybe she wants to use it on her husband."

Ada smiled even though she didn't get the joke. "We have some lovely ones over here. They are all made locally by Amish craftsmen."

She led the customer to the display of rolling pins. From here she could see into the showroom, where Amos and the girl were looking at dining room tables and chairs.

The woman selected a rolling pin, then chose some place mats from another display. Ada took her selections to the cash register while the woman continued to browse through the store. Rose came back from her lunch as more customers came in, and the afternoon became as busy as the morning had been.

Ada tried to be pleasant as she waited on the customers, but her mind was on Amos and the mysterious girl in the furniture showroom. What were they looking at? What was taking them so long? And who was that girl?

Finally, Amos came into the store to find Rose. Ada was busy ringing up another customer and couldn't hear what he asked, but Rose followed him into the showroom, her order book in hand. Several customers later, Amos and the girl left, and Rose returned, but the store was too busy for her to ask what Amos had ordered.

By the end of the day, when the last customer was gone and Rose had flipped the Open sign to Closed, Ada was exhausted. The store was a mess, with ice melt tracked in and the displays in disorder. Rose leaned on the counter by the cash register, leafing through the order book and recording each entry in her ledger.

Ada glanced at the bakery display, glad that it was empty. Every time she thought of Amos and the girl, she was tempted to eat something. Anything. As long as it was sweet.

Matthias came in from the workshop, pulling on his coat. "You girls were busy in here, weren't you? It seems like the only thing I heard all day was that bell over the door ringing every time it opened."

"It's the Christmas season," Ada said. "And as much fun as it is to be busy, I'm ready to sit down and put my feet up this evening."

He walked over to the bakery display. "The cookies are all gone?"

"We sold out by three o'clock."

"I thought I'd take a couple home for Mamm, but I'll have to wait until Monday."

Ada stepped around the counter and straightened the display of rolling pins. "If you let me know that you want some, I can set them aside for you."

"What kinds will you have?" Matthias untangled some Christmas ornaments on the display.

"I was thinking of making some of those molasses crinkles for the store. It would be something different from our usual." Ada moved to the place mat display next to Matthias.

"Those were delicious cookies."

Ada looked up. Matthias was still straightening the Christmas ornaments. "Did you really like them?"

"I think I liked them even better than your sugar cookies."

She waited for him to give her his usual smile, but he only straightened a set of place mats.

"Then it's decided. I'll make them for Monday, and I'll save some for you to take home. How many would you like?"

"Two . . . no, three. I know I'm going to eat one on the way home." He pulled on his gloves. "I need to get going or Mamm will worry."

"I'm glad you don't have to ride your bicycle. It's cold out there tonight."

"I'm thankful to have Nellie Belle for the winter. I appreciate your Dat thinking of us." He started for the door. "I'll see you at church tomorrow."

He had just closed the door to the workshop when Rose giggled. "I told you the two of you are friends."

"All right, maybe we're becoming friends. But I don't want to encourage anything more. That would ruin my chances with Amos."

Rose bent her head over the day's furniture orders. It wasn't like her to stay silent.

"What is it?"

"I think you need to forget about Amos."

Ada's fingers grew cold. "What do you mean?"

"Amos was here this afternoon." Rose still didn't look at her.

"I know. He came in while you were at lunch."

"He had a girl with him."

"I saw her. I figured she must be his sister or a cousin. . . ." Ada let her voice trail off as Rose shook her head.

"They were much too friendly. They were very friendly."

Ada's stomach turned. "What do you mean?"

Rose put her pen down. "They were choosing furniture to furnish their home. Amos bought a bedroom set."

Ada's eyes blurred, but she kept her hands moving, straightening the place mats again, as if Rose's words didn't change anything.

Rose walked over and pulled Ada into a close hug. "I think the Great Cookie Campaign is over."

CHAPTER SIX

The next Tuesday morning was Christmas Eve day. Matthias brushed Nellie Belle, getting her ready to drive to work. On Sunday, he had ended up staying home rather than going to the church meeting. Mamm had refused to ride in the buggy, and the day had been much too cold for her to walk the two miles to the Planks' house, where the G'may met.

Leroy had noticed his absence and talked to him about it at work yesterday. When Matthias had explained the situation, Leroy had told him he would talk to Mamm. Leroy and his wife had visited yesterday evening, talking in the kitchen until after Matthias had gone upstairs to his room.

This morning, Matthias took his time in the barn, delaying having to deal with Mamm's reaction to their visit until he couldn't put it off any longer.

He picked up the morning milk pail steaming in the frosty air as he crossed the drive, and he opened the kitchen door with caution. Mamm's moods had been mercurial over the last couple weeks. He couldn't tell what he would meet when he opened the door.

This morning, Mamm sat at the kitchen table, a cup of coffee in front of her. Yesterday, she had been banging pans on the counter. On Saturday morning, she had been in the living room, moving the furniture around. Today, her peaceful expression and the quiet house made Matthias uneasy. What was going on?

As he moved into the kitchen, she smiled. "Your breakfast is almost ready. I made an egg casserole last night and put it in the oven this morning."

Matthias set the milk pail on the kitchen counter. "Are you feeling all right?"

She snorted. "Why wouldn't I be?"

"It's just that ever since Leroy brought the horse and buggy, you've been upset."

Mamm nodded. "You're right."

She got up and poured another cup of coffee for him, then checked the casserole before sitting down again. He joined her.

"It's hard to say this, but I was wrong."

Matthias spooned sugar in his coffee. "About the horse and buggy?"

"About you." She sighed. "When your Dat passed on, I didn't realize how much it affected me."

"It was very sudden." Matthias poured a bit of cream in his cup and watched the white and black blend into a warm brown as he stirred it. "Making the adjustment was hard on both of us."

"That isn't an excuse." She pressed her lips together, then went on. "I guess I wanted things to stay the same. I didn't want anything to change, but everything was out of my control. Selling the farm, giving up on our dream, moving back here to this house . . ." She looked at him. "Do you think this house is too small?"

Matthias nodded. "It is, but I don't want to complain."

"I don't think it's a good idea for you to have to sleep in the attic. It must get cold up there."

He grinned. "As cold as it can be. But I have enough blankets to keep warm."

Mamm shook her head, her eyes closed. "I can't believe that I've been treating you like a little boy. You're a grown man. Franny was right."

"What made you change your mind?"

"Something Franny said yesterday when she and Leroy came by to visit. She was talking about her daughters, Rose and Ada. She said she thought Rose would be getting married soon, but she was glad that Ada would always be with her. I pointed out that Ada might very well marry one day, too, and we both had the same thought at once. It was clear to me that she wasn't giving Ada the freedom to grow, and she saw that I was doing the same with you." She took a sip of her coffee. "We cried about it at first, and then we laughed at what silly women we are."

Matthias's face warmed when Mamm mentioned Ada, then realized that she had said something about him. "What was that?"

"I said I've been thinking about it. I was wrong to let Simon take charge when your Dat passed on. You are nearly twenty now—"

"Mamm, I'm twenty-one."

She smiled at him, her old mischievous look back. "I know that. I was only teasing you."

Matthias laughed. "You don't know how much I've missed your teasing."

"I feel like I've been living in a cloud this year, but now I'm ready to be myself again."

The timer on the counter dinged and Mamm took the breakfast casserole out of the oven. She continued talking as she cut the casserole into servings and brought it to the table.

"David and Elizabeth offered their *Dawdi Haus* when we

moved back here, but Simon said we should invest the money we had left in another house, so I let him buy this one. I'm regretting that decision now."

She set plates and silverware on the table, then sat down again. After their silent prayer, she went on.

"I want to move to the Dawdi Haus. David lives in our district, so I wouldn't have to leave my friends. Then you could live here."

Matthias's fork stopped halfway to his mouth. "Alone?"

"Not for long. Talking with Franny made me realize that it's time for you to marry, and no girl would want to share this tiny house and kitchen with her mother-in-law. That isn't the way to start a marriage."

"If you're sure that's what you want to do, it would be fine with me." Matthias took another bite of the casserole.

"It isn't only what I want to do—it's what I need to do. I'm not so old that I need to be taken care of, but when I do get that old, I don't want to be living here with my bachelor son. I want to be near one of my daughters."

Matthias ate the rest of his casserole and took another helping. This house was small, but he could live in it for a few years yet. He could even live here with a wife. But the only girl he had ever met who he would want to marry had her eye on someone else.

"Life is only as short and hard as we make it," Mamm said. "The moments come and go, but we can take it."

"Is that from one of your poems?"

"It just came to me." Mamm's face brightened. "Did you like it?"

He shook his head. "It was terrible."

She laughed. "You're right. It was pretty bad. I'll have to work on it. But what I was trying to say was that if you have a girl in mind to be your wife, don't delay. Tell her. Ask her to marry you."

"What makes you think I've found someone to marry?"

Mamm shrugged. "You're the right age. Most young men have their eye on someone."

Ada's lovely face came to mind again.

"There is someone, but I don't think she likes me. I thought we were friends, but then I said something that she took offense to. She hasn't really been friendly to me since then."

"Don't delay in mending fences. Bad feelings quickly become offenses."

Matthias grinned as he rose from the table. "That one needs work, too. I need to go. Leroy is closing the workshop early tonight because of Christmas Eve, but I don't know when I'll be home. I might take your advice and mend those fences."

Ada was working in the kitchen long before dawn, just as she was every morning, but she did her tasks automatically. She couldn't find any pleasure in rolling out the cookie dough or baking the double chocolate brownies. And it was Christmas Eve. She looked out the kitchen window at the dark yard as she washed the bowl from the brownie batter. Ever since she had seen Amos with that girl on Saturday, she had felt drained and angry at herself. How could she have thought she was in love with Amos?

Rose came into the kitchen, trying to suppress a yawn. "How do you get up this early every morning?"

"It's a habit. What are you doing up? It isn't time to start the chores yet."

"I thought I'd help you," Rose said, pouring herself a cup of Ada's coffee and sitting at the table. "You've been moping around for three days, but it's Christmas Eve. I want us to have fun in the store today, but we can't if you're still pining after that Amos. He proved that he wasn't worthy of you."

Ada's eyes itched, and she blinked fast to hold back the threatening tears. "I'm just not good enough for him. Mamm is right. I'll always be single, living here at home with the folks."

Mamm appeared in the doorway, tying her apron.

"I was wrong about that, Ada," she said. "It was just wishful thinking, as the Englisch say."

Rose was silent as she sipped her coffee, watching Ada. Mamm poured a cup of coffee for herself, then sat at the table with Rose and laid her pencil and old envelope within reach, ready to start the day's list.

"You girls will understand someday, when your own children get older. I made the mistake of trying to hold on to the days when you were all little and the house was filled with activity."

Mamm turned her coffee cup, staring at the steaming liquid.

Ada sat next to her. "But we have all grown up, and now you have grandchildren."

Mamm nodded. "Essie and I talked the other day, and what I said to her has been pestering me ever since." She squeezed Ada's hand. "I think I've been holding on to you too tightly, only because you're the youngest. There is no reason why you shouldn't have a beau, and eventually a husband and a family of your own. You are a very loving and giving young woman, and I've selfishly wanted you to be with me for the rest of my life."

Ada blinked. She had never thought that Mamm could be wrong about anything.

Rose leaned over the table. "I have an idea. Maybe you should keep going with the Great Cookie Campaign. You should make the jam thumbprint cookies, just like you planned."

Mamm looked at both of them. "The Great Cookie Campaign?"

Her cheeks growing hot, Ada went to the oven to check on the brownies. "It was just a silly thing."

"It was my idea," Rose said. "But I guess it backfired, like all of my ideas. Ada wanted to attract Amos's attention, so I thought cookies would do it."

"But why is it over? Amos isn't the only boy in the world."

Ada shook her head. "It's over. Who would I make the cookies for? I'm a terrible baker anyway. No one likes my cookies."

Mamm rose, her list in her hand. "That isn't true." She gave Ada a hug. "Everyone loves your cookies. Why else would you sell so many at the store? You keep baking, and you'll find your beau." She squeezed Ada's shoulders once more. "I have to go talk to your Dat about tomorrow, but don't let anything I've said in the past keep you from the life the Good Lord has for you."

As Mamm left, Rose put her cup down. "You are a wonderful baker. Amos is a fool, and you know it. You liked the gingerbread cookies, didn't you?"

Ada took the batch of brownies out of the oven and slid the next trays of cookies in. She never wanted to think about gingerbread cookies again.

Rose stood between Ada and the bowl of cookie dough. "He hurt you badly, I know that. But it wasn't your fault. Amos was wrong."

Ada pushed past her sister and started rolling out more sugar cookie dough. "He wasn't completely wrong. You know I'm . . . I'm fat and clumsy. No man will ever love me."

"Now you're the one who is wrong. I know for a fact that there is at least one man who likes you. He might even love you."

"Who?"

"Matthias."

Ada sighed. She missed Matthias. Missed talking to him and eating lunch with him. She hadn't realized how much she looked forward to him coming to work each morning because she was too focused on Amos. She had been so blind.

"I think our friendship is over. We used to talk about all kinds of things, but ever since—"

"Ever since he tried to warn you about Amos and you got angry with him, things haven't been the same between you. But on Saturday the two of you seemed to be getting along."

Ada pressed the star-shaped cookie cutter into the dough. She looked at Rose. "He was as friendly as ever, but, well, something was missing. Do you think he could forgive me for being so mean to him?"

"There's only one way to find out. You need to ask him."

Ada turned back to the cookie dough. "I don't know how I can do that. He must hate me for how I treated him."

Rose stirred her coffee, the spoon clinking gently against the side of the cup.

"That's why I thought you should continue the Great Cookie Campaign. But this time, don't let Amos and Vernon know about the cookies. Make them only for Matthias."

As she transferred the stars to the cookie sheet, Ada thought about Rose's suggestion. She glanced at the recipe card she had placed in her holder last week, in preparation for baking the jam thumbprint cookies. She had never wanted to be too bold when it came to making cookies for Amos, but Matthias was different. He would appreciate the gift, and it might even help to mend the broken place in their friendship. Her eyes grew wet when she thought about it. She had caused that rift, but could she fix it?

Later that morning, after breakfast was over, Ada started mixing the dough for the thumbprint cookies. Since she hadn't planned to make them, she hadn't had time earlier this morning, but Rose offered to open the store by herself. Ada hummed a Christmas hymn as she mixed the dough.

She had just put the first cookie sheet in the oven when someone knocked at the kitchen door. Matthias was waving at her through the window as she went to open it.

"Aren't you supposed to be at work?" she asked him. His smile encouraged her. Perhaps they were still friends, after all.

"I was going to ask you the same question." He pulled his gloves off as he walked in. "When I saw you weren't at the store this morning, I thought you might be ill. Rose sent me over to see how you were feeling."

Ada poured a cup of coffee for him and set it on the table. "Rose knows I'm not sick. I got behind on my baking this morning."

Matthias poured some cream in his coffee. "I wanted to talk to you and apologize for how I've been acting."

"You don't need to apologize." Ada sat across the table from him. "I'm the one who was so kerfuffled that I treated you badly. I'm sorry."

He grinned. "Does this mean we're friends again?"

A warm feeling started in Ada's middle and spread. She smiled at him. "I hope so. I've missed talking with you."

The timer dinged, and Ada jumped up. "Sorry. I have to take care of these cookies right away."

She took the cookie sheets out of the oven as Matthias came to look over her shoulder.

"Is this a new kind?"

Ada nodded, carefully pressing her thumb into the middle of each cookie while they were still hot. Then she spooned a bit of raspberry jam into each indentation and returned them to the oven.

"Thumbprint cookies?" Matthias asked. "They are my favorite."

"I think every cookie is your favorite," Ada said. She paused. How much should she say? Silently, she passed him her grandmother's recipe card.

"'My Ben's favorite,'" Matthias read. "Who is Ben?"

"Dawdi Ben, my grandfather." Ada moved another tray of the cookies to her cooling rack. "These will be ready to eat in a few minutes."

"As delicious as they look, I don't want to eat the cookies you plan to sell."

"These aren't going to the store. I made them for you."

"You mean for Amos, Vernon, and me?"

Ada shook her head, her face growing hot. "Just for you. They are your Christmas present."

When she dared to look at him, he was smiling. "That is the best present ever."

Matthias walked across the drive to the workshop, ready for his next project. The first, to mend the rift in his friendship with Ada, had ended up better than he could have hoped. Not only were they friends again, but he had seen a glimmer in her eyes that gave him hope that she might feel the same way about him that he did about her.

But first, he must talk with Leroy.

He found his boss in his office. Matthias closed the door behind him when Leroy invited him in. "I've been thinking about your offer."

Leroy pushed aside the papers he had been working on. "I'm glad to hear that."

"But a partnership usually means that each party puts money into the business, and I can't afford to do that."

"I don't expect you to buy in to the business," Leroy said. "We can talk about the details later, but the main part of it is that I thought you could work with me and learn how we operate. Learn the fine points of Heritage Amish Furniture while working here."

"That's what I was hoping you would say."

"I look forward to working with you," Leroy said. "You are everything I would have wanted a son to be."

"What would you like me to do first?"

Leroy grinned. "Finish up the Christmas orders that are still pending so that we can take a few days off this week."

Matthias spent the rest of the day following up on the tasks Leroy had assigned to all three of them. By noon, Amos and Vernon had finished everything on their lists and were out delivering the last-minute orders.

Finally, three o'clock came. Matthias went into the store, where Rose had just turned the sign on the door to Closed.

"It has been a busy day, hasn't it?" he asked as he helped Ada straighten up the displays.

"But it was fun." Ada smiled at him and his heart pounded. "Everyone was in good spirits. It makes the time go by quickly."

"Rose." Matthias cleared his throat. "If you want to go home, I'll help Ada close up the store."

"Are you sure?"

Ada waved her toward the door. "You have a date tonight. Go get ready for Johnny." She leaned close to him, her blue eyes shining. "She thinks he might ask her to marry him tonight. Isn't that romantic?"

"You're glad she's getting married?"

"For sure." Ada moved to the display of rolling pins, straightening them on their rack. "It will make her happy, and that's what I want for her."

Matthias glanced at her. They were friends again, but would she be willing to consider more? He pulled her present out of his pocket.

"I have a gift for you." He handed her the small bundle wrapped in tissue paper. "It isn't anything as special as cookies, but I think you'll like it."

As she unwrapped the paper, she gasped. The cardinal he had carved for her lay in her hand, the colors perfect. She stood the little bird on the counter, and it seemed to cock its head, as if it was asking for some sunflower seeds.

"It's beautiful, and so lifelike. I'll treasure it forever."

Matthias took her hand. "Will you? Do you really like it?"

Ada gazed into his eyes. Her expression was trusting and peaceful. "I like it because you made it. It will always remind me of you."

He tugged at her hand, pulling her closer. "I've always liked you, Ada, even when we were in school together. Since I came back to Shipshewana and we've gotten to know each other better, I've found that I still like you. I treasure our friendship." He paused. "Is it too soon to tell you that I think I love you?"

Ada's voice shook. "It isn't too soon. I have been so stupid, thinking that I wanted to be in love with Amos, but what I had in mind wasn't love at all."

Matthias leaned even closer. "I think love is looking forward to a lifetime together." He kissed her cheek. Her skin was soft, and a sweet fragrance surrounded him. "And working together." He kissed her other cheek. "And spending every moment together that we can."

Ada hesitated, then wrapped her arms around his waist as

he drew her closer. He tilted her chin up with one finger and looked into her eyes.

"Holding you like this feels very good."

She smiled. "You are being very forward."

"Someone told me that I shouldn't wait to take hold of God's blessings. I want to spend time with you, talk with you. Learn everything about you."

"That might take years."

He leaned his forehead against hers. "I'm ready to take as long as I need to."

When she smiled again, he captured her lips with his. He was finally home.

Jam Thumbprint Cookies

(MY BEN'S FAVORITE)

1½ cups	all-purpose flour
¼ cup	ground almonds, or commercial almond meal
½ teaspoon	baking powder
½ teaspoon	salt
¾ cup	butter, softened (room temperature)
½ cup	sugar
1 teaspoon	vanilla
1	egg
	raspberry jam

Mix flour, ground almonds/almond meal, baking powder, and salt together in a small bowl. In a medium bowl, cream together butter, sugar, and vanilla. Beat the egg into the butter/sugar mixture until fluffy. Add the flour mixture to the butter/sugar mixture and mix well.

Form the dough into 1-inch balls and place on a cookie sheet. Bake at 350 degrees for 12 minutes, or until the tops of the cookies are no longer shiny.

Remove the cookie sheet from the oven, then quickly and gently press your thumb into each cookie to make a depression. Put a scant 1/2 teaspoon of raspberry jam into the depression.

Return the cookie sheet to the oven for another 3–5 minutes. Let the cookies cool for 5–10 minutes, then remove them to a cooling rack.

Makes two dozen.

AN
UNEXPECTED
Christmas
GIFT

KATE LLOYD

To Kathleen Kohler

CHAPTER ONE

The moment I saw the sign for Miller's Quilts and Gifts through the onslaught of snow, my throat constricted as if I'd swallowed a handful of salt. I jammed on the brakes, but the car glided through the white flurry, slid into a ditch, and came to rest with a metallic crunch against a fence.

My brain spun with uncertainty, as if I'd gotten onto a roller coaster ride and changed my mind. But it was too late to turn around and drive back home to Hartford, Connecticut. This car wasn't going anywhere until I called a tow truck. I cut the engine.

At least the airbag hadn't inflated, making it possible to move. But when I reached for the door handle, I shouldered the door without success. I was trapped.

The snow fell so quickly that my windshield was soon covered with a blanket of white. The setting sun cast a gray shadow. What on earth was I doing here? Who in their right mind would travel to Lancaster County on the day before Christmas Eve?

Me, apparently. Because I wasn't planning to celebrate Christmas. Ever again. Not since my sister and I took our DNA tests and found out we weren't related in any way, flipping my world upside down.

We'd gone to our father, as our mother had died two years

earlier. The corner of his mouth had lifted a skosh. *"Uh . . . we adopted you, Maria. I'd wanted a boy, but your mother said it was too late to change our minds. And then she got pregnant with Trish four years later."*

My sister and I looked at each other with new eyes. I recalled her as a toddler and remembered my mother's jubilation as they decorated her nursery. *"I'm just like Hannah in the Bible,"* Mom had said years later. *"God answered my prayers."* Her hand moved to the nape of her neck. *"He answered them—twice."*

I heard a knock on my window, saw a man's glove swipe across it. "Are you okay?" came his muffled words. "Unlock the door."

I fumbled to unlock it as a hefty form tugged at the door and pulled it open past snow-covered grasses.

"Kumm." He was Amish, dressed the way I'd seen in books and movies, but never in real life. He assisted me in escaping my dungeon.

"Oh! Thank you so much." With the wind whipping particles of snow into my eyes, I squinted at the shop's sign, way down a fence-lined lane and what looked to be an impossibly long distance. "I need to go to the quilt shop."

"It's not open, but the owners live next door." Snow accumulated on his black felt hat and shoulders. "It's five o'clock and tomorrow is Christmas Eve."

"Yes, I know, but that's where I'm headed." I'd have to check the damage to my car later. "Will you help me?"

"Yah, of course."

When I stood, I found my legs shaky. The man, who looked to be in his upper twenties like me, took my elbow and helped me climb out of the ditch. I chided myself for thinking I could drive my Toyota in the snow. But the weatherman hadn't predicted this humongous accumulation.

A gust of wind blew the man's hat off, and he bent to retrieve it. After a shake, he set it squarely on his head.

There wasn't another vehicle in sight. I felt chill air invading my clothing. "Wait, maybe I should call a tow truck first."

"I doubt you'll get help tonight." He straightened his hat, but the wind threatened to toss it away again. "My friend and I can assist you tomorrow."

"Really? I heard Amish don't drive."

"My friend's Mennonite, so he can."

"Oh, okay." But where would I sleep? I'd planned to find a cheap motel room in town. Well, I'd come this far and would not be deterred. As the sky darkened, I was losing sight of the quilt shop. I couldn't afford to wait any longer. I took a step and felt icy snow creeping over the tops of my socks.

He proffered a hand. "The snow's deep, so you best let me give you support."

"Nah, I'm fine." A moment later I lost my balance, but he caught me in midair.

"Thanks again," I said, even though Mom taught me never to trust strangers. Wait, she hadn't even been my mother. How could I believe her words of advice?

"What's your name?" I asked, my words muted by a gust of wind.

"Isaac Stoltfuz. You want to borrow my coat?"

"No, that's okay." I should have thought to wear warmer clothes.

"And what's yours?"

Did I want to tell a stranger anything about myself? A first name couldn't hurt anything. "Maria." I looked around expecting to spot his buggy but saw nothing. I'd heard the Amish used horses and buggies, and I wouldn't mind getting a look at one. But evidently he was on foot.

I started my trudge toward the sign for the quilt shop and saw a spacious home. A hurricane lamp in a window cast yellow light across the white lawn. Now that I thought about it, there were no streetlights leading up to the house, and the sky was draining of color.

"Change your mind?" Isaac asked.

I hadn't realized I'd slowed my pace. I sped up. "No, the quilt shop is my destination."

"Like I said, it's closed tonight. But it's next to the Millers' home."

"Okay." I headed for the house's front door, but he beckoned me around to the back past a barn. We crossed the barnyard and climbed the back stairs to a small porch. He rapped on the door, then stomped his feet.

The door swung open. "Isaac," said an Amish woman who looked to be in her early twenties. She wore a calf-length dress, a black bib apron, a white heart-shaped organza head covering, and an expectant grin. She grabbed his arm and pulled him inside. "What a lovely surprise."

"Hullo, Nancy. I'm not coming in but for a moment. I brought a stranger named Maria."

"Oh?" Nancy's smile flattened. "What are you doing out on such a *greislich* night, Isaac?"

"Looking for *Mamm*'s favorite goat." He glanced at me. "I was just about to give up when I noticed Maria's car skidding into the ditch out front. It looks like the bumper and fender are dented, but there's no way to tell in that snow."

The corners of her mouth angling down, Nancy gave me a good look-over. "Probably driving too fast."

"No, I wasn't," I said through the snowflakes. "As a matter of fact, I was trying to slow down, but my car kept going."

"Because you were driving too fast."

No use arguing with her when in fact I'd been creeping along, all the while second-guessing myself. I shouldn't have acted so impulsively to begin with. No matter my hurt feelings.

"You best come in." She frowned at my soaked Adidas. "Please stomp your feet first." I glanced down at my snow-covered shoes and realized she was right.

The ambrosia of baking breads beckoned us forward as Isaac and I followed her through a dimly lit hallway. We passed a utility room with an old-fashioned wringer washer and then a small sink by a closed door. Nancy opened the door, and I found myself inside a beautiful kitchen, not what I expected of an Amish home. I'd heard they didn't use electricity.

Nancy pointed to a towel on the floor and told me I could leave my shoes there. Fair enough, no need to get their lino-leum wet. But still, I felt unwelcome. I'd never been more out of my element.

I scanned the room, expecting to see Christmas decorations. A few fir-tree sprigs perched on a shelf. Huh? I guessed the Christmas tree was in the living room. My gaze latched on to muffins on a cooling rack, and two loaves of bread sitting on the counter were emitting a luscious aroma. I hadn't eaten for hours, and my stomach growled with hunger.

Nancy introduced me to her mother, Naomi, and her younger sister, Anna. Both women, dressed the same as Nancy, gawked at me but seemed friendly. Naomi insisted I join them for sup-per. "We've got plenty of sliced ham, cold meat loaf, cheeses, pickled beets, and applesauce." She turned to her daughters. "What's keeping you, girls? Set the table and slice the bread. Your *Dat* will be in from the barn in five minutes. He's been working all day and the table isn't even ready."

"I'd best be going." Isaac repositioned his hat.

"Please stop back again soon," Nancy said.

"Yah, okay." His gaze caught mine for a moment and then he looked away, but not before I noticed his sky blue eyes and clean-shaven chin. Even with a hat and long bangs, he was good-looking. No wonder Nancy obviously had a crush on him. But he didn't seem to notice or was purposely ignoring her when he wished us all a good night. I listened to his departing footsteps and hoped he really would come back and help me with my car. I didn't belong to AAA or have towing coverage in my driver's insurance. I doubted I had enough money in the bank to cover the deductible if my car was damaged. Thank goodness I'd paid off my credit card.

"Where are you headed tonight?" Naomi asked me. "Last-minute shopping?"

Nancy lifted her chin. "We closed our store early because of the snow, but I suppose I could walk over there with you. Eventually one of us will have to lock it up."

"Uh, sure. Thanks." I felt my cheeks warming. "The truth is—and I really am so sorry to bother you—but I guess this house is my destination."

"Why on earth?" Naomi asked.

Before I could answer, the back door opened and a man's deep voice spoke to Isaac. More stomping of boots, and then the door closed with a thud. The young women sped into action, like synchronized swimmers: one wiped down the rectangle table covered with a red-and-white-checkered vinyl cloth, while the other brought out plates, cutlery, and napkins. Naomi placed the items around the table. I noticed there were five places, meaning she was including me, for which I was grateful. I should have brought a snack to nibble on as I drove or stopped at a café along the way.

I heard running water just outside the kitchen; I assumed someone was washing their hands. The water snapped off, then the kitchen door blasted open, bringing with it a gust of frigid air. A burly, bearded man entered, wearing a stern expression that told me he was fatigued and not in the mood for chitchat. Wearing a hat and slippers, he must have shed his jacket and boots in the back hallway.

Naomi introduced the man. "This is my husband, Silas." Nancy and Anna remained silent. Were they afraid of their father or was their behavior for my benefit?

Without looking my way, he removed his hat and hung it on a wooden peg.

Naomi's voice was filled with delight. "Looks like we have a dinner guest tonight. Silas, this is Maria. What did you say your last name was?"

I purposely hadn't. "Um—Romano." What could it hurt?

"Italian?" Silas was obviously not impressed.

"Yes." I ran my fingers through my damp shoulder-length hair and found a tangle.

"Her car slid off the road, and she's got nowhere else to go," Naomi said. "We can't turn her away in this storm."

Silas's tense features softened. "I suppose not."

Nancy sliced cooling bread, and the other sister arranged ham and cheese on platters, and then scooped beets, condiments, and applesauce into dishes. As I watched them, I observed an eerie family resemblance to myself. How could I have been so stupid all these years? My father had dark brown eyes and hair, and Mom's hair wasn't much lighter. My hair was caramel-colored and my eyes blue.

Minutes later, we all bent our heads as Silas led us in a silent prayer from his end of the table. I guessed God could hear my thoughts, but He certainly hadn't answered my prayers. If anything, He'd tossed me into a sinkhole.

Mom died of ovarian cancer two years ago; Dad had rushed into a new marriage with a woman who had no interest in getting to know me. I found out my boyfriend was cheating on me three months back. Then I'd been canned at the library—replaced by technology. Since losing my job, I'd been living off my savings, which were shrinking.

Why had I studied philosophy in college when I knew I couldn't make a living from it? I'd been replaced by a computer at the library—not that I'd earned the required master's degree to become a real librarian. Much as I loved reading, returning to college to earn my master's held no appeal. But my future was bleak without a good-paying job. I felt defeated.

Finally, Silas cleared his throat—a guttural sound—and all heads raised. Arms reached out to spoon food onto plates and silverware clattered. I grabbed a muffin, tore it in half, and slathered it with butter.

Still, there was no conversation until Naomi said, "You never did finish telling us what you're doing in this area, Maria."

I hesitated as I tried to decide whether to reveal the truth. But it was too late to turn back. "I took a DNA test and found out that I'm possibly related to someone in this room."

Silas sputtered into laughter. "You've been reading too many Amish romance novels."

"No, I haven't." But I wished I'd read something about the Amish. My mother had always discouraged me from visiting this area or reading what she called "fluffy Amish romance."

Naomi looked up at me with interest, but Nancy's head remained bent, not looking at either of her parents.

Naomi gave her head a shake. "I can promise you I haven't taken a DNA test, nor will I ever."

"Nancy and Anna?" Silas's voice turned harsh. "Is there something you want to tell us?"

"*Nee*, don't force me, Dat." Nancy buried her hands in her lap. "It'll only make you mad."

Naomi's eyes widened. "Nancy, if you've done something sinful, you must come clean."

Nancy's face scrunched up. "Please, Mamm."

Silas bolted to his feet, his large hands resting on the table, supporting his weight. "I can tell that you're lying, so spit it out."

Nancy blinked several times. "Four years ago, when I turned sixteen and went into my *Rumspringa*, some *Englisch* friends and I got on a computer at Troy Bennett's family's furniture store. We went on a website where they trace your DNA."

"But why on earth would you do that? Do you not believe that you're Amish through and through?"

"Yah, but I thought it would be fun."

"And what did you find out?" Silas leaned forward.

"Just what you said. I'm Amish. Our ancestors came from Switzerland."

Silas thudded back onto his chair. "I do not approve of this in any way, but I suppose it has harmed no one."

"Except me." As the words sprang from my mouth, all heads turned in my direction.

CHAPTER TWO

gulped a mouthful of water to give me time to gather my courage, then spoke to Naomi. No way could I look into Silas's penetrating stare.

"Like I said, I took a DNA test recently that directed me to a furniture shop, which led me here." I wouldn't mention the guy I'd spoken to, for fear of starting a dispute.

"I will not listen to this." Silas rapped the table with his spoon handle. "How dare you insinuate my wife—I can't even say it."

Naomi's face grew pale. "Never, ever would I be unfaithful to you, Silas."

"Hush, we mustn't speak of personal matters in front of a stranger."

Naomi sliced the meat loaf and served Silas first, then sat and passed the platter around the table. "Our daughters could be Maria's cousin, certainly not her sister."

"Since when do you know so much about DNA testing?"

"I've read about it in the newspaper. It's all the rage in the Englisch world. Ancestry.com and 23 and Me. Nothing I've ever contemplated or ever would."

Silas balled his fist. "We are admonished to stay apart from the Englisch world."

"If you like, I'll confess to the whole congregation. But I know many women who scan the newspaper when they're in Walmart."

"Two wrongs don't make a right." Silas glared at her, then his daughters. "Don't you realize my position as a minister? I'm supposed to set a good example for the rest of the district."

"It's all my fault." Nancy stared at her plate. "I knew I was sinning and hanging out with the wrong crowd. I figured it was a chance to use a computer before I get baptized. . . ." Her voice sounded strangled. "I never should have given the furniture store's number as a way to contact me."

"What were you thinking?" Naomi asked.

"I guess I wasn't."

"*Ach*, I shudder to think of other tomfooleries you've dabbled with." Silas's eyes bore into hers. Then he glanced to me. "We best talk about private matters without Maria here."

Naomi appeared visibly relieved, her shoulders lowering. "Yah, we should wait." She glanced at Nancy. "But there is no way we can ignore the situation. What if Maria is indeed one of our relatives?"

"We've got plenty of those." Silas tossed his napkin on the table. "How would we ever figure out which one it is? And do we really want to know?"

His question speared into me like an arrow. Did I want to know the truth? I pictured myself returning home and pretending everything was the way it was before. Maybe this was all a terrible mistake.

No, my gut told me it wasn't. And my father had already admitted to adopting me. My parents' betrayal was the worst part. Dad never paid much attention to me. He'd often mentioned he wished he had a son. I'd figured that was why he'd gone to my sister Trish's soccer and softball games and opted out of my piano recitals.

The family consumed the rest of their meal in silence. Upset as I was, I savored the food.

"Is anyone ready for dessert?" Naomi attempted an unconvincing smile.

"Nee, I've lost my appetite." Silas pushed back his chair. "I've got more chores to do in the barn." Wind rattled the windowpanes as he frowned at me. "When Maria has gone, we'll finish this conversation."

I squirmed in my seat as swirls of white blew past the window. The storm was turning into a blizzard. I second-guessed my every action since I'd learned the truth.

Once Silas exited the room, I turned to Naomi. "I'm sorry to just show up like this. I left a couple of messages on the quilt shop's phone, but no one returned my call."

"Ach, that recorder is old and needs to be replaced. And we don't have a phone in the house."

"Well, in any case, I shouldn't have arrived without warning and ruined your evening."

"You haven't. It's Nancy who Silas is mad at." She smiled as Nancy winced. "He'll settle down. When he's not stressed, he's gentle and easygoing."

"Yah, sometimes he has us in stitches," Anna said.

"*Mei Man* often goes back to the barn after dinner." Naomi aimed her gaze at Nancy. "As for you, we still have much to talk about. Why would you take a DNA test? Are you not planning to join the church?"

"Yah, I am. I'm so sorry. But . . ."

"And what else did you experiment with?"

"Well, I drank alcoholic beverages a couple times that made

224

my mouth pucker and burned all the way down my throat." She paused, as if wondering how much to divulge. I remembered experimenting with smoking and alcohol in high school and college, and still regretted it.

"Ach, this Christmas will not be a celebration when your Dat finds out." Naomi folded her napkin.

Nancy gazed at her mother with pleading eyes. "Maybe he won't."

"You want me to lie to your Dat? I can't. But I suppose it can wait a few days." She expelled a lengthy sigh as she stood up. "First we should get Maria situated."

"Is there a B-and-B close by? Or do you rent out rooms?" I asked.

"Sometimes, but you'll spend the night here as our guest." Naomi rested her hand on mine. Her skin was warm and surprisingly soft for a woman who must do plenty of labor.

"I don't feel right about staying here without paying," I said. "I have a credit card."

"Since I refuse payment, what are your choices?" Naomi shrugged. "With this storm increasing, you'll not be driving anywhere. How would you get into town to find a hotel—if there's even an empty room?" She stood and turned toward her daughters. "You two clear the table and put away the food. Now follow me, Maria. Leave your plate where it is."

I tried to think of ways to stall the inevitable but came up empty. A branch scritched against the side of the house as the wind picked up. I pictured my car entombed in snow. I'd be lucky to locate it in the morning.

I was stuck.

I had no one to blame but myself for acting impetuously, venturing out two days before Christmas. If I were back home, my family would be finishing up shopping and wrapping presents.

But they weren't really my family. My dad was not my real father, and my new stepmother never welcomed me into their home. I felt a twinge of guilt for my resentful attitude toward him, but he'd never treated me with unconditional love. I could not get over my parents' duplicity. Sadness and confusion more than anger had spurred me on this journey.

I followed Naomi through a sizable but sparse living room with a huge stone fireplace. Where was the Christmas tree and usual holiday decor? There weren't even paintings on the walls—only a calendar and a white candle in a glass hurricane lamp on the windowsill. Well, I was in no mood to celebrate Christmas this year anyway.

As we traveled toward a hall lit by one propane gas light, all I saw out the front windows was white. Poking up here and there were a few snow-covered fence posts.

"Ach, what a storm, and it's only getting worse." Naomi pulled a flashlight from her apron pocket, flicked it on, and led me up a staircase and toward the back of the house. I followed in her wake, my stockinged feet padding across the wooden floors. The farther we stepped from the living room and kitchen, the colder it got. I felt goose bumps erupting on my arms.

"No heat back here?" I asked.

"We like the family to stay together in the kitchen or living room." She paused and turned to me. "Especially now that our three older sons are married and have places of their own in Ohio, and Nancy and Anna are in Rumspringa—their running-around time—meaning they have much more freedom to come and go as they wish."

Stopping near the end of the hall, she opened a door. She lit a propane lamp by the bed with a Bic lighter after we stepped inside. The air hung damp and heavy. She fluffed the quilt. "We'll get you nice and warm. Lots of quilts in this home."

I actually preferred sleeping in a cold room but wondered what it would feel like to wake up and slide out of bed, my bare feet hitting the icy wooden floor. "Uh, would it be all right if I borrowed a nightgown?"

"Yah, of course, the girls and I have plenty. And I'll find a pair of slippers."

"Thanks, but I still don't feel right about this. Please let me pay you for the night."

"I wouldn't accept it, so don't even try. After all, we seem to be relatives."

Now was my chance to speak to her. "Can you think of anyone who had a child out of wedlock about twenty-eight years ago?"

"If they did, I can't imagine them putting the baby up for adoption. There are plenty of families who would take the child in. I would have, myself. An Amish family can never be too large."

"How big is yours?"

"Besides my husband and our children, I have many cousins, aunts, and uncles. Both my parents are alive and live with my eldest *Bruder*. My sister has no children, and her husband passed away soon after they wed. No cousins for my girls at her house. Surely I would've heard of an unmarried woman in such a quandary." She paused and rubbed her chin in thought. "Gossip is a sin, but it's hard to contain. We may not have telephones in the house, but news travels through the Amish community like a flock of chattering starlings."

I looked into her lovely face, devoid of makeup, and thought we could indeed be related. Same sandy gold hair, although I saw gray streaks peeking out of her head covering. Same blue eyes.

But why should I believe her? My own parents had lied all

my life. I recalled the look of derision on Dad's face when my sister, Trish, and I told him about the DNA tests. Our parents had pounded into us the importance of honesty, yet Mom and Dad were blatant liars.

An idea took root in the back of my mind. Maybe Naomi was my mother. Maybe as a teen she'd given birth to me—not out of the realm of possibilities. If so, she didn't seem happy to reclaim me, which made me think Silas was not my father. Or had Naomi had an affair and ended up pregnant? Although that didn't make sense either, because she had five children. Certainly someone would have noticed.

I took in her attire: the plainest of plain coffee-brown dress and a black apron. Would someone be able to hide a pregnancy under that copious fabric?

As if reading my mind, she said, "I wish I could say you were mine." Her kindness made me feel as if I were melting into a puddle. "I'd be delighted with a daughter like you." She dabbed the corners of her eyes. "Well, we know someone who does know the truth: the Lord Almighty. He will reveal it when He's ready."

Not that I didn't believe in God entirely, but He'd never spoken to me or made a whit of difference in my life. I chided myself for the hundreds of prayers I'd given up to heaven when most likely no one was listening. Or else I wouldn't be in this crazy, confusing mess.

Bubbles of laughter erupted from the kitchen; the clattering of dishes and flatware drifted up the stairs.

"The girls are just about done cleaning up," she said. "Come in and see your room, and then we'll join them."

"Are you sure I can't pay you?"

"Your room and meals will be our Christmas gift to you. I insist."

"I feel terrible for interrupting your Christmas. I was rude to just show up out of the blue."

"When Christ was born, there were many interruptions." Her lips formed a concerned smile. "Don't worry about us. It's you I worry about—a lost lamb. But the Father will leave His flock and come looking for you."

I realized she was trying to be kind, yet her words brought me no solace. I was just as lost as when I arrived. But at least I had a good meal in my belly. "Did I thank you for your delicious supper?"

"I'm glad you enjoyed it."

"I'm afraid Silas wasn't happy to have me there."

"He's a good man, but sometimes at the end of the day . . . well, he's been up working since before dawn. We have three dozen Holsteins, and he was racing around trying to salvage anything left out in the snow. Plus, as a minister, he has a second non-paying full-time job."

What? I must have misunderstood her. "I assume he'll take Christmas morning off."

"Our cows need milking every day of the year, not to mention feeding. On a farm there is no day off."

She pushed down on the single bed against the wall. I heard springs creaking. "I'm afraid this mattress may be lumpy."

I admired the meticulously sewn quilt with its geometric shapes of bold colors. "This bed looks a lot more comfortable than my car." A branch flipped against the side of the house; I was thankful to be out of the storm. "This room will be perfect. You're very kind to bring in a stranger."

"We would do this for anyone in need. Let's go back to the kitchen and have dessert."

On our return through the living room, I noticed Silas sitting in an easy chair reading a magazine. He didn't look up. Fair enough.

The man must be exhausted. Naomi and I reentered the kitchen, and much to my surprise my suitcase sat near the back door.

"Isaac brought it in." Nancy's exuberant voice revealed her pleasure at seeing him.

Isaac sat at the table with a cup of coffee and a wedge of pumpkin pie. "I should have thought to bring the suitcase in when I first came." I couldn't read his expression. Was he annoyed or happy to be here? The latter, no doubt. Two lovely sisters both pouring on all the attention, rather than washing the dishes, which were scraped and stacked in the sink, soaking.

Naomi arched a brow. "You're always welcome here, Isaac, but these dishes need washing, girls."

"We were just about to, Mamm. Honest." Nancy poured more coffee for Isaac.

"Thank you for bringing in my stuff," I said to him. "I was so shaken up I forgot about it."

"I should have thought to ask you earlier." He took a sip from his mug. "You left the car unlocked, so when I passed by, I could easily get into the trunk."

I knew there was nothing easy about going outside this evening. We had miserable snowstorms in Connecticut, but nothing like this. Well, if the electricity went out, we were all set here.

"Have a seat." Naomi pulled out a chair for me in the middle of the table.

"I could help with the dishes." It would give me a small way to pay them back.

"They are quite capable." Her voice was no-nonsense yet carried with it the melody of love and humor. "Now, girls, get to work." Naomi probably figured Isaac had returned to see one of her daughters. Flirtatious Nancy was the obvious choice. Fetching my suitcase was just his excuse to return, but I was glad to have my clothes.

"Thanks again for bringing in my things, Isaac." I couldn't help but admire his attractive features, even if his haircut was a little outdated. Make that very outdated, with those long bangs. Was he trying to look like one of the Beatles from decades ago?

"It was no trouble, although the snow is accumulating quickly."

"Won't you miss your supper?" Naomi asked.

"Not really. I found the goat and took her home, then grabbed a quick snack. My Mamm and five sisters are preparing pies, cookies, and cakes. They chased me out of the kitchen."

"You're welcome to stop by any time." Nancy spoke over her shoulder. She turned to the sink and squirted in liquid soap, her face flushing from the hot water or from her nerves. "Even on Second Christmas."

"You celebrate it twice?" I couldn't help but be surprised.

"Christmas Day will just be immediate family." Naomi crossed her arms as she surveyed the cluttered sink. "The day after Christmas we invite extended family and friends. Isaac's family lives just across the road."

"How about Aunt Linda?" Anna asked as she swabbed a pan.

"I invited her for tomorrow since she's all alone." Naomi glanced out the window. "But with this snow I can't imagine how she'll get here."

"I'll go fetch her," Isaac said. "I'll bring out our sleigh."

"You best ask your parents about that." Naomi wore an amused smile.

"Can I come with you?" Nancy's voice sounded hopeful.

"Me too, me too," Anna chimed in.

"Now, girls, let's wait and see if his parents give him permission," Naomi said.

"I think they will." Isaac turned to me. "Maybe Maria will want to come, too."

I would have liked to go with them, but my mind was awash

with uncertainties. I'd come here on a mission: to find my birth mother. "I didn't bring warm enough clothing."

"We can lend you some." As Naomi passed behind me, her hand brushed my shoulder in a loving fashion. "We've got plenty of boots, bonnets, and wool coats."

Nancy frowned. "Are you sure we can all fit?"

"Fit in where?" Silas's head poked through the kitchen door. He lumbered to the end of the table and sank down on his chair.

Naomi set out a plate of pumpkin pie for him and dolloped on whipped cream. "We're trying to decide how to pick up my sister tomorrow on Christmas Eve. Isaac very kindly offered to fetch her in his family's sleigh."

"And we want to go, too." Nancy twisted the ends of her cap's string.

"My daughters will not go gallivanting around the county on the day before we celebrate the birth of Jesus."

"But—" Nancy appeared crestfallen.

He turned to Naomi. "Didn't your *Schweschder* Linda come last Christmas? Can't she visit one of your brothers?"

"Travel to Ohio during a snowstorm?" Naomi paused for a moment, as if collecting her thoughts. Her voice softened. "Silas, *Lieb*, we already invited Linda to spend the night on Christmas Eve. You said it was okay months ago."

He tugged his profuse beard. "I suppose. But our daughters aren't going with Isaac to fetch her. If Maria wants to, I say let her. If Isaac's parents don't mind."

CHAPTER THREE

Silas told the girls to bundle up and make sure the shop was secure when they were done with the dishes.

"There have been break-ins in the area," Silas explained for my benefit, his solemn face appearing pained.

"In this kind of weather?" Nancy asked him. "No one will be out." The two young women got busy scouring the pots and pans and wiping down the counters. I wandered over and began towel-drying the clean dishes.

"I can go there with them," Isaac said. "I finished my chores for the day, and, like I said, my house is filled with jabbering women."

"Maria might enjoy going over there, too," Naomi said.

"I would, thanks. I am interested in the quilt shop. The building looked huge." This might be my only chance to see the store's interior. I set the towel aside and looked down at my skinny jeans. What was I thinking when I left my apartment earlier today? I should have checked the Lancaster County weather forecast. "But I'm not dressed for the snow."

"The girls can help you with that." Naomi looked to Nancy. "You will, won't you?"

"Yah, Mamm."

Nancy brought me a navy blue dress to cover my legs. I thanked her as she adjusted the waist so it wouldn't be too long. Since I was only five-four, the hem still dragged on the ground. Naomi insisted I wear one of her black wool coats and a scarf, which she wrapped around my neck. She plopped a black bonnet atop my head. I imagined I looked weird, but what did it matter? And Isaac smiled at me in a way that told me he approved.

Anna volunteered to finish cleaning the kitchen while Nancy bundled up. I thought Nancy might wriggle out of making the trek when she looked out the window and saw the snow driving down, but I figured she didn't want me to be alone with her love interest.

"Too bad you don't have a dishwasher, Anna." I knew this was a lame statement but reached for levity.

"We do." Anna sent me a crooked smile. "You're looking at her. But I'd rather do this chore than leave the house tonight."

Naomi handed me a flashlight. "Here, you'll need this."

Nancy grabbed another one off the counter. Isaac extracted a flashlight from his jacket pocket, tested it, and found it working. I noticed Nancy and I were wearing matching coats and bonnets. At the back door, we slid into matching tall rubber boots. Isaac grabbed a shovel.

Moments later, I grasped the railing as I descended the back steps. Icy particles of snow bit into my cheeks. I covered my face up to my eyes with the scarf, but gusts of wind blasted, making me squint. Ahead loomed the quilt shop, which looked more like a metal-walled quadruple-garage.

Snow slammed against the structure, accumulating up to three or four feet in places. I was curious to get inside and see what the business was all about. Isaac immediately started clearing the snow with his shovel so the door could swing open. He leaned the shovel against the building, tried the knob, and found it unlocked. He said something, but I couldn't hear him above the moaning wind.

Nancy scurried inside through the narrow opening, and I followed. Isaac stepped in after us and immediately halted. "Wait, I smell cigarette smoke."

"Ach, I smell it, too." Turning on a propane gas light, Nancy scanned the vast interior.

I sniffed the air. "So do I." Proof positive we were not alone.

Isaac told Nancy and me to stay by the door while he looked around.

"Be careful." Nancy took hold of his elbow. Clearly, she was afraid for his safety. Or was that just an excuse to be near him?

"No," I said. "I think we should all stick together." I noticed a six-foot metal flagpole and grabbed it to use as a weapon of defense.

Nancy and I crept along behind Isaac. Shining the flashlight for guidance, I inched past a cash register on a counter with a telephone sitting next to it. I canvassed the room. Never had I seen such beautiful quilts and quilted items, such as potholders and purses. This shop really was something to behold.

The smell of smoke grew in volume. No doubt about it, we were not alone.

A grubby boy in his late teens wearing a knit cap sprang to his feet and nearly fell back to the floor as he attempted to maintain his balance. "Get—away from me!" His words were slurred.

"Bart? Are you drunk?" Isaac asked.

"Or stoned?" Nancy stepped closer. "What are you doing here?"

"My parents kicked me out again. I have nowhere to go." The young man looked as if he hadn't bathed or changed his jeans or jacket in days. His greasy dark hair, cut in that funky Amish style the same as Isaac's and Silas's, clung to his forehead.

"Now what?" I turned to Isaac. "Call the police?"

"Nee, I haven't broken any laws. The door wasn't locked." The guy balanced himself against a post. "And I know you wouldn't throw me out in the cold. I've slept in the Millers' barn many times."

"But this is my parents' business." Nancy's voice came out with unexpected force. The young man sprang up, stumbled forward, and knocked her to the floor.

"Hey, cut it out." Isaac came to her side and helped her to her feet, but did not push Bart in retaliation.

I looked to Isaac with questioning eyes.

"We must always turn the other cheek," he told me.

"But shouldn't we call the police?"

"Please don't. My parents wouldn't like it." Nancy straightened her bonnet.

"Then you'd better get Silas to handle this," I told Isaac.

A moment later, Silas opened the door. I'd never been more happy to see someone. "I thought I'd check to see what was taking you so long." I assumed he'd seize the guy by the scruff of the neck and toss him out, but instead Silas said, "Hello, Bart. Out you go to the barn, if you like. You know where the sleeping bag is. And no smoking, ya hear?"

"But it's too cold out there. I'll freeze to death."

"I wish I could let you spend the night in here, but I dare not take the chance." He stroked his bushy beard. "I tell you what, since it's such a gruesome night, I'll let you sleep in our basement."

"In the basement?" Bart's pale face twisted. "Where my parents used to make me sleep when I was a bad boy?" He looked like he might cry. "Or they locked me in the closet."

"Now, now, I won't lock the door to the outside." Silas's voice grew gentle. "You can leave if you want to."

"Please let me stay in here." He wiped his mouth with the back of his hand. "I won't take anything."

"Why did you come in here?" Nancy asked.

"When the snow started up, it seemed like the best place," Bart whimpered. "I promise not to steal anything."

I didn't believe him for a minute. What was there to stop him?

"Come on." Silas wrapped an arm around Bart's shoulder. "I'll take you in the house and feed you before we decide what to do."

"*Denki*. I haven't eaten a decent meal in days."

"We have leftovers in the refrigerator. But you'd better be on your best behavior or my Naomi won't want you in the house at all."

"Yes, I will be. I promise."

I was floored. Bart had to be lying, but Silas didn't seem to care. He spoke to all of us. "Let's get back to the house. Nancy, make sure the door is locked, okay?"

"You want me to stick around?" Isaac asked Silas.

"Yes. Please walk the girls back to the house. Denki." He and Bart strode out the door at a fast clip.

Isaac, Nancy, and I followed them out into the blizzard, the snow blasting. Nancy locked and bolted the door, then dropped the keys in her coat pocket. Isaac walked on Nancy's side, his arm draped across her shoulder like an anchor. She snuggled into him, and I linked arms with her to keep myself upright. I was afraid I might get blown away as we forged the storm.

Nancy and I slogged up the back stairs, with Isaac close behind. "I best be on my way," he said when we reached the door. "Good night, Nancy. Maria." He turned and faded into the flurry of snow.

Bart sat at the kitchen table, scarfing down a meat loaf sandwich and drinking coffee. Anna stood close by, offering him ketchup and pickles. She seemed delighted to have a visitor, even if he was, in fact, a vagrant.

"Dat said Bart could sleep on the couch for the night," she told Nancy. She extracted a jar of applesauce from the refrigerator and scooped some into a dish. "Is one sandwich enough?" she asked Bart, placing the dish in front of him.

"I'll take another, if it's not too much trouble." Bart spooned into the bowl of applesauce. He seemed comfortable sitting at this table, even though he'd been caught as an intruder. I wondered why his parents had thrown him out—if he was even telling the truth about that.

As Anna sliced homemade wheat bread and Nancy the meat loaf, they chatted in what must be Pennsylvania Dutch, then switched to English when they saw me staring at them with curiosity. "Mamm put blankets and PJs on the couch for Bart, for after he showers," Nancy said.

Anna assembled another sandwich and placed it in front of Bart, who didn't say thank you. But she seemed pleased with her hospitality and lacked resentment, as far as I could see. The Amish were a conundrum to me.

Thirty minutes later, while Bart showered and Anna went to her room to wrap Christmas presents, Naomi and Silas said good night and climbed the stairs. Nancy and I settled into chairs at the table, slices of pumpkin pie before us.

"Why would your father allow Bart to stay here?" I asked her before taking my first bite.

"We've known Bart for years, before his family moved to another church district north of us. That lad has always been in trouble for something and kept returning and asking to sleep in our barn. His family is a mess, so I can't blame him. His father beat him until Bart grew taller than his dat and finally punched him back. It was a game changer. His dat never hit him again."

"I take it they're Amish."

"Yah, Amish." She chuckled. "Bart's sixteen and in his Rum-springa. We Amish are not perfect, but we are taught to obey our parents. Everyone is a sinner. Right?"

"I guess so." I thought about how picture-perfect my family had looked from the outside, while a cesspool of secrets lurked in its core. An itchy feeling invaded me. Was I a sinner, too? Of course, I was.

To change the subject, I asked, "How do you live without electricity?"

"It's not so bad. If you've never had it, you don't miss it. Our refrigerator is run by propane gas. Since Anna and I are not yet baptized, we sometimes . . . well, never mind. What you don't know won't hurt you."

"I found out the hard way that isn't true."

Her expression sobered. "I'm so sorry for your terrible predicament. And to think you tracked me down from one silly little blood test. How can that be?"

I flashed back to my calling Bennett's Wholesale Furniture, which Nancy had listed as her contact information. I'd spoken to a guy named Troy for a few minutes, and he'd reluctantly given me the Millers' address. His baritone voice had intrigued me. I wondered where the furniture store was in relation to the quilt shop, and if I'd have a chance to meet Troy before I left.

"Your name popped up as a relative," I told Nancy. "We're related by blood, some way or another."

She sucked in her lips. "I never should have taken that test, but having me for a cousin wouldn't be so bad, would it?"

"No, I like you."

My proclamation brought a grin to her face. "But, Nancy, I don't know what to believe. I took three separate DNA tests, but still, there's a possibility they were wrong. The lab could have made a mistake. I'm not a scientist."

"I feel terrible for taking that DNA test, the cause of all your sorrow."

"Please don't hold yourself responsible for my parents' lies." Once again, I felt like a kid discovering Santa Claus wasn't real. I'd had plenty of disappointments in life but never experienced anything comparable, even with my ex-boyfriend. Kevin had said he wanted to marry me—until he found a long-legged blonde at work who apparently had more to offer. I'd felt like a discarded washrag. Not good enough to be loved. I hadn't dated since.

Nancy stood and took our empty plates to the sink. "I have an idea," she said. "We could set the table for tomorrow morning. A surprise for Mamm."

Nancy proceeded to set the table using green paper napkins she said she'd found on sale at Walmart. "I suppose I should wrap my presents tonight, too. Ach, I'm sorry I have nothing to give you, Maria."

"Don't worry about it. I'm not celebrating Christmas this year. Or maybe ever again." There was only one gift I wanted. I clamped my lips together before I could spout out my disappointments and heartache. I realized I was acting like a juvenile, but the child deep inside of me wanted to cry.

I needed to change the subject. "Is your mother's sister really so awful?"

"No, although she and Dat have never gotten along all that well. Of course, neither of them speaks badly of the other. I love her, even if she is a bit eccentric."

"What do you mean?"

"She's not like the other women in the district. She goes to church and dresses plain but isn't afraid to speak her mind. It's no wonder my dat doesn't approve of her. He's a minister and commands respect from everyone in the district."

"He went to divinity school?"

She wagged her head once. "No, he was chosen by lot. By the hand of God."

I resisted smirking. Silas didn't look like any minister I'd ever seen. And he was chosen by random chance?

"Maybe that's how childless widows act." Nancy scanned the room, I assumed to make sure we were still alone. She lowered her volume. "I can't let that happen to me." She cupped her hand around her mouth and whispered, "If you'd really like to give me a Christmas gift, then please let me come with you and Isaac tomorrow."

I grinned. The way she said his name, like it was a chunk of Milky Way melting in her mouth, told me she was sweet on him, which I'd guessed earlier. He hadn't seemed to pay her much attention, but maybe that was an act for me and her parents. I hoped.

Nancy straightened one of the napkins and seemed pleased with how festive the table looked. "I guess I'll be turning in, too. Did my Mamm show you that the bathroom is across the hall from your room?"

"Great."

Nancy escorted me to the bedroom, where I found a clean and pressed nightgown and bathrobe on the bed. A moment later, she slipped out the door, and I was left alone in a frigid bedroom with green shades. Why hadn't I brought along reading material? What was I to do with no TV? I took out my cell phone but realized there was no one I wanted to speak to. It needed to be charged anyway, and I didn't want to use up its remaining juice since there was nowhere to charge it.

The room was too cold for me to unpack my suitcase, and

besides, I'd be leaving in the morning if the snow let up. In fast-forward I undressed and snuggled into the nightgown and bathrobe. The sheets were cold but soft and carried with them the aroma only line-dried sheets could. When I pulled the quilt up around my neck, they warmed quickly.

I glanced at the bedstand and saw a black-and-white magazine called *Family Life*. As if there would be anything in there for me. I had no family and no life. But out of sheer boredom I opened it to the first page and started reading well-written letters to the editor. Several were more interesting than I'd expected, but my lids drooped. I felt drained. I figured most of my fatigue came from the aching in my heart. And yet I felt comforted by this lumpy mattress and quilt.

During the night, in the depths of my dreams, my mind explored the possibility of meeting my real mother. Why go to all that trouble to meet someone who didn't even care about me enough to track me down herself? My whole existence now seemed to pivot around the fact that she'd abandoned me. Hey, who was I trying to kid? Of course, I wanted to meet her.

The what-ifs and could-have-beens melted away like an ice cube in a cup of warm tea. In what seemed like a moment, I awoke refreshed. The smell of breakfast wafted under the door, telling me someone had made coffee and was preparing eggs and bacon. And corn bread. Yum.

I clambered to my feet and showered in lovely warm water, then dug through my suitcase. None of my clothes seemed appropriate, since the Miller women all wore dresses, black aprons, and white head coverings. I let out a sigh. Nothing to be done about it now, so I grabbed a pair of jeans, a long-sleeved T-shirt, and a fleece vest. Wearing the slippers Naomi had lent me, I headed for the kitchen. I was suddenly starving again, even after that delicious supper.

Passing through the living room, I slowed to look out the window at the ocean of white snow sparkling like lavender- and peach-colored diamonds in the brilliance of the sunrise.

Bart wasn't sleeping on the couch, and the blankets were folded. The door from the living room to the kitchen was shut, but I opened it and entered. Naomi stood at the stove turning bacon, with Nancy at her elbow, scrambling eggs.

"Good morning, dear." Naomi placed the bacon on a plate and set it on the table. "I'm sorry if we woke you."

"This house smells so scrumptious I couldn't resist getting up." I glanced over to Nancy, who looked exhausted and had dark rings under her eyes.

"Silas is still out in the barn. Bart and Anna are helping him. They'll be in any moment." She glanced at Nancy and asked, "Why are you so long in the face?"

Nancy stifled a yawn just as Anna plodded through the back door. "Ach, why do I always have to go out and help Dat with the milking?"

"You're so good at it." Naomi sent her a sly smile. "You want me to ask one of your brothers to leave his family in Ohio and come home to help?"

"But it's so cold out there. My fingers are like icicles." Anna rubbed her hands together.

"Then you'd better not marry a farmer." Naomi's voice was upbeat. I figured she was teasing Anna, not that I understood what the joke was about. After all, who would want to be a farmer's wife? Especially an Amish farmer. I felt sorry for Naomi, for all her strenuous work. And yet she seemed content, perhaps even delighted to be living in this big old farmhouse without electricity. I couldn't live without it, that's for sure, which reminded me of my cell phone. How and when would I get it charged?

"I'm glad Bart decided to spend the night and then stay." A smile bloomed on Naomi's face. "In truth, he didn't have much choice. Ach, his clothes were so filthy I put them in the wash immediately. Then I climbed up to the attic and sorted through our sons' old clothes until I found things that fit. He had to dress Amish today, much to his displeasure. At least he has his knit beanie."

Anna tittered. "He was fit to be tied when he found out his clothes were in the basement drying on the line, but I think he was glad to help Silas and me in the barn."

"I promised Bart all the breakfast he could eat as soon as they were done." Naomi placed an array of jams and jellies on the table.

"Those look delicious," I said. "Did you can them?"

"Yes, with my daughters' help."

"We grew all the fruits and berries in our garden." Anna's enthusiastic voice was a testament to her satisfaction. "The honey is from our hives."

As Silas and Bart entered the room, they were speaking Pennsylvania Dutch. I could make out bits of words here and there, thanks to studying German in high school. My father had insisted I switch to Italian in college. He was proud of his heritage.

But, alas, his heritage wasn't mine.

Silas and Bart's conversation sounded cordial but serious. I wondered what they'd been talking about while doing the milking and feeding the livestock.

Naomi and Nancy placed more food—eggs, bacon, corn bread, toast, and sausage—in front of me. Silas hung his hat on a peg and took his place at his end of the table. I reached for a square of corn bread, but his glare stopped me. Oops. We hadn't prayed first.

He cleared his throat and lowered his head. Bart removed his beanie and the women ceased conversation. I did the same. Silas's minute-long silent prayer seemed to last five minutes. I wondered if he had much weighing on his heart or if he was trying to teach me a lesson by making me wait to eat. Or could he have something else against me? Perhaps he thought Naomi should be charging me for my room and this meal. Not that I blamed him. I tried to think of ways I could make it up to them.

Or maybe he was tired from his farm work. I calculated what time he, Bart, and Anna must have gotten up to go out and milk and feed the cows. No wonder he was grumpy. Yet I got the oddest feeling he was scrutinizing me.

CHAPTER FOUR

"How may I help you this morning?" I asked Naomi as we cleared the table thirty minutes later.

"Now, Maria, you're our guest."

"But today is Christmas Eve. I feel as if I'm intruding."

"Well, then, if you'd like to help me with my baking I'll gladly accept your assistance."

"I'll try. In the meantime, I'll wash the dishes." I got busy scraping the uneaten food into a container I assumed would be put to good use by pigs or the compost. I knew little about farming, except that nothing went to waste. I filled the sink, squirted in the liquid detergent, and watched the bubbles expand. Leaning against the sink's lip, I realized that despite my worries I felt at peace in this home. Why couldn't Naomi have been my mother? She would have been perfect.

Rapping sounded at the back door. "I'll get it." Nancy flew to turn the door's handle and swung it open. "Hullo, Isaac." The name flowed like a melody on her tongue. "And Troy. What brings both of you by?"

"Troy is going to help me pull Maria's car out of the ditch with his pickup truck." Isaac rotated toward me. "If that's okay with you, Maria."

I wasn't ready to leave this house yet, but I turned to meet Troy. His hazel-brown eyes locked on to mine in a most delightful way, sending a buzz of attraction through me. He wasn't dressed Amish; he wore jeans, and his turtleneck sweater revealed wide shoulders and defined biceps. His brown hair was cut short. "Hi, Maria, remember me? Troy Bennett. We spoke on the phone."

"Uh—yes. Hi." I must have worn a surprised expression because Troy said, "I have a winch on my pickup at work. I'll be extra careful with your car."

"I hate to trouble you."

"No trouble at all. But it will have to wait until the snow lets up. I drove my Suburban today." He stepped toward me and put out his hand to shake mine. His dreamy eyes never left my face. "My family lives next door, and my father owns the wholesale furniture factory down the road. I work there, too. Well, actually, I manage the place since my father suffered a minor stroke."

I was delighted to see him but wore my best poker face. "Nice to meet you, Troy."

"Odd we've never met in person." He held on to my hand a beat longer than needed. "I thought I knew everyone."

As I withdrew my hand, an idea snaked through my mind. If he knew everyone in the area, he might know about my mother. No, that didn't make sense. He was only a couple years older than I was—thirty-two, at the most. Which meant he was most likely married. I glanced down at his left hand and was pleased not to see a wedding band. Yet, if he worked with machinery, he might take it off during the day for safety reasons.

"Naomi, I hear you need someone to pick up your sister," Troy said. "I could do that, no problem. That way Isaac won't have to use his family's sleigh."

"Yah, my Dat doesn't want me driving it very far," Isaac said.

"Troy, that would be wonderful. But do you know where she lives?"

Isaac stepped forward. "I'm pretty sure I know the way."

"I could go with them and make sure they don't get lost." Nancy's face beamed up at Isaac.

"Only if you bring Maria as a chaperone," Naomi said.

"Sure, glad to." Troy's wide smile told me he was delighted.

"But will there be enough room for *Aenti* Linda if we all go?" Nancy asked.

"We can fit in my bench seat in the front. And back. There's even a third bench seat. I have shovels and a broom back there in case we need them."

Silas stepped into the kitchen from the living room, where he must have been eavesdropping.

"But the roads will be slippery." Naomi clasped her hands together.

"They're not that bad," Troy said. "The snowplows were out all night."

"Well, then, we'd best be on our way," Isaac said. "The weather forecaster said there's more snow moving in this afternoon."

Naomi spoke directly to Troy. "I'm not sure my sister will even come with you. She's a bit of a recluse, living on her own all these years."

"But she knows me," Nancy said. "And if she's low on food she might be willing."

"Maybe you should just bring her food," Silas said.

"No." Naomi's hands clasped her hips. "One more reason for her not to come with them."

Silas leaned against the counter, crossed his legs at the ankle. "If she decided to stay home it wouldn't break my heart."

"How can you say such a thing?" Her eyes narrowed, Naomi flashed a look of anger in his direction. "She's my sister and I can't desert her today, of all days. What would the bishop say?"

Silas stiffened. "Don't use that tone of voice with me. Maybe we should just leave things as they are. It seems your sister never has a good time over here anyway. Plus, she always brings her little dog, which I won't allow in the house."

"How can you say that? She loves coming to visit her nieces." Naomi worked her lower lip. "We must make sure she has food. We can't desert her just because of a little snow."

"You call this a little snow?" Silas folded his arms across his barrel of a chest.

"All the more reason to get her. She can spend the night until it's safe for us to bring her home. We are admonished in the Bible to take care of widows."

"Don't ya go quoting the Bible to me." Silas's voice grew hard. "It also says in the Bible that a wife should submit to her husband's wishes."

"And what is your wish? That Linda be all by herself, possibly out of food and wood for heat?"

Silas's face reddened, and he seemed to be containing a surge of anger. "Okay. I know you put up with my family when they visit, too."

"I love your family."

Silas clamped his lips together, I assumed to mask his irritation. "We appreciate your help, Troy," he finally said. "But please use extra caution."

"Absolutely, I will." He glanced to me. A grin tugged at the corner of his mouth. My, what a handsome man. But the last thing I needed was a relationship with anyone. Yet without him today my chances of meeting this woman who might be a relative were slim. I cautioned myself not to let my hopes get too high. I couldn't take another disappointment.

Isaac shifted his feet. "We'd better leave before the next snowstorm."

"Then come by for coffee and cookies later." Naomi brought me the same black wool coat, bonnet, and scarf I'd worn yesterday. "Use a pair of boots by the back door. You know the drill."

"But did you need my help in the kitchen this morning?" I asked, feeling guilty that I'd offered and now was leaving.

Naomi patted my arm. "There will be plenty of baking to do when you get home."

"Perfect." Troy rubbed his palms together.

"What about these dirty dishes? I can't just leave them in the sink."

"Anna will take care of them." Naomi practically scooted us out the back door.

Silas called after us, "Nancy, I expect you home when Troy comes back. You hear me?"

"Yes, Dat."

"*Hmmph*, you'd better."

As I stepped outside, icy air bit into my cheeks. Someone had shoveled the back steps, yet I tread carefully for fear of slipping. In the barnyard stood Troy's gray metallic Suburban with snow tires—or maybe all Suburban tires came with gigantic treads. At least someone in Lancaster County owned a vehicle that could brave the storm.

Troy opened the passenger door and helped me climb inside. A gentleman. Nice. I clicked on my safety belt as Isaac and Nancy slid in the back seat.

"I sure appreciate this, Troy." Isaac glanced up at the house.

"They're watching us from the kitchen." Nancy giggled.

"There isn't anything I wouldn't do for your folks." Troy

gave them a wave. "They've been good to my family—especially when the electricity goes out—even though we're not one of you." Troy craned his neck to see over his shoulder as he backed out of the drive, the tires crunching on the snow.

The moment we were out on the road, Nancy slid over to sit next to Isaac. She leaned against his arm and gazed up at him.

Troy glanced into the rear mirror. "Nancy? Where exactly does your aunt live?"

She straightened her back. "Not very far. On the other side of Route Thirty."

An enormous snowplow headed our way from the opposite direction, shooting cascades of white onto the side of the road. Troy slowed down and swerved to let it pass, then pulled in behind several other vehicles and a horse and buggy.

Nancy leaned into Isaac to look out his window. "If I could ride around like this all day, I might not tell you where she lives. No heaters in our buggies."

Troy chuckled. "In that case we'll run out of gas."

Finally relenting, she gave Troy the directions. "After we cross Route Thirty, head north for a few miles."

"This is the perfect vehicle for a day like today." My gaze swept the landscape. "Look, there's another horse and buggy."

"You'd better get used to seeing them."

"My parents never brought us down here as children." And now I knew why.

Troy glanced my way and gave me a quizzical look. But I wouldn't give him personal information about myself. This could be a wild-goose chase for all I knew. Still, I was glad to get away from Hartford, which no longer felt like home. And this area was beautiful, what with its magnificent barns and towering silos. Troy edged around a pickup covered with snow, no doubt abandoned last night. Several cars sat in ditches near it.

After ten minutes, Nancy leaned over the front seat. "Take a right here on this little lane."

Troy slowed, then maneuvered around the corner. Up ahead stood a cottage surrounded by pine trees. Snow concealed the bottom half of the front door and all windows were hidden behind shades. Only a thread of smoke ribboned out the chimney, alerting us to the presence of a person.

Troy and Isaac hopped out. As Troy opened the rear hatch and removed a couple of shovels, a block of icy air entered the SUV. He handed one shovel to Isaac, and the two men got busy digging out the front steps and door. Finally, the door cracked open a few inches.

"Who's there?" Trepidation filled the middle-aged woman's shaky voice. Then she coughed.

In my excitement, I opened the Suburban's door and slid out so I could hear.

"It's Isaac Stoltfuz and my friend Troy Bennett, who drove us here. Your sister asked us to fetch you for Christmas."

"But I'm not ready. I haven't done my baking." She had Naomi's eyes, but her face looked weathered and her hair was graying at the temples, beneath her black scarf.

A scruffy pint-sized black-and-white pooch scampered to Linda's feet. "There, there. Everything's okay, Saucy."

Isaac leaned down to pat the dog, but it yapped at him. He retracted his hand and straightened his spine.

"Naomi will have my hide if we don't bring you with us, and we needed to come before the next storm rolls in." Isaac glanced to the Suburban. "Nancy is here."

"And who else?"

"A guest who's staying with the Millers."

The woman covered her mouth with her hand as she coughed. "Well, like I said, I haven't done my baking. You can just leave me here. I'm perfectly fine by myself."

Through relentless icy snowflakes, I strode to the front door, mounted the three steps, and stood next to Isaac. Without an invitation, we moved into the cottage. The air inside was scarcely above freezing and felt damp. A moment later, Nancy joined us.

"Brrr." She rubbed her upper arms. "Aenti Linda, it's freezing in here."

"I'm low on wood and propane for my space heater."

"You should have let us know."

"The phone shanty is buried in snow. . . . And it's so far away."

I inched toward Linda. "Hello, there." I peered into her eyes, hoping for some sign of recognition, but saw none. She scooped up what appeared to be a terrier mix and cradled it.

"How old is this little *Hund*?" Isaac asked.

"I have no idea. She straggled here several years ago not wearing a collar or identification tag." The woman's mouth formed a half smile, but she didn't actually look at me.

I scanned the room. Her home was the opposite of Naomi and Silas's in size and content. And temperature. One small fire burned in the fireplace of the cramped living room. A kerosene lamp illuminated the space, but the shades kept the room dark. I guessed they also prevented frigid air from penetrating the windowpanes.

Nancy stood at my side. "Come stay with us over Christmas, Aenti. We have plenty of room now that my brothers are gone."

"They're gone?"

"You went to their weddings, remember? They and their new wives all moved to Ohio."

"Vaguely." She stepped back. "Nancy, I don't want to give you this cough."

"How long have you had it?"

She glanced to the threadbare throw rug. "A couple of weeks."

"I'm not worried about it." Nancy brushed the air with her hand. "Everyone in our family has had a cold over the last few months." She draped a lap-blanket over Linda's birdlike shoulders. "Have you met our friend and neighbor Troy before?"

"I can't remember." She squinted up at Troy.

I waited for someone to introduce us but decided I'd let Nancy and Isaac first orchestrate the expedition, lest Linda change her mind about coming with us.

"Hurry and pack your bag," Nancy said. "I'll help you."

"I can't leave my little Saucy."

"Dat doesn't like dogs in the house. Especially one that's bitten him in the ankle." Nancy turned to Isaac. "I guess we can put her in the barn."

"Nee, that will be too cold." Linda hugged Saucy. "And I can't leave her here."

"We won't let her starve or freeze, Linda." Isaac strode into the kitchen and came back with a sack of dog kibble. "Nancy, please pack your aunt's bag. We've come all this way."

"I appreciate it, but I'm better off right here." Linda made no move. I wondered if she was mentally ill or just kooky.

"We won't leave without you." Nancy stood akimbo. "Mamm is expecting you, and it's much too cold." She moseyed into the small kitchen and opened the refrigerator. "You hardly have any food."

"I have enough."

Nancy disappeared into the bedroom and came back a few minutes later, holding an aged suitcase. "I've packed some clothes and you can borrow anything you need from me, Anna, or Mamm, who will have a fit if you don't come with us right now. Please."

"Your Dat will have a conniption when he sees my Saucy again." Linda cracked a smile.

I had to chuckle to myself about the dog's name. Perhaps at one time that dog was saucy, but not anymore.

Linda put the dog down, and it wandered over to me. I'd always loved dogs but felt wary about petting this one. Yet when I put out my hand it snuggled up to me.

"Well," I finally said, "is anyone going to introduce us?"

"Ach, I'm sorry, Maria." Nancy checked for stray hairs escaping her white cap. "This is Saucy."

I contained a smirk. "I was referring to your aunt."

"Sorry. This is Maria Romano. Maria, this is our favorite Aenti Linda."

Linda stiffened and looked away from me, as if she'd been slapped in the face. Apparently, her temperament was the opposite of Naomi's, too. Not a woman I'd wish to know. But I reminded myself that she'd been stuck in this icy house all night and might not have even had coffee or breakfast. Judging from her hollow cheeks, she was underweight, with no spare body fat to help warm her.

"Oh, I almost forgot the presents." Linda spun around, gathered wrapped presents, and stuffed them into a couple of brown paper bags.

"So many." Nancy passed the bags off to Isaac. "You shouldn't have."

"Not bring gifts?" Linda glanced to the ceiling. "I hope I didn't forget anything."

My gaze tracked to the corner of the room, where bookshelves housed dozens of stacks of neatly folded fabric and a rack containing a plethora of thread. Next to them stood an old treadle sewing machine.

"Aenti Linda provides quilts for the shop," Nancy said, noticing my stare. "Hers are the absolute best."

"Now, now, you mustn't exaggerate." Linda's eyes met mine for the first time.

"And she sews clothes for Anna and me." Nancy wrapped an arm around Linda's shoulder. "Don't tell Mamm, but she makes the best clothes."

"Naomi is busy, and I'm glad to fill in for her, my only sister." A moment of silence filled the air, and I wondered if Linda would refuse to go with us after all. But she finally consented.

Five minutes later, Isaac and Troy helped her down her front steps and into the back seat of Troy's Suburban between Isaac and Nancy. I carried the dog, as no one else offered. I wondered how Naomi would feel about having this scruffy pooch in her house, especially if Silas didn't allow dogs.

"Here you go." I set Saucy on Linda's lap, and her arms encircled her. Still no thank-you or even a smile in my direction. I reminded myself not everyone was going to like me. I was a complete stranger and this woman was standoffish, to say the least.

Troy opened the back hatch and tossed in the shovels and Linda's suitcase. He didn't seem to be disappointed that she hadn't acknowledged his kindness, so I decided to act the same way. Never mind that it was Christmas Eve. I was not in the holiday mood. I had little to rejoice about.

Troy fishtailed as he turned the Suburban around and progressed down the road. Every bump made Linda start, but Nancy attached Linda's seat belt and leaned into her to give her comfort. On the main road, the Suburban seemed to glide along on its own several times, but Troy maneuvered it like a pro. We passed two horse and buggies. In spite of the cold, I hoped to get a ride in one before I left.

When we arrived at the Millers', I was once again struck by the size of the sign of the quilt shop at the end of the lane, like a beacon calling me. My car still lay buried in the ditch. I was thankful to have Troy and Isaac's promise to help me later, as a tow truck would be expensive.

Troy drove us into the Millers' barnyard and stopped at the bottom of the stairs to the back porch. I held Saucy again as he and Isaac helped Linda climb the ice-covered steps. The door burst open, and Naomi greeted her with a hug.

"Ach, I was so worried for all of you. But especially you, dear Schweschder." Then her eyes took in the little dog I was carrying, and she let out a sigh.

Linda's demeanor stiffened. "If you force my little Saucy to sleep in the barn, I'll turn around and go home."

"And how are you going to get there?" Silas stepped around Naomi.

Linda coughed. "I knew this was a bad idea."

"Hold on." Naomi looked up to Silas. "May the dog sleep in the utility room?"

He lowered his brows. "What's the use of having rules if they're broken?"

Anna squealed as she wriggled between Silas and Naomi. "Let me give Saucy a bath, Dat. I can tell she needs one."

He sniffed the air, flared his nostrils. "She needs a dose of good manners more than anything." Silas's voice was firm, yet I could see his demeanor relaxing.

"Please, please, Dat." Anna tugged at his elbow.

"The last time that little mongrel was over here it bit me."

"She won't do it again, will she, Aenti Linda? We can make her a leash."

"I'll find a piece of rope," Naomi said.

Troy and Isaac lugged Linda's suitcase and bags of Christmas gifts up the stairs behind us.

"Are you moving in permanently?" Silas's voice was laced

with humor. I had the feeling they'd had this conversation before.

"I'll be out of your hair before you know it." Linda stepped into the kitchen. "Ach, it's so nice and warm in here."

Naomi draped an arm around Linda. "You look pale as a ghost."

"Her house was like an icebox," Nancy said.

"What happened to all the wood we brought you?" Silas asked.

"Buried under the snow." Linda didn't remove her coat. "I should have brought more in before the snowfall. No one to blame but myself."

Silas showed a look of remorse. "We should have thought to do that ourselves. I got so busy . . ."

"Of course you did." Linda's cheeks still hadn't filled with a blush of color. "You already do too much for me."

"We're glad to help." Naomi took Linda's coat and replaced it with a woolen shawl. "And we're delighted to have you here on Christmas Eve. Maria and I are going to make use of our culinary skills, so you can just sit and watch."

No answer. Was this woman intentionally snubbing me because I wasn't Amish?

"Linda? Is there a problem?" Naomi felt her forehead. "Ach, you're burning up." She helped Linda take a seat at the table and insisted she drink a glass of water. "Did you have breakfast today? Can I get you some coffee?"

"I have no appetite. You know, Christmas Eve is the day my Jonathan died."

"Sorry, I forgot." Naomi turned to me. "Linda's husband passed away only three years after they were married. No children."

"Why would you tell a stranger such a thing?" Linda said sharply.

258

Ignoring her sister, Naomi continued talking. "He was a fine young man. A buggy accident on the highway took his life too early."

The pieces of the puzzle were beginning to assemble themselves. Linda was a widow and had no children. She'd never married again. And she'd lost her husband on Christmas Eve. No wonder this day was so sad for her. I admonished myself for judging her without having the facts first. I wondered why she never remarried but wouldn't dare inquire. Well, maybe no other man found her attractive. She was not sweet-natured. Yet Anna and Nancy adored her. Nothing made sense with this family.

"Come with me." Naomi took hold of Linda's elbow and guided her toward the living room. "I'll get you settled on the couch in front of the fireplace." Naomi returned and prepared some kind of herbal tea I didn't recognize. "Will you please bring Linda this tea?"

"Sure." I carried the mug into the living room. Linda lay blanketed on the couch, pillows propped behind her back.

Linda took a couple sips of tea, then her head drooped back into the pillows. I heard Silas's voice and the clicking of a dog's paws on the kitchen's linoleum floor. A still-damp Saucy raced into the room and licked Linda's hand.

"Ach, not in the living room." Silas thundered in but stopped short when he saw Linda and heard her cooing over Saucy. "Well . . . I suppose he needs to dry off somewhere warm. Better here than the kitchen." Silas shook his head in slow motion. "Just this once. I will not allow a hund to take up permanent residence in this house."

Back in the kitchen, wearing an apron, I washed and dried my hands, then stood at the counter with Naomi, taking a lesson in making piecrusts. "Your mother never taught you to bake a pie?" She sounded like she was asking me if I'd ever gone to the moon.

"Nope," I said. "And I'm not much of a cook, either."

As Naomi directed me on how to measure out flour into a bowl, sadness wafted over me as I realized how much I missed Mom. She was the woman who'd raised me. But the truth was, she'd always favored my sister, who I loved with all my heart. When Trish got married and moved away, there'd be nothing left for me in Hartford.

"Being with you is fun, but I can't imagine growing up this way or living your life. No TV, no Internet, and I can't help but notice those straight pins around your waist."

She grinned. "And yet a lot of *Englisch* people wish they were Amish. I know of only a few cases where that actually worked out and *Englischers* were baptized into the Amish church. Even then, two of the people I know left the church."

"Do all the women have to wear the same dress and apron?" I glanced down at my own black apron—without the pins, thank goodness. "It's sort of like a uniform."

"Yah, we are not supposed to try to outdo each other. Be prideful. Although sometimes that happens . . . Never mind, I must not judge others."

"What's this Rumspringa all about?"

"When Amish children turn sixteen, they may experiment with the world before they get baptized, which is a lifetime commitment—so we don't pressure them. For the most part."

"Is that why Isaac gets to hang out with Troy?" I dipped my hands in the apron's deep pockets.

"Yes and no. Those two have been friends all their lives. Troy's parents live next door, so the boys played and fished together often. They even attended the same one-room school-house until the eighth grade. However, Troy is Mennonite and went off to public high school and then college to study business, while Isaac stayed home to help his father on our farm. That's the Amish way."

"Do you think Isaac would've been happier with more schooling?"

"I have no idea. But I'll ask you this question: Do you think Troy would have learned more staying home and working in his father's business, which he now manages and will someday own?"

"I don't know." The thought of Troy's dreamy eyes caused a jolt of electricity up my spine. But the last thing I needed to do was get involved with Troy or any other man. Still, I recalled how gently he'd treated Linda and how he'd ventured outside with Isaac to inspect my car in the ditch. My ex-boyfriend never would have done either. He certainly never would have dragged a car out of the snow when he could call AAA. And he'd told me once he didn't like being around uneducated people. His snobbish attitude had always irked me.

I heard coughing from the living room. "How sick do you think Linda is?"

"I'm not sure." Naomi filled the kettle with more water and set it over the flame on the stove. "I'll make her more herbal tea, a blend used by my family for decades."

"What if she gets worse?"

"If she doesn't improve by this afternoon, we'll have to do something. Depending on the weather."

I glanced out the window and saw fluffy snowflakes drifting down. "I should tell Troy not to bother with my car until this snow stops."

"*Gut* idea," Naomi said. "I hope that means you'll stay with us all through Christmas." She placed a cinnamon roll on a

261

plate. "Would you mind taking this to Linda? She never could resist these."

"I get the feeling she doesn't like me."

"She's sick and she's probably surprised to see an Englischer in the house."

"But I'm not English."

"We call anyone who isn't Amish *Englisch*." She sliced into the butter and laid a slab and a knife on the plate. "Please don't take offense, as none is meant."

"Okay, I won't."

I expected to find Linda asleep on the couch, but she sat staring at the flames in the fireplace. "Naomi asked me to bring this in." I set a tray with tea and the roll on the low table before the hearth. She made no move to drink or eat. "Is there anything else I can bring you?" I heard a rustling sound in her chest as she breathed.

"No. I have no appetite."

I plunked down on the couch next to her. A snoozing Saucy awoke and sniffed at my hands, then turned her nose to the roll and sniffed the air.

"She's a consummate beggar." Linda furrowed her brow. "We brought her kibble, didn't we?"

"Yes, and there's a bowl of water out in the kitchen for her."

I lifted the mug and put the handle in her hand. "Naomi said this tea is an herbal remedy. I'm sure she wants you to drink some."

She put the mug to her lips and sipped. "Denki—I mean, thank you. I shouldn't take my poor mood out on you. For me, this is the worst day of the year."

"This isn't exactly a great day for me, either."

My statement garnered her attention. "Why not? Why aren't you with your family?"

I stumbled on my words. "My sister is staying with her girlfriend and planning for her wedding, and my mother died a couple years ago."

"And your father?"

"He's married to a woman who doesn't like me."

"How could that be?"

"It's a long story." My throat closed, cutting off my words.

Silence filled the living room, broken only by the crackle of the fireplace. Now what would we talk about?

CHAPTER FIVE

*N*aomi called me into the kitchen and asked if I'd like to assist in the preparation of the Christmas cake, although it seemed she had plenty of help. I noticed Anna chopping nuts and Nancy browning butter in a saucepan.

"Isn't there a saying about too many cooks in the kitchen?" I asked.

"Not in an Amish kitchen." Naomi added sugar and butter to a large ceramic bowl.

"Really, I'm happier watching."

"As you like, Maria." Naomi commenced creaming the sugar and butter. "We'll eat this cake tomorrow. If you like, I'll give you a copy of the recipe. It's the family's favorite Christmas cake."

"That would be nice, although I can't promise I'll use it."

"Sure, you will. You'll get married and have a husband and children to feed."

"First I need the husband."

"Troy seems sweet on you."

I felt warmth moving up my throat to my cheeks. "Unlikely. I hardly know him." I wouldn't mention our previous chat on the phone or that he'd given me their address. Or how attracted I was to him.

"Not only that, I think Isaac likes her, too," Nancy said with a whine in her voice.

"He does not," Anna cut in. "You're his obvious choice."

"Do you really think so?" Nancy's eyes brightened.

"Yah, to him I'm invisible. Why else would he come back and visit you last night?"

"Shush," Nancy said, her finger to her lips. She and Anna burst into giggling laughter.

"What's going on?" Silas sauntered into the kitchen from the utility room, followed by Bart, whose cheeks and nose were scarlet. He removed his damp beanie, then rubbed his hands together.

Linda stepped into the kitchen from the living room. "What are you talking about? Is there a problem with my being here?"

"Not at all. We want you with us." Naomi grasped Linda's hand. "Ach, you're still too warm. You should rest. Have a seat." She led her to a rocking chair near the stove.

"I'll make more tea." Nancy added water into the brass kettle.

"Maybe she should go to the doctor's office." But one glance out the window showed me that the snow was increasing; I realized it was almost impossible to go anywhere.

"Let's wait a few hours to see if her fever breaks," Naomi said. She turned to Bart. "You look half frozen. I'll make you hot chocolate. How did you two get along in the barn?"

"Great." Silas patted Bart's back. "He's an excellent worker. Now that our sons are gone, I'd like to hire him. If he wants a job." Silas brought his face close to Bart's. "How does that sound?"

"*Wunderbar*." Bart sent him a lopsided grin.

"We're all done for the day, Bart, if you want to head back

home after you have your hot chocolate," Silas said. But that statement made Bart shrink back.

"He's not going anywhere in this fierce storm," Naomi said. "We can't turn him out in the cold."

"I think he should be with his parents for Christmas."

"My Dat told me not to return." Bart's words came out in a whisper.

"Ever?" Silas asked. "Are you sure?"

"That's what Dat said after the accident. I left the gate open and his favorite draft horse wandered out onto the road, where he was struck by a truck." All of us cringed. "The horse recovered, but Dat is still furious." Bart hung his head. "It was my negligence. I've always been a disappointment."

"I don't recall hearing about this," Silas said. "Where do they live now?"

"Up by New Holland."

"They must be worried sick about you." Nancy poured milk into a small pot, set it atop the stove. "But let's not fret about it right now."

Five minutes later, Naomi escorted Linda back into the living room. I brought a fresh cup of tea to Linda, who sank down into the couch as if the cushions could swallow her.

Naomi draped a shawl around Linda's shoulders and a blanket across her lap. "Linda needs to eat," Naomi said. "She's skin and bones."

"I could bring her a tray when there's something ready," I said.

"Denki. I'd appreciate that."

As Linda sipped the tea, her gaze latched on to mine. When Naomi returned to the kitchen, I decided there was no time like the present. Linda's cough could spiral into pneumonia. She could end up in the hospital tonight and pass away.

"Linda, please forgive me for being so forward, but I have a question for you." My heart pounded in my ears as I formulated my words. "My adoptive parents lived in Hartford, Connecticut. Have you ever been there?"

"I don't recall." Her face twisted. "What gives you the right to ask me personal questions?"

"I'm sorry." How could I have been so thoughtless on the anniversary of her husband's death? "I won't trouble you again."

I returned to the kitchen to see Naomi arranging slices of whole wheat buttered toast upon a plate, along with blackberry jam. She placed them on a tray and I carried it into the living room. But Linda would not allow me to place the tray in her lap.

"I'm still not hungry."

"Maybe later." I set the tray on the coffee table. "Naomi says you should try to get some food in you. I can bring you more tea if you need it."

"No. Now leave me alone."

The snarl in her voice startled me. I tried to decipher my warring emotions. I needed to accept the fact that Linda was not my mother either. Did I even want a mother like her?

Laughter and chatter erupted from the kitchen as the back door opened and shut.

"Hey, there. How's it going?" Troy asked as he entered the living room with Nancy in tow.

"What brings you back out in this terrible weather?" I said.

"I wanted to find out if Linda feels better. And I brought my mother, who's a nurse practitioner."

"I'm fine," Linda answered, followed by a cough.

"Too late, Linda," Troy said, his voice upbeat. "My mother's in the kitchen. Her office is closed today. Would you mind if she gives you a quick exam? She brought along a stethoscope."

"I'm sure I'm fine." Linda glanced toward the women's voices in the kitchen.

A moment later, a tall lady strode through the door and into the living room. "I think we've met, Linda, but in case you don't remember me, I'm the Millers' neighbor, Charlene Bennett." She shook Linda's limp hand. "How about if I check you over?" Charlene, who must have been in her early sixties, wore her dark hair pulled into a bun, slacks, and a red cardigan over a turtleneck.

"I don't want to put you to any trouble." Linda's voice waned to a whisper.

Charlene extracted a thermometer from her bag and put it under Linda's tongue, then palpated her upper neck.

"Is your throat sore?"

Linda nodded.

Charlene checked the thermometer. "You're running a low fever, so nothing to worry about—yet. But we need to keep an eye on you."

Charlene used a tongue depressor and flashlight to check Linda's throat. "You poor thing, that's got to hurt."

"Well?" Troy said as we hovered in silence. "How is she?"

Charlene raised her brows. "Patience has never been your virtue, son." She glanced at me as if she'd been including me in the statement. I wondered if he'd told her about me, and if so, what he'd said.

Charlene brought out her stethoscope and listened to Linda's lungs, first in the front and then her back. "Please take a deep breath." A moment later, she said, "Now another."

Linda sputtered a few times, trying to cover her mouth.

"I suspect you're getting laryngitis, Linda," Charlene said. "Don't try to talk or whisper. It will only make your larynx worse."

In my mind, I prayed for Linda. Being around the Millers,

who wore their faith on their sleeves, must have been rubbing off on me. I felt as though I'd been brought to this house for a reason. Why else would God hurl me into this zany situation?

Naomi entered the room. "What do you think, Char?"

"You know I'm not a physician and this isn't an official call, but my opinion is that she has a nasty cold verging on bronchitis. Probably a virus. For today, I recommend you keep her quiet and hydrated. I'll come back tomorrow and give her another looking-over. I'm not worried about catching it. At work, I'm around sick people all day."

"But tomorrow is Christmas."

"Then consider it my gift to you."

"I'd better come, too." Troy set his gaze on me. When his mother smirked at him, he said, "Well, don't you want a ride, Mom?"

"Sure, although we're only next door."

"But the storm's so bad. And it's a bit of a walk."

"Okay. I will certainly want to see how our patient's doing." She turned to Naomi. "If she gets any worse, please call us. Troy or my husband can drive her to an urgent care facility."

Linda started to protest, but nothing came out of her mouth.

"Save your voice," Charlene said. She turned to Naomi. "Do you have a thermometer?"

"Yes. I should have thought to use it immediately."

"Take her temperature again in a few hours, and let me know if it's gone up."

"All right, I'll call you from the phone shanty."

"That little shack is buried in snow." Troy looked at me. "Maria, do you have a phone with you?"

"I do, but it's probably dead by now."

"If you give me your phone, I'll charge it and bring it back in a couple hours. And check on Linda's temperature."

I nodded, then went upstairs and retrieved my phone. I hesitated as I handed it to him, not that it was doing me any good right now. Did I actually expect an important call? No. And I wanted to see Troy again.

Linda's eyelids drooped. Naomi scooted her around so that Linda could stretch out on the couch, then she and Charlene covered her with the blanket. Naomi beckoned us all to come into the kitchen.

Charlene put her stethoscope into her bag. "I wish I could do more for her, but if what she has is a virus, it will have to run its course." She closed the bag and fastened the latch. "Promise to call if you need me or call 9-1-1. But my guess is they're running behind on a day like today."

"We can't thank you enough." Naomi embraced her.

"My pleasure. You know that." Charlene shoved one arm into her down jacket. "See you tomorrow morning."

"And thanks for the holly." Naomi helped her with her other arm. I looked to the counter and saw sprigs of red-berried holly and evergreens, giving the room a festive look and emitting a lovely aroma.

"That was Troy's idea. He braved the storm to clip them."

"I ran it past Silas to get his approval," Troy said.

"Yah." Silas, sitting at the table with Bart, nodded.

"They're beautiful," I said. Glancing at Troy, I felt another zing of attraction.

"Glad you like them." Troy grinned.

"I'd better run. I have my own baking to do." Charlene nudged Troy. "And my husband's in front of the TV watching football and will want a snack."

Troy's eyes locked on to mine for what seemed like forever. "See you later, Maria, after I charge your phone."

Maybe it was my imagination, but chemistry was buzzing between us.

Knuckles rapped on the back door, then the door swung open as Isaac let himself in. He entered the kitchen, carrying a brown paper bag full of greenery. "Sorry to stop by uninvited, but I cut these for you. I didn't figure anyone in this house would wish to forage around outside."

He scanned the counter. "Ach, looks like someone beat me to it." He zeroed in on Troy, who seemed to be suppressing a satisfied smirk.

Nancy shot to her feet. "Thank you so much. We can decorate the whole house this afternoon." She addressed her father. "Dat, could we have a decorating party, since we won't be out caroling this year?"

"Yah, as long as you don't go overboard."

"Did you hear that, Anna?" Nancy clapped her hands. "We'll decorate the house, bake cookies, make popcorn, and play board games. Since Troy and Isaac brought the decorations, they can help."

"That okay with you, Mom?" Troy asked. "We open our presents tomorrow morning anyway."

The corners of Charlene's mouth tipped up. "Sure, although I thought you wanted to watch the game today."

"I did, but this will be more fun." He slipped on his jacket. "I will see you all later."

As he and Charlene headed out the back door, I felt a sense of loss. What was happening to me?

CHAPTER SIX

This kitchen was beginning to seem familiar, as if I'd always lived here. Naomi had insisted Isaac stay for coffee and pumpkin muffins. Nancy's voice tittered each time Isaac spoke, but she grew taciturn when he talked to me. I wanted to tell her there was no way I was interested in Isaac. It wasn't like I was going to become Amish and join their church.

However, would that be so bad? Amish blood flowed in my veins and here was a ready-made community, even without my biological mother living in it. I needed to learn that never knowing her would have to be good enough.

"We'll put Linda in one of the downstairs guest rooms." Naomi's statement harpooned me back to the present. She glanced at Bart. "Don't worry, we won't turn you out into the blizzard. This big old house has plenty of room." She sighed. "Our sons and their families won't be able to make it this year. There go all my plans for a big family Christmas celebration."

"Mamm, what about Nancy and me?" Anna asked.

"Yah, don't we count?" Nancy planted her hands on her hips. "And Aenti Linda and Maria and Bart."

I was touched she'd included me, but Silas seemed ill at ease. "Bart should spend Christmas with his family."

"Ach, I should have asked Charlene to leave a message on their phone shanty," Naomi said. "Once Bart gives us the number."

"They don't want to hear from me." Bart raked a hand through his mop of thick hair. "My Dat has a terrible temper, and I doubt it's simmered down yet."

"When the snow lets up, I'll bring you home," Silas said, frowning at the snow piling up on windowsills. "But you might be celebrating Christmas with us here."

Bart shrank lower in his chair. "I wish I had presents to give you in return for your generosity."

"No need." Silas crossed his arms. "Christmas is about celebrating our Savior's birth."

I'd been so consumed by my personal agony and confusion, that I just then realized I had nothing to give them. I'd only bought my sister, Trish, a sweater online, which would be delivered to her by tomorrow. I didn't have a clue what Nancy and Anna would want. I figured they couldn't wear makeup or wear trendy fashion items. A gift card to Amazon would be out of the question without a computer.

I nudged Naomi under the table and spoke in her ear. "Later, could I beg you to open the shop so I can buy a few items for Nancy and Anna? Or is that just silly?"

"Not so silly." She turned to her husband. "That okay with you, Silas?"

Silas tugged his beard. "I s'pose. Bart has done several hours' work, but not Maria."

"I have a credit card in my purse."

"In the meantime, free room and board," Silas muttered.

I held up my hands. "Hey, I offered to pay several times."

Naomi sent him a weary look that told me they'd already had this discussion. "No room at the inn, Silas?"

He glowered. "Don't use the story of the birth of Jesus to manipulate me. Where have you been picking all of this up?"

"From your sermon last Sunday."

Nancy came to her mother's rescue. "It was such a good one, Dat. Really, it was."

The corners of his mouth curved up—what I could see of them under his shaggy beard. And his shaved upper lip revealed his appreciation. "Denki, Nancy. I'm glad to hear you were listening. And you, too, Naomi. I won't allow Satan to bring strife into the family." He looked my way as if I might be the bad influence.

"I'm sorry if I'm making things difficult." I squirmed in my chair. "I made a terrible mistake by coming without an invitation. I should have contacted you first."

Silas seemed to weigh the sincerity of my statement. "Never mind," he said. "There may be no room at the inn, but there's always room around the manger."

For the first time in a very long time, I felt the Lord's love descend upon me. Linda wasn't my mother, but I was where I was supposed to be.

Several hours later, Naomi brought out a bubbling cheese casserole from the crammed oven while Nancy sliced bread and Anna brought out condiments for dinner. We all sat, Silas initiated a silent prayer, then we devoured our meal without much chitchat. I figured each of us was deep in thought pondering his or her own burden. We all had them.

After we polished off our coffee, Naomi elbowed me. "Bundle up and let's take a look in the shop."

"Sorry to make you go out in the snow."

"It seems to have stopped for the moment. I need to check the building anyway to make sure no pipes have frozen."

Minutes later, the two of us slogged through the knee-high

snow. It was not a long distance from the house but quite an arduous trek. Once inside, Naomi flicked on the propane gaslight to illuminate the room. "Go ahead and choose a few things. Please, nothing for me or Silas, as he won't appreciate it and I don't need anything."

"That leaves Nancy, Anna, and Bart."

"And a young man?"

"Maybe." Could she tell I'd developed a crush on Troy? "It looks as though most of these items are for women though." I noticed a bookrack of Amish paperbacks. Tables of potholders and glorious quilts I could never afford. One hanging on the wall with a red diamond in the center, trimmed by green on a navy blue background, caught my eye.

"Isn't that one marvelous?" Naomi's gaze followed mine. "Linda sewed and quilted it. It's an Old Order Amish pattern. Not many quilters sew them anymore. And the hand-stitching on the back is meticulous."

I stood staring at the bold shapes and patterns for a minute, then turned my attention to my task. I noticed a display of honey. A sign above it stated that the amber-colored nectar was from the Millers' hives. I selected a jar and, on a whim, selected a jar of peach preserves.

Naomi picked up a pair of potholders. "I remember when these came in. Anna loved this fabric and made a big fuss." A grin widened her mouth. "I'll give you the special family discount."

"That's not necessary."

"Yes, it is. I insist."

I peered around the room. "What do you think Nancy would like?" I noticed some quilted purses and moved over to them. "Would she use one of these?"

"Her father may not approve, but she loves the color purple."

"I don't want to get her in trouble."

"She's in her Rumspringa. So far, she hasn't even tried wearing Englisch clothing or jewelry."

I selected a shoulder-strap purse of purple and lavender hues I wouldn't mind owning myself. Naomi snipped off the price tag before I could see it.

I scanned the plethora of quilted items. I could spend all day in here. I pulled out my wallet, but Naomi shook her head. "I don't want to have to get out the credit card slips."

"Okay." I put away my wallet. "Please be sure to make me a receipt so I can pay you back."

"We can worry about all that later." She wrapped the items in tissue and placed them inside an opaque plastic bag. "Are you satisfied Linda is not your mother?"

"Yes."

"I wish it could have been so." Naomi passed me the bag. "I'm afraid I didn't pay much heed to Linda when she was a teenager." Her cheeks brightened. "Once I met Silas, all my attention turned to him. We married early, and God blessed us with a son right away, followed by another. We had our own farm, so I spent little time at my parents' home." I noticed her features growing sad.

"Understandable," I said. "You must have been extremely busy."

"Yah, I was. And Linda was busy with a housekeeping position. I didn't see her for months." She handed me the bag. "We should get back in the house and check in on her."

Ten minutes later, she and I stomped our boots off at the back porch and then stepped out of them and into our slippers. Not that the slippers were actually mine.

Nancy and Anna had cleaned up the kitchen. Nancy stood by the stove, stirring the caramel frosting for the Christmas cake in a saucepan, while Anna assembled the other ingredients.

Naomi discarded her jacket and hurried into the next room to check on Linda. She knocked on the bathroom door when she didn't find her in the living room. "Are you in there?"

No answer.

Naomi tried the knob, but the door was locked. "Please rap on the door if you're in the bathroom." Finally, the door handle rotated, and Linda toddled out. She pointed to her mouth and shook her head.

"I understand," Naomi said. "You've gone and lost your voice." As she exited the bathroom, Linda glanced over to me, but her features remained flat. I wondered if she'd really lost her voice or if she'd found a convenient way not to communicate with me.

"Charlene said to keep you hydrated." Naomi picked up Linda's empty mug from the tray. "I'll make more tea."

I trotted up the stairs to my room and stashed the bag in a closet. I'd worry about wrapping things later. I spun around and jogged down the staircase just as Linda was settling herself on the couch. Saucy jumped into her lap and Linda cuddled her.

I settled on the easy chair nearest the fireplace. "Linda, Naomi showed me some of the quilts you sewed. They're marvelous." My words hung in the air. Had Linda even heard me? "I wonder if I could learn to quilt." I'd never thought of quilting before, but when viewing the masterpieces in the shop, the idea circled through my mind. "Do you think you could teach me?"

Linda seemed to be nodding, but then she coughed.

Naomi swished into the room carrying a cup of tea and placed it on the table. "Is your throat feeling better, dearest Schweschder? No, never mind, don't answer me. Save your voice."

"We were having a one-way conversation," I told Naomi.

Linda's nod was barely visible.

"Yoo-hoo." Troy poked his head into the living room. "Silas said to come right in."

The sight of Troy ignited a warm buzz in my chest. Yes, I was infatuated with this guy.

"Here you go." He handed me my phone. "All charged. Thought you might need this to call your family."

"Thanks." I slipped it in my pocket. "I do want to wish my sister a merry Christmas."

Troy turned to speak to Naomi. "Mom wants to know if you've taken Linda's temperature."

"I will right now, before she has her tea." Naomi bustled to the bathroom, then returned with the thermometer and placed it under Linda's tongue. Moments later, Naomi announced, "It's lower."

"Great. I'll call Mom with that information." He pulled out his cell phone as Silas entered the room.

Silas grimaced, his shaved upper lip lifting. "Using cell phones is *verboten* in this house."

"Sorry." Troy shoved the phone in his pocket. "How about on the back porch? I'd like to tell my mother that Linda's temperature has fallen."

"Yah, I suppose that would be all right under the circumstances." Silas aimed his stare at Troy. "As a minister I'm supposed to be a role model to the community. I mustn't disobey the *Ordnung*."

"I understand." He nodded at me. "I'll be right back."

Silas, Naomi, and Troy left the room. Linda and I sat in silence until Troy returned.

"What is the Ordnung?" I asked him as he sat down in a chair.

"The Ordnung is their set of unwritten rules they must obey, along with the Bible."

"Oh. Okay." Being Amish was a lot more complicated than I'd imagined. And yet I was attracted to their way of life, their love of family and community. I figured I could survive without electricity, and maybe even learn to drive a horse and buggy. I'd taken horseback riding lessons as a girl and adored the animals. But all other obstacles seemed insurmountable. Wearing straight pins around my waist and not being able to understand Pennsylvania Dutch would be too hard. I dismissed the idea. Why waste my time thinking about what would never be? No way would I give up my cell phone and the Internet. A website had brought me here in the first place.

I listened to the clock on the hearth's mantel ticking and the flames crackling and popping. Linda had fallen back to sleep, her lids closed. Her scruffy little dog lay in her lap. Seeing Saucy made me grin. That little canine must be more of an irritation to Silas than I was.

Well, at least I'd picked a good place to skip Christmas. I didn't miss the jolly Christmas songs on the sound system at the mall nor the never-ending merry-Christmas-happily-ever-after reruns on TV.

"Is there anything more I can do to help you, Maria?" Troy said. "We haven't really had a chance to talk since our phone conversation."

"Maybe. You and your family must know most of the Amish in this area."

"Except for going away to college for four years, this has been my home. Why do you ask?"

"I came here on a fool's mission, thinking I could find my mother." Gathering my thoughts, I paused for a moment. "I keep thinking about that DNA test. In fact, I took the test three times using three different companies because I didn't want to be in the idiotic position I find myself now."

"I shouldn't have let Nancy use our Internet," he said. "I knew her father wouldn't like it, especially being a minister and all. But I figured since she's not yet baptized it was okay. And she begged me like crazy." He flattened his palms together. "I never dreamed anything would come of it. She gave the website permission to post her contact information, using the business's email and phone number."

I couldn't help but smile in return. "Believe me, no one was more surprised than I was."

"I've heard that sometimes people who get tested find out more than they expected."

"That's for sure."

"What do your parents have to say about it?"

"My mother died a couple of years ago. The whole time she was sick she never mentioned a thing. Dad's the one who admitted I was adopted, as if it was no big deal."

"Maybe it isn't to him. Maybe he loves you as his own daughter."

"Possibly, but growing up it always felt as though he favored my sister. In fact, I know he did. I sure wish my parents had just told me the truth as a child."

"Would that knowledge have helped?"

"I don't know." I shrugged one shoulder. "With so many Amish in this area, not to mention those who have probably moved away, I may never find my bio mom." Speaking this reality made my heart feel as if it were caving in.

"Hey, Maria." Troy reached over and took my hand, as if my fingers were the most delicate things on earth, then let go. "I'm not sorry I helped Nancy. Without that DNA test, you and I never would have met."

CHAPTER SEVEN

*M*inutes later in the kitchen, Isaac's arrival ignited a robust blast of chatter through the back door. I assumed from Nancy's and Anna's elevated voices speaking Pennsylvania Dutch that they were both thrilled to see him. I could understand why. Except for that funky hairdo and his clothes, he was a fine-looking man.

I decided I needed to put a stop to Nancy's worries now. I slid my arm through Troy's bent elbow as we stood up and walked into the kitchen. "This is for Nancy's sake," I whispered in his ear.

"You don't hear me complaining, do you? But I must warn you, the Amish don't outwardly show their affections. Dating is all very hush-hush."

"All the better." I retrieved my hand and glanced at Isaac, who looked surprised. But not Nancy. Exuberance fluttered through her like a spring breeze.

Isaac puffed out his chest. "Sorry, Troy, but there isn't room for all of us in the sleigh."

"Why don't you just take the girls?" I sidled up to Naomi, who stood measuring out flour into a ceramic bowl. "I promised Naomi I'd help her with the cooking."

Both Nancy and Anna grinned, but Isaac said, "You're missing out on a chance of a lifetime."

"You may be right. I do want a ride in a sleigh someday. But I'd better stay here to help care for Linda, too."

"I'm so excited." Nancy punched her fists into her coat sleeves. One step ahead of her, Anna was already buttoning her coat.

"There's still much to get done this afternoon," Naomi said to Anna and Nancy.

"But, Mamm, we'll be the envy of every girl in the county." Anna's eyes sparkled with excitement.

Naomi's brow furrowed. "Shush, you want your father to hear you? Eliciting envy is nothing to be proud of. Pride in itself . . . Well, you know it's a bad thing, so I won't give you another one of your father's sermons."

"No worries, Naomi, I'll fill in for them," I said. Not that I knew my way around a kitchen. Certainly not when it came to desserts. "Too cold out there for me anyway."

Part of me wished I'd taken Isaac up on that ride as I listened to their laughter exiting the back door. I peeked out the window and watched as they climbed into the sleigh. The horse gathered speed, and the sleigh departed. I hoped Isaac found Nancy to his liking.

Troy said, "I'd better go help shovel my parents' driveway, although it seems to be a never-ending battle."

"Are you coming back later to decorate?" I didn't want him to leave.

"Sure, I don't want to miss out on all the fun."

"Did I thank you for charging my phone?"

"Yes, you did. Glad to." He turned to Naomi. "I might go outside and help Silas for a few minutes."

"Even if he says he doesn't need help, don't believe him,"

Naomi said. "I know he'd appreciate it, even if he doesn't act that way."

"Yeah, I know Silas well enough." Troy chuckled. "My dad's the same way."

As he left through the back door, I was tempted to run after him and hug him good-bye, because I figured I might never see him in private again. When the snow stopped, I'd be forced to leave—not that I knew my next destination.

"Maria, would you do me a favor?" Naomi's question yanked me into the present.

"Sure. Anything."

"Would you please go sit with mei Schweschder? I feel uneasy about leaving Linda out there by herself. If one of the girls were home, I'd ask them."

I would have rather stayed in the kitchen with Naomi, but I said, "Okay, if you're sure you don't need my help."

"Sitting with Linda is the help I need the most. Seriously. And take your cell phone with you, just in case." She handed me a scrap of paper. "Here's Charlene's telephone number."

"But Silas made such a fuss about using the cell phone."

She winked. "I don't recall him telling you anything."

"But—"

"Please encourage her to drink fluids. She has always been a strong-willed person. Well, not as a child. She was the most compliant in the house, but when she became a teenager something changed her. I have no idea what."

As I entered the living room with more tea, I felt mean-spirited as I acknowledged I didn't particularly like Linda, although I admired her spunk, her ability to live by herself all these years with no man to help her.

Don't judge a book by its cover, I kept reminding myself as I set the tea down on the table.

Linda lay sprawled on the couch, her face buried in a pillow. Her shoulders shook.

"Linda? Are you all right? Is there anything I can do?"

"I'm fine," she croaked, dabbing at her cheeks with her handkerchief. "Just feeling sorry for myself, which is a sin."

"I feel sorry for myself all the time," I said in an attempt to elevate her mood. "At least recently." Now what should I do? "Are you sure you're feeling all right physically? I can call Charlene."

"No, don't." Her voice was barely a squeak. "I deserve to die. God is punishing me, as He did before when He kept me barren and then took my husband away."

"But why?"

Her words were too slurred for me to understand.

I felt her forehead. Her skin seemed warm. "Naomi," I called. "Please come in here."

She hustled into the living room. "Did she pass out?"

"I don't know. She was talking just a minute ago." I decided not to reveal the subject of our conversation. "Do you think we should call Charlene?"

She glanced toward the kitchen. "Yes, go ahead."

"But what about Silas?"

"He's out in the barn . . . Never mind." She took the phone from me and tapped in Charlene's number. She and Charlene had a short conversation, then Naomi said, "Hold on," and set the phone aside without hanging up.

"Linda?" Naomi shook Linda's shoulders gently. "Can you hear me?"

Linda's eyes opened halfway. "I guess I fell asleep."

I had a difficult time believing anyone could fall asleep that quickly, even if they were ill, but maybe I was being overly critical. I recalled my mother accusing me of playing possum when I was a child.

Naomi spoke into the cell phone. "Hi, Char. Linda's awake. What do you think? Give her another couple of hours to rest?" A long pause ensued. "Okay, if she's not better by tomorrow then I'll ask Troy to take her to the urgent care clinic."

Naomi hung up and gave the phone back to me. "Charlene said to keep watch on her. She said to let Linda sleep. When Silas comes back in the house, we'll put her to bed."

An hour later, Silas and Bart carried Linda to one of the first-floor bedrooms, then sat at the kitchen table, enjoying hot chocolate. Isaac returned with Nancy and Anna. Jubilation and laughter filled the room as they described their ride.

"Everyone stared at us," Nancy said, removing her bonnet and wriggling out of her coat. "Not that we were trying to make anyone jealous, Dat."

Troy appeared at the back door, carrying a platter of assorted cookies and candies. I felt a wave of giddiness traveling through me.

"Take these plates into the living room and bring out the board games." Naomi seemed as excited as the girls. Maybe she really was happy to have extra people over on Christmas Eve. She must miss her sons and grandchildren.

After supper, Nancy, Anna, Isaac, Troy, Bart, and I played Monopoly, Chutes and Ladders, and other board games from my childhood. We laughed and joked, and I forgot my troubles.

During a lull, while Nancy cooked more popcorn, I stepped out into the utility room with my cell phone to call my sister. She'd been worried about me but was excited to share her updates about her wedding ceremony to her longtime boyfriend, who had a job waiting for him in Texas. I told her I'd be delighted to be her maid of honor, all the while thinking how much I would miss her when she left. We assured each other that we would keep in touch, but of course I knew it wouldn't be the same. I was both happy for her and forlorn at the same time.

Back in the living room, we played more games, decorated with the greenery, and nibbled on snacks until ten. Bart fell asleep on the couch. I recalled my childhood fantasy that Santa Claus would arrive at midnight with a bag full of presents, knowing ahead of time exactly what each child would want. I realized I'd have to be content not receiving my most treasured gift, and I asked God to give me peace.

As Troy and Isaac prepared to leave, Troy took my hand for a moment. I felt like sinking into his arms and relying on his support. I wasn't strong enough to make it on my own anymore.

CHAPTER EIGHT

Sometime in what must have been the middle of the night, I heard rustling and then a door shut. An intruder? Isaac paying Nancy another midnight call? Was that what the sisters had been snickering about?

Ordinarily, I would have gotten up to find out what was going on. But the chilly air persuaded me to snuggle in my bed. Who in their right mind would break into this Amish home? And I hadn't heard a car's engine.

The next morning, the tantalizing aroma of coffee, sizzling bacon, and baking muffins traveled up the stairs and under the crack beneath my door. I checked the battery-operated clock on my bedstand and was amazed that I had slept in until nine. Had I missed all the Christmas morning festivities? Then I reminded myself I wasn't even planning to celebrate Christmas this year. Yet, being in this unique home with its quaint customs and charming people, I wanted to.

I wondered how Linda was doing. The staggering thought that she'd succumbed to death's jaws gripped me. Had that been what I'd heard last night? Had they taken her to the hospital while I slept?

I showered, dressed, and trotted down the stairs. I passed

Bart's tousled blanket in the living room, but he was nowhere to be seen. Silas stood, stoking the fire in the hearth.

"Bart's Dat fetched him at eleven-thirty last night. I told him what a wonderful help Bart had been to me and his Dat was most pleased." He expelled a lengthy sigh. "I also reminded both of them that we are to forgive one another as the Lord forgives us. Bart lives in a different district, so I'll have to leave their problems to their own deacon and ministers to sort out. I'll send word to them in a few days." Silas seemed sad as he smoothed his upper lip. "I promised Bart a job when the weather clears and it's time for plowing. Or maybe earlier."

Strolling into the kitchen with Silas on my heels, I was delighted to see the family sitting at the table, drinking coffee. Including Linda.

They all grinned at me. A chorus of "Merry Christmas!" resounded through the room.

I couldn't help but smile. "Merry Christmas to you." I looked out the window to see blue sky and a frozen world cloaked in glittering white.

Naomi sprang to her feet and told me to have a seat. She fixed me a plate of food, including eggs, sausage, bacon, toast, and freshly baked blueberry muffins, while Anna poured me coffee and offered me milk. I scooted into a vacant spot across from Linda.

"Thanks. This looks fabulous."

Anna set the cup before me. "Hurry up so we can open our presents."

"Hush, Anna." Silas silenced her, and she found her seat.

I guessed they'd already prayed, so I took a moment and bowed my head. When finished, I gazed across the table at Linda. "You look much better today."

"Denki, I feel better, too." Her voice was still scratchy but sounded stronger.

Naomi steepled her fingers. "And her temperature is back to normal."

"That's fantastic." Although now Troy and Charlene would have no excuse to come over. Phooey.

Under Anna and Nancy's scrutinizing stares, I consumed my breakfast as quickly as I could.

Searching for scraps, Saucy wandered over, then sat with her full attention on me. I'd forgotten how much I liked dogs. Trish was allergic to them, so my parents had never gotten one. Plus, Mom had complained about any kind of animal hair. Saucy didn't look like she'd shed much.

"You can have more to eat later," Naomi assured me as I took my last bite. "The girls are excited to open their presents. We can clean the table after."

"Okay." I dashed up the stairs to retrieve my gifts. The fresh white tissue paper would suffice as wrapping paper. I wished there was something I could give Naomi, Silas, and Linda, but it was too late to worry about it.

When I returned minutes later, the family had gathered in the living room by the hearth. The girls ripped open their presents from their parents and squealed with excitement.

Nancy marveled at her plush purple velour bathrobe. "Just what I wanted." She stroked the robe's fabric and brought the softness to her cheek. She'd also received an assortment of books, both fiction and nonfiction. I saw horses on the front of several.

Anna dug through a handled wicker basket holding a silk floral arrangement in a glass vase with a battery-operated light inside it, and an abundance of soaps, shampoos, and lotions. "Denki, Mamm and Dat."

They opened presents sent from Ohio from their brothers and their wives, and several other relatives. All were utilitarian items such as towels embellished with embroidered trim, but the girls were delighted and couldn't contain their glee.

Finally, they came to my gifts. "These are the potholders I loved so much. Denki." Anna glanced to her mother, who had obviously helped me select them.

Nancy opened her quilted purse and hugged it. "I love it." She looked to her father. Fortunately, Silas said nothing negative.

The girls presented me with a meticulously wrapped present, much to my surprise. A teal-colored scarf and a pair of matching mittens. Finally, Naomi gave me a large gift from the whole family: the incredible quilt I'd admired at the shop.

"This is too much," I exclaimed, although I found myself clasping it. Now I needed a bed. But where would I land?

Naomi's gaze flitted to her sister. "Linda wanted us to give it to you."

I turned to Linda, who looked away. My guess was that Naomi had talked her into giving it to me. Still, I needed to show gratitude. "Thank you very much, Linda, I will treasure this the rest of my life." I felt salty moisture pricking the backs of my eyes. More than ever I wanted to be a member of this loving household.

An hour later, Anna and Nancy trundled up to their bedrooms with their gifts, leaving Naomi, Linda, Silas, and me to sip coffee together.

Naomi brought out a box. "Linda, you haven't opened your gift from Silas and me."

"I can't accept a gift until I've made a kneeling confession." Linda looked at Silas. "May I make it to you right now, seeing as you're a minister?"

"Nee, that's not the way we do it. I'd need a deacon or another minister with me to hear a confession. And a kneeling confession is made before the whole congregation. You know that."

"Now open our present." Naomi scooted the box closer to her.

Linda cleared her throat. "I don't deserve gifts. Not after what I've done. A lifetime of deceit." She seemed to be shrinking. "But I have something I need to tell all of you."

Silas stroked his beard. "Can't it wait?"

"What could be so terrible?" Naomi asked.

Linda wrung her hands. "Many years ago, I worked for a couple in Connecticut as a housekeeper."

"I seem to recall that, now that you mention it," Naomi said. "When you were a late teen."

Linda looked like a frightened rabbit trying to seek camouflage in the couch.

"How did you meet them?" Silas leaned forward, his elbows on his knees.

Linda strained to get the words out, as if her body were wracked with pain. "I was working in Bird-in-Hand. Somehow this Englisch woman surmised I was in a motherly way."

"You mean with child?" Naomi's voice rose in pitch but not volume.

"I was seventeen years old." Linda paused so long I wondered if she'd continue. I didn't dare speak, couldn't inhale.

Finally, she said, "Not even our mother suspected a thing. She was busy helping you and your new baby, Naomi." Through her chalky white skin, a dark stain erupted on her cheeks. "I was so naïve. I never should have been alone with that boy, even if he was Amish." She stared at the floor. "Anyway, the woman said that she and her husband wanted to adopt my baby and would give it the best of homes. In the meantime, I could live with them and do light housekeeping, so no one would be the wiser. I agreed on the spot. I didn't even pack a bag. I just quit my job, asked my boss to tell our parents I was okay, and left with them." She fluffed Saucy's fur and received a lick. "She and her husband were very kind, so I have no regrets as far as they go. They were fine people."

"Well, did you give birth to a child?" I asked.

"Yes, and I left my baby with the couple." Her voice grew weak. "I promised never to contact them again as long as they took care of my dearest little child."

"A girl or boy?"

"A—a girl." Her face contorted. "I was afraid to hold her for fear I'd change my mind and want to keep the baby. I'd already promised to give her away. And I'd agreed never to reveal anything to anyone."

I felt as though a giant hand was squeezing my heart. Could this woman who looked so innocent be playing me for a fool? Maybe she didn't want me for a daughter.

"The couple lived in Connecticut?" I couldn't stop myself from asking.

"Yah."

Silas broke in. "I demand you tell us the truth. No more deceit."

"Yes, please," Naomi said. "Why would you keep such a secret? Silas and I would have helped you raise the child."

I felt light-headed. "What was the couple's last name?"

"Romano." Her moist eyes found mine. "Maria, if you're my daughter, I'm so very sorry. If you're not, I'm even sorrier."

I hadn't planned on this scenario. A cyclone of emotions whirled through me. White noise filled my ears.

Naomi wrung her hands. "Maybe we should do another DNA test."

"No more tests." Silas seemed to be containing a volcano of anger.

"How about if Charlene administered it?" Naomi beseeched him.

"I'll give it some thought after I've spoken to the deacon and the bishop."

"In the meantime, I float around in a state of limbo?" I sounded pitiful, even to me. "I need to know if Linda is my mother."

"I'm sure of it." Linda turned to face me. "The moment I saw you it was as if God Himself had brought me the greatest gift I could ever receive."

Silas shook his head, but Naomi shushed him before he could speak. "I felt it, too," she said.

How about me? What did I think? Now was not the time to get swept away into emotional decisions. I stared at Linda until her eyes met mine. "Who's my father?"

"I don't know for sure. I had a crush on an Amish boy my age. We went to a party with the wrong crowd. Ach, I drank too much. When I awoke in the morning, I was alone."

"You have no idea what happened?"

"I remember drinking too much and feeling fuzzy-headed. I vaguely recall the young man . . . I must have passed out." She blinked away a tear. "He was probably so drunk he doesn't remember either. Can you see why I've not told anyone?"

"There's never a good excuse for lying." Silas's balled fist rested on his knee.

"I know that." Linda bowed her head. "If only I could turn back the clock, I would." She took my hand. Hers was soft and gentle; her fingers tightened around mine. "Can you ever forgive me, dear *Dochder*?"

What other choice did I have? Did I really need a DNA test to prove she was my mother? No. Yet, I'd been duped before.

As if reading my mind, Linda spoke. "You had a birthmark . . ."

With a trembling finger, she pointed to her forearm. "Right here."

All eyes turned to me. I rolled up the sleeve on my left arm. I'd always hated that inch-long wine-colored birthmark. But today it was like discovering a vein of gold.

CHAPTER NINE

*L*inda reached out and gently took my wrist. She ran two fingers across my birthmark with care, as if it was the most precious thing in the world. Then her eyes found mine. "Can you ever forgive me?"

Regret and sadness roiled inside me like an ocean wave against a jagged cliff. "I don't know. I don't know what to think anymore."

"I wouldn't blame you if you never did. I haven't forgiven myself." Her face blanched. "I wouldn't blame you for hating me."

I had no answer for her. I turned to Silas and asked, "What now?"

"We must forgive others as God forgives us. That's all there is to it."

"Honestly, I don't even know if I believe in God." And yet a wonderful world of possibilities spread out before me.

"Then we will pray for you, Maria." He turned his gaze to Linda. "And we'll pray for you, too, that you can accept God's never-ending mercy."

As her reality became three-dimensional in my mind—what she'd endured living without her only child—my heart softened. She'd made a promise to a stranger at age seventeen that she had no doubt regretted hundreds of times. Thousands.

Affection for her expanded in my heart. "I wish I had a Christmas present to give you." I took her small hand and felt fragile fingers.

"You just did. I can never thank God enough for you—my unexpected Christmas gift." She reached out to embrace me, and I slid over closer to hug her. With my arms around her, I felt as though I was finally whole. Could a one-day-old baby remember her birth mother? A deep sob inside threatened to erupt, but I held it in. Yet a moment later, we were both crying decades-worth of tears.

Naomi brought over a box of tissues. "I'm glad you told us, Linda. And we're happy to include Maria into the family. She can continue to stay here with us for as long as she likes."

"Yah." Silas nodded, his beard moving up and down. "We have plenty of room. I feel certain you're one of us, Maria. It's not as if we don't rent out rooms every once in a while, anyhow."

I took a tissue, blotted my eyes, and blew my nose. Linda did the same. Her eyes, rimmed with pink, gazed at me as if I were the most cherished person on earth. Mom never saw me that way. Trish was always the center of her universe. Not that I held animosity toward our mother; she'd done the best she could.

"I've always loved you, dear daughter." Linda's voice quavered. "Never has a day gone by when you've not been on my mind and in my heart." Her words were a balm to my soul. "God's hand was in this. I know it." She blew her nose again. "The Lord must have orchestrated this whole reunion."

"I guess you're right." No way could it be random.

"Then you'll eventually come live with me?" Linda asked.

I was speechless, unable to formulate an answer. Wasn't this what I wanted—why I'd come here? What was holding me back? Fear of more disappointment?

I looked into Linda's face and saw myself twenty years from now. I had no doubt she was my biological mother. I experienced her encompassing love. But I felt like a child unsure of herself.

"I don't know." A rogue tear slipped down my cheek. "Shouldn't I get to know you first?"

"Yah, Maria, we should get to know each other first."

"All things work for good for those who love God," Naomi said.

Silas harrumphed. "Who's the minister in this household anyway?"

"Sorry, Silas. It just popped into my mind. But it's true, isn't it? I heard you saying that at church last month."

As they spoke, I turned to Linda. Should I start calling her Mother or Mamm? I'd have to ask her later, after the colossal shock subsided and we were alone. We had much to talk about. Years to make up. I wanted to hear every detail of her life, without judgment. I inched closer to her, and we hugged each other again.

I could have stayed in her arms forever but heard, "Yoo-hoo." I recognized Charlene's cheery voice. When she saw Linda and me embracing each other, she stopped short. "Oh dear. Am I interrupting?"

"No," Naomi and Silas said in unison.

Charlene's lips turned up into a smile. "How is my patient doing?" Carrying her bag, she moved closer to Linda and felt her forehead. "I'll take your temperature and listen to your lungs in a few minutes, but you feel cool. And there's new color in your face—a glow, really."

Troy stood in the doorway, his tall frame and broad shoulders filling the space.

"Come in, Troy." Naomi got to her feet. "We have incredible news. Linda is Maria's biological mother."

"Really?" Troy sounded skeptical—not that I blamed him. "You had another DNA test already?"

Silas got to his feet. "We have all the evidence we need."

"Does that mean she'll be staying?" Troy asked.

"Yah," Silas said. "Right here for now."

Troy's smile stretched from ear to ear and he sat down on the couch next to me. "In that case, I need to talk to Maria before I leave." He swiveled to face me. "I know you want to spend time with Linda, but I need to speak to you. Okay?"

"Sure."

Later, as the others chatted in the living room, my mind was still gyrating, as if the earth had propelled me into a new orbit. A better one. I had a new family!

Troy and I exited the kitchen and made our way through the chilly utility room for privacy. When we neared the back door, he stopped and turned to me.

"Are you cold?" he asked.

"I should be, but I'm not."

His arms slid around my shoulders. "Now that we're alone, I can do what I've wanted to do ever since the moment I first saw you." His face moved closer until his lips brushed mine. A short and simple kiss I knew I'd never forget.

"Maria, may I court you, as the Amish would say?"

My jaw dropped. "Huh? What do you mean?"

"Date you. See each other exclusively."

"I don't know what to say." Yet I felt myself being drawn to him more than any man I'd ever met. "Everything is moving too quickly. So many changes."

"I've been praying to meet the right woman. You're just what I'd envisioned, and my mother agrees."

"You know I have a lot of strings to unravel."

"I won't pressure you." He kept hold of my hand, brought

my fingertips to his lips. "But if you tell me there's a chance, I will continue to pursue you."

My heart swelled with the thrill of hope. In my mind I thanked God for Linda, my mother, and my extended Amish family. And my new beau.

"Yah," I said. "All right."

I was open to whatever came next.

Caramel Christmas Cake

⅔ c	butter, softened
1⅓ c	sugar
3	eggs
2¼ cups	sifted cake flour
½ tsp	salt
2 tsp	baking powder
⅔ c	milk
1 tsp	vanilla extract

Cream butter; gradually add sugar, beating until fluffy. Add eggs, one at a time, beating well after each addition. Combine flour, salt, and baking powder; add to creamed mixture alternately with milk, beginning and ending with the flour mixture. Stir in vanilla.

Pour batter into two greased and floured 9-inch round cake pans. Bake at 350 degrees for 25–30 minutes until a toothpick inserted in the center comes out clean. Cool in pans for 10 minutes. Remove from pans and cool completely.

Caramel Frosting

½ c	butter
1 c	firmly packed brown sugar
3 T	milk
3 cups	powdered sugar
1 tsp	vanilla extract
⅓ c	chopped pecans or walnuts

Melt butter in a medium saucepan. Add brown sugar and cook one minute over low heat. Stir in remaining ingredients except nuts and beat until smooth. Add more milk if necessary for proper spreading consistency. After frosting the cake, sprinkle chopped nuts on top.

ABOUT THE AUTHORS

Leslie Gould is the #1 bestselling and award-winning author of over thirty novels, including the COURTSHIPS OF LANCASTER COUNTY series, the NEIGHBORS OF LANCASTER COUNTY series, and the SISTERS OF LANCASTER COUNTY series. She holds an MFA in creative writing and enjoys research trips, church history, and hiking, especially in the beautiful state of Oregon, where she lives. She and her husband, Peter, are the parents of four adult children.

Jan Drexler brings a unique understanding of Amish traditions and beliefs to her writing. Her ancestors were among the first Amish, Mennonite, and Brethren immigrants to Pennsylvania in the 1700s, and their experiences are the inspiration for her stories. She is the author of several books from Love Inspired, as well as *Hannah's Choice*, *Mattie's Pledge* (finalist for the 2017 Holt Medallion), and *Naomi's Hope*, all a part of the JOURNEY TO PLEASANT PRAIRIE series from Revell. Jan lives in the Black Hills of South Dakota with her husband of thirty-five years.

Bestselling author **Kate Lloyd** is a passionate observer of human relationships. A native of Baltimore, Kate spends time with family and friends in Lancaster County, Pennsylvania, the inspiration for the LEGACY OF LANCASTER TRILOGY and the LANCASTER DISCOVERIES series. Kate is a member of the Lancaster County Mennonite Historical Society. She and her husband live in the Pacific Northwest, the setting for Kate's novel *A Portrait of Marguerite*. For relaxation and fun, Kate enjoys walking with her camera in hand.

Sign Up for the Authors' Newsletters!

Keep up to date with latest news on book releases and events by signing up for their email lists at:

lesliegould.com

jandrexler.com

katelloyd.com

More from the Authors

Leisel left her Amish roots for a career in medicine. She has an English boyfriend and big dreams—but these come crashing down when her sister is diagnosed with cancer. Soon nothing is going as planned. With difficult choices to make, will she stick to the traditions of her past or learn from the story of a WWII ancestor and embrace a life of uncertainty?

A Faithful Gathering by Leslie Gould
THE SISTERS OF LANCASTER COUNTY #3
lesliegould.com

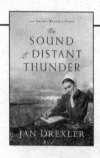

Despite war being at odds with the teachings of the church, Jonas Weaver is taken in by the romance of the soldiering life, especially for the abolitionist cause. And when his married brother's name comes up in the Civil War draft list, he volunteers to take his place. But can the commitment he made to his sweetheart survive the separation?

The Sound of Distant Thunder by Jan Drexler
THE AMISH OF WEAVER'S CREEK #1
jandrexler.com

BETHANYHOUSE